Crossing the street, Eva jumped over a stagnant puddle while behind her a horn blared rudely. She took no notice. Argentineans used their horns constantly. It meant nothing.

But the tall, imposing man walking in front of her obviously didn't know that. He turned to look. She hadn't noticed him until this very moment, but now she wondered why. He looked unlike anyone she'd seen so far in Comodoro. His appearance—clothing, demeanor, attitude—set him apart from everyone else on the street.

Taller than anyone around him, he seemed prosperous and sleek, his dark clothing expensive and expertly tailored. Beneath the clothing, she was sure there were broad shoulders and well-toned muscles. He walked with a very particular gait that was both sensual and graceful. Straight but fluid…almost military-like.

He could only be American.

The realization hit her, slamming into her brain with a visceral abruptness, the results immediate. An instantly dry mouth and hands that were suddenly freezing. A stomach that churned and fought against the breakfast she'd eaten hours before. An American? Here? Who was he? What did he want?

Was he looking for her?

Dear Reader,

Recently, I spent two years living in a very remote town in southern Argentina. My favorite form of entertainment was to sit at the front window of my living room where I could watch everyone pass on the bustling sidewalk below.

I saw everything, Gypsies who read palms, beggars asking for money, even a man who came once a month to sell books, which he would carefully display on the hood of his car.

Looking out one day, I saw a man walking down the sidewalk. He was clearly a stranger. Tall and well dressed, obviously urban in appearance, he stood out among the local residents. I instantly wondered who he was and what he was doing in our isolated town. He disappeared quickly in the crowd and turned the corner.

I never found out who the man was, but the image stayed with me. Soon I had a story to go with it. The result was *The Ends of the Earth*.

I no longer live in Argentina, but split my time between my home state, Texas, and a new residence in Santa Cruz, Bolivia. I'm sure, however, that Bolivia will yield just as many fascinating stories as Argentina.

Kay David

THE ENDS OF THE EARTH
Kay David

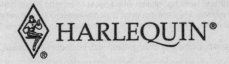

TORONTO • NEW YORK • LONDON
AMSTERDAM • PARIS • SYDNEY • HAMBURG
STOCKHOLM • ATHENS • TOKYO • MILAN • MADRID
PRAGUE • WARSAW • BUDAPEST • AUCKLAND

ISBN 0-373-70798-3

THE ENDS OF THE EARTH

For the best critique group in the world:

Thank you, Pat, for making me act saner than I really am.
Thank you, Heather, for making me more logical than I want
to be. And thank you especially, Marilyn, for always
accepting me when I want to be neither sane nor logical.
You guys are wonderful, and I love you all.

CHAPTER ONE

"THESE GUYS ARE DANGEROUS as hell. They'd just as soon kill you as look at you." Thomas Solis uncapped the can of charcoal lighter fuel he held in one hand and looked up.

Standing by the picnic table, a startled Eva Solis jerked her head up and met her brother's gaze. Overhead, the pine trees and bent cedars were green and full of light, a bright summer sun shining down, the country air full of nothing but sharp, clean smells. The setting made Thomas's expression—dark and tight with worry—and his words—troublesome to say the least—more incongruous than ever.

"They're ruthless *and* international," he went on. "The influence they wield goes beyond Houston...beyond the United States even. They aren't the usual gunrunners—"

He broke off abruptly, his words stopping in midsentence as he looked over Eva's shoulder. Turning around to follow his stare, Eva saw Thomas's wife, Sally, coming toward them. Behind her, in the Texas piney woods, was the tiny cabin where they'd come to spend the weekend. Through the open window, Eva could hear the pings and pongs of her nephew Daniel's latest computer game.

Thomas snapped his mouth shut. An undercover agent for a special department of the U.S. Treasury, he never talked about his cases in front of Sally. *Never.* He'd share things with Eva—she worked for the Treasury, too, as a translator—but he always protected Sally from that world.

She waddled toward them, a bowl of potato salad clutched in her hands and resting unceremoniously on the swell of her belly. She was eight months pregnant.

"What are you two whispering about out here? You're not talking work, are you? We're supposed to be on a vacation." She put the bowl down on the table and stared accusingly at them. "And it's Daniel's birthday, too. Can't it wait till Monday morning?"

Eva went over to Sally and put an arm around her. Squeezing her sister-in-law's shoulder and smiling with all the encouragement she could muster, Eva said, "Don't you have better things to worry about than our boring old conversations? Like that address list? I bet you haven't even worked on it at all, have you? We're going to have a baby shower next week and we'll be the only ones there!"

Sally's hazel eyes widened, the distracting ploy working easily. "Oh, my gosh, I haven't! But I brought all the stuff." She raised one eyebrow.

Eva threw up her hands as if in surrender. "Okay...okay. Go inside and get it, and we'll work on the addresses together. How's that?"

"Great!" Sally smiled, then turned and headed for the house.

As soon as she was out of earshot, Eva wasted no time. Looking at Thomas, she spoke again, urgency deepening her voice. "So what are you saying? What's really going on?"

He glanced toward the house first. When his eyes came back to Eva's, they were even more concerned than before. "I'm saying these are really bad guys, and they don't care who they kill. In fact, they enjoy it. I don't plan on providing them any entertainment."

Her mind was already putting the pieces together. "That's why you brought us up here early, isn't it? Instead of next month, like we'd planned..."

"I just thought it might be a good idea to get everyone out of Houston for a while. Could you stay here with Daniel and Sally for a few days? At least until I get this investigation sewn up?"

"Well, sure I can. I have plenty of vacation time coming. I'd be happy to stay here with them, but..." She frowned. "Do you think the situation is that bad?"

"I don't know, but it doesn't matter. If there's any chance at all that things could go south, I don't want any of you around town."

Their eyes locked. They were so much alike, it almost felt as though she were looking in a mirror. Strangers always thought she and Thomas were twins, but they were two years apart in age. Eva had heard all the explanations—they looked alike, they spoke the same way, their hair was the same color—but she knew what it really was.

They thought alike and they always had.

Even before their parents had divorced when they were just little kids, she and Thomas had shared an empathy that bordered on the psychic—they were that close. After the divorce, when Thomas had become the "man" of the family, they'd grown even closer. Some people might think it was corny, but she didn't care—Eva looked up to her brother. He was her hero.

She shook her head, the unhappy frown still on her face. "I wish you hadn't taken this assignment."

"I know, I know." His voice held an uncharacteristic note of regret. "But I didn't have a choice. I was the only one in the office who had the kind of Spanish they needed for the job."

"This is the Mexico City deal, right? *Los militares?*"

That was all she really knew about the current investigation. It involved people who were selling guns, guns that had been stolen from the Mexican government. Eva and Thomas always referred to them as *los militares,* but in fact the men doing the actual selling were Americans and they were determined to make as much money as quickly as they could regardless of who got in the way. Like all the people Thomas dealt with, they were bad. Very bad. In her many years with the Treasury, she'd translated thousands of pages, but few had been as horrifying as the ones associated with these guys.

"Yeah, that's the case." Thomas looked down into the flames of the grill with a worried stare before he faced her again. "I'm getting close to making some arrests, and I don't like the way it's going down. The whole thing smells bad. I asked for extra security, but the request was denied. I was told we don't have the budget."

"Extra security…" Her chest tightened with a band of apprehension.

"Just a precaution," he reassured her. "They might know more than I want them to."

Alarm flooded her. "They know who you are?"

"Oh, hell, no." He vigorously shook his head. "If I thought that, we wouldn't be standing here right now. We'd be in a safe house."

"But…"

"But…" He glanced toward the cabin before looking at her again. "Something's not kosher at the office. Could be a leak, could be something else, I'm just not sure. If it *is* a leak and it's at the level I'm talking about, then there's going to be problems that won't stop here. It could mean H.P.D., too."

"The *Houston* police?"

He nodded grimly.

"Jack, too?"

"I'm not sure. Maybe…"

Frowning, Eva crossed her arms over her chest. She hated Jack Finely, Thomas's boss. Since Thomas had moved back to Houston from Washington, Finely had been convinced Thomas was there to replace him. Insecure and incompetent, the man had taken every opportunity he could to undermine Thomas, it seemed to Eva, even putting him into dangerous assignments like this one. Thomas's last job had gone wrong, and he'd barely survived. It'd been impossible to trace responsibility for the problems directly back to Finely. But Eva was certain who was behind it.

"He could be involved. He definitely insisted on my taking this job." Thomas's expression went grim. "Right now, I don't know who to trust."

"What's Ridley say?"

Ridley Holt was Thomas's best friend at the office. They'd met when Thomas had been transferred to Texas and they'd clicked almost immediately. A long-time agent, Ridley wanted to go up the ladder just like Jack, but Ridley's approach to success was completely different. He was nice. He'd taken Thomas under his wing from the first day out and they'd been friends ever since.

"Ridley understands." Thomas paused, then spoke again. "I've contacted a guy by the name of Williams in the Washington office about it, but I didn't tell him that much."

"And this Williams fellow—you feel like you can trust him?"

"Until I get more proof, solid proof, I can't trust anyone. He sounds decent enough, but I don't really know him. He could be as involved as the next guy." Thomas met her worried stare. "Basically, we're on our own. We'll have to look out for each other."

"That's nothing new." She smiled. "We can handle it."

"You and I—for sure." He glanced again toward the little cabin before turning back to Eva. "I don't want to tell Sally, though. After her two miscarriages, I just can't risk it. On the other hand, if I didn't say anything, and then something happened…" He shook his head, his jaw clenched. "I'd never forgive myself. That's why I wanted to let you know what was going on. You understand, don't you?"

"Of course I understand." Eva moved closer to Thomas and put her hand on his arm. The feelings they'd always shared filled the space around them with warmth and unspoken love. "I'll stay here with her and Danny as long as I have to. Don't worry about it."

He nodded, started to say something else, then stopped. Starting again, his voice was husky. "If something should happen to me—"

"Nothing's going to happen to you," she said firmly.

"Well, that's certainly *my* plan," he answered, "but if it did… You'd need to leave here, Eva. You'd have to take Sally and Daniel and run as far away as you could get and as quickly. I keep money in my briefcase, the one with my computer. It's not a fortune, but it *would* get you out of the country, and that's a good place to start." His eyes pinned hers in a steady stare. "You understand what I'm saying? There's no one you could trust. Not at the office, not at H.P.D., not in Washington. No one. You'd have to disappear for a while."

She nodded, her eyes never leaving his face. "But we're safe here."

"Yes, we're safe here." His expression lightened. "That's why I picked it."

"Right." She smiled, trying to match his easier attitude. "The way I see it—our biggest danger is your cooking."

He grinned, and again she felt as if she was seeing herself. "My cooking? Dangerous? I'll need more lighter fluid for that. How 'bout going to the barn and getting me some? I want to get this blaze really going."

Eva was rolling her eyes before he even finished speaking. "What is it about you men and the size of your blazes? I just don't understand it."

"Well, if you'd get married again, you could figure that out. You know Ridley—"

"Stop right there. I don't want to hear any more of your matchmaking." Her divorce several years ago had left her wary, and she had the feeling she'd be that way for quite a while to come. Ridley was nice enough, but she wasn't interested. Not a bit.

"You just didn't have the right guy the first time," Thomas said.

"Sure, sure." Waving her hand, she started walking down the path that led to the barn. Before she could reach the first tree, though, Thomas called out to her, using her Spanish name.

"Evita..." He waited for her to stop and turn,

which she did, halfway expecting another smart-aleck remark and preparing one of her own. He grinned at her. "I love ya, okay?"

Touched, she grinned back. "Well, I love you, too. But I'm still not marrying your best friend!"

A second later, she reached the tiny building that was almost hidden in the trees. Danny had nick-named it "the barn," but it wasn't much more than a toolshed. She struggled with the rusted handle Thomas had nailed to the door, then finally managed to wrench it open, her thoughts returning to Thomas's words of warning as the hinges screeched a protest.

Sally and Thomas and Daniel were Eva's only family. They held her steady, kept her sane. Without them, she wouldn't even know who she was. All through her horrible divorce, their support had been her lifeline.

Stepping inside the shed, Eva paused, her eyes ad-justing slowly to the musty, dark interior. After a moment, she spotted the red-and-white can of lighter fluid. She reached for it, brushing off a spiderweb, then froze, the silence of the forest suddenly shatter-ing in cacophonous noise.

"What the hell...?" She swirled, hitting her head on a rake as she stumbled to the door, the terrible sound continuing to erupt. Pausing for a heartbeat, she understood now, the noise finally registering.

It was automatic gunfire.

"Oh, God... Oh, God..." Dropping the can, she immediately ran out of the tiny building, heading for the cabin. She crashed through the woods, ignoring the path for the quickest way, tree limbs snatching at her, thorns raking her legs. The confusion of sound continued as she ran, but it changed abruptly as she got closer, turning into squealing tires and someone yelling. Above her labored breathing, she prayed, a useless mantra, over and over. "Oh, please, God... Please, God..."

A second later, she skidded out of the trees and fell to the ground in her haste, her nails digging for traction into the bark of the nearest pine, but missing, skin peeling off her fingers as she crashed to her hands and knees. Tumbling down, she lifted her eyes at the last minute and caught a glimpse of a black Explorer thundering out of the rutted drive. The faces inside were a blur behind darkly tinted windows. She caught a fleeting impression of someone with black hair, but nothing more. The vehicle screamed down the unpaved lane and disappeared, the trees swallowing it.

Scrambling to her feet, she ran into the clearing.

Thomas lay by the grill, blood blooming on his chest. Sally was nearby. Even to Eva's untrained gaze, it was clear she was already dead. A movement near the back door caught Eva's stunned and disbelieving stare. She whirled and crouched automatically, but it was Daniel. He was huddled near one of the wild gardenia bushes, his face so white it matched the incandescent blooms surrounding him.

Glancing over his shoulder to the road where the truck had raced, he lifted one trembling hand and pointed at Thomas. "Th-those men…th-they shot my daddy…."

The words jarred Eva into action. Flying to Thomas's side, Eva threw herself on the ground beside him. "Thomas! Thomas!" She yanked off the sweatshirt she'd been wearing and tried futilely to stem the blood gushing from his chest.

He pushed her hands away and pulled her closer toward him. "Did…did you see them?"

"No, no…I didn't see them! But…I think Danny did." She looked up. The little boy hadn't moved. He seemed frozen in his spot beside the flowers, then suddenly—as if he couldn't take it a moment longer—he jumped and ran inside the cabin.

"Oh, damn…" Thomas's eyes sagged closed.

"Oh, God, Thomas!" she cried, her heart clenching in an agony of disbelief. "Stay with me, please! Don't do this!"

"Got to leave," he mumbled. Lifting his hand, he reached for Eva's arm. "You've got to leave."

Danny reappeared at Eva's side, his skinny chest moving up and down with exertion and fear. "I called 911! They're sending an ambulance…police, too."

Thomas's eyes flew open, their green depths filled with horror. Reaching up, he gripped Eva's shirt with a strength she couldn't believe.

"Leave…leave now. No police… You…have to take Danny…get out of here." His dying breath smelled hot and was filled with fear and urgency. "Do like…like we planned. Grab my briefcase, take off. Don't stop…don't pack. Don't trust anyone. Just run!''

Three weeks later
Somewhere in Houston

THE MAN BEHIND THE DESK threw down the black-and-white photos, scattering them across the desktop like so many oversize cards. He looked up, an expression of disgusted impatience crossing his face. ''That's her and the kid. We took those at the company picnic last month. Don't let the innocent look fool you.''

Michael Masters studied the photos with a cool and dispassionate eye. She was a petite woman, five-four or less, he judged. Dark, sleek hair worn short and smooth. An intelligent face with black eyes that hinted at her Hispanic heritage. A slim figure, but proportioned just right. She wore shorts and a matching blouse. They looked like silk and fitted her well, showing off a flat stomach and an athletic build.

Michael looked up from the photos to the man behind the desk. ''How deep is she into it?''

''Why do you care?''

''I don't. But it will make a difference to her and to how far she decides to run.''

The man snorted. ''Then let's just say she's in it deeper than anyone. She might have even set him up—we're not sure.''

''Her own brother?''

''How else would they have found him?''

"But why?"

The man shrugged. "Who knows? She went through a pretty nasty divorce several years ago—rumor has it he left her with a lot of debts. She coulda needed the money."

Michael focused on the photos again. There wasn't anything outstanding or unusual about Eva Solis, but there *was* something there…something he couldn't quite put his finger on. He studied the photo more closely, trying to define what had caught his eye. Finally, abruptly, he dismissed the impression just the way he'd dismissed the shrink he'd seen right after Amy's death. The crazy doctor who had told him that he'd look for his dead wife in other women's faces.

Michael's gaze went to the other photos in the stack. A kid, this time. Six, maybe a small seven. The boy looked ordinary, too, his hair long and straight over almost shaved sides. In one photo, he was in-line skating. In another, he was pitching a football to a man, his right knee covered in a small bandage, his clothing rumpled and loose. The man about to catch the ball looked at him with the obvious love and affection only a father could manage.

Tapping the photo with his finger, Michael asked, "This Solis?"

"Yeah." Leaning back in his chair, Michael's contact lit a cigarette, then shook out the match, the tiny office filling with smoke and an acrid smell. "That's him."

Michael stared. The man in the photo reminded

him of himself…back in the days when he'd believed in truth and justice, back in his own government days. "Was he good?"

"Not good enough to keep himself alive. Or his wife, either, for that matter." Michael raised his eyes, his cold gaze reaching painfully out across the desk. For a heartbeat, the man behind it looked back, then realizing what he'd just said, he let his chair fall forward and he stubbed out the cigarette nervously. "Oh, damn, Masters. I didn't mean… He wasn't…"

The man continued to stumble in embarrassment, but Michael tuned out the awkward words of apology and heard nothing else. It was easy. In the past few years, he'd become adept at hearing only what he wanted to.

"How long have they been gone?" he broke in.

"Three weeks," his contact said, relief at being interrupted obvious in his voice. "Maybe less. We think she headed to Mexico."

"Why there?"

"She was a translator in the Houston office—she speaks the lingo. Besides that, she goes down there in the summers to do volunteer work. Lives in a hut and helps the locals dig ditches—that kind of shit. Seems logical she'd head that way. Lots of places down there you could lose yourself."

"Did you check all the consulates for visa applications? There are other countries in the world where Spanish is spoken, you know."

Lighting another cigarette, the other man paused, his expression now scornful, his voice sarcastic.

"No, we didn't check the other consulates. That's what we're hiring you for. We've got better things to do than chase down some stupid broad and a kid."

"I'd be careful who I called stupid. She managed to leave the country without your knowing about it."

The man's face flushed. "Just find her," he barked. "It's life and death."

"It's always life and death...to someone." Michael stared again at the photos. The woman looked happy, self-assured. The little boy seemed carefree and just as cheerful. They looked like ordinary people enjoying their lives and looking forward to the future. But looks could be deceiving, couldn't they? Once upon a time, his own life had appeared that simple, that casual, but beneath the surface, things hadn't been that way at all. And they never would be again.

"The powers-that-be want this finished. Can you do it?" The contact's voice broke into Michael's reverie. "Can you find her?"

"Oh, I'll find her." Michael slipped the snapshots into a folder and put it into the black leather case at his side, the sound of the snapping locks menacing in the tiny office. He waited one long moment, then he looked up and met the other man's eyes with a piercing black gaze. "I always do. The question is— what are you guys going to do once you have her?"

CHAPTER TWO

Eight months later
Comodoro Rivadavia, Chubut, Argentina

THE WIND NEVER STOPPED.

Eva had once read in a guidebook that the early settlers of Patagonia, Welsh people for the most part, had frequently gone mad because of the wind. She hadn't understood that statement until now. The wind in this part of Argentina howled constantly, pushing people around corners and stealing their scarves, even destroying their homes and automobiles on occasion. The city was on the Atlantic coast, but the violent gusts sucked the humidity from the air and made the whole region dry, dirty and extremely inhospitable.

The exact reason Eva had chosen to come to Comodoro.

No one in their right mind actually came here to live. They passed through the area as quickly as they could and hurried without a backward glance to the prettier regions of the country: the snowcapped mountains where they could ski, the blue-tipped seas where they could swim, the urban sprawl of Buenos Aires where they could be entertained endlessly.

They didn't come to Chubut.

Rounding the street corner and barely missing a stray dog huddled halfway in a doorway, Eva told herself once again that she'd done the right thing. Done the only thing she could. The night Thomas had died, she'd grabbed Daniel and they'd run, just as her brother had told her to do. Inside the briefcase he'd told her to take, there had been his laptop computer and money, enough cash to keep them going for quite a while. Buying two one-way bus tickets to Brownsville, she'd stuffed the remainder of the money back into the case. At the border the next morning, they'd simply walked across and grabbed a second bus for Mexico City. Confused, filled with grief and horror, she'd hidden them there in a small out-of-the-way hotel.

Then she'd had second thoughts. What had she done? What did she *think* she was doing? She'd opened the file in Thomas's computer marked "notes," and her vision had gone red. She'd had to decipher them, but to her, their meaning had been clear.

Thomas hadn't told her everything. Someone in the office, probably another agent but he didn't say who, had been feeding Thomas information... information that Jack Finely, his boss, had been taking payoffs from the people out of Mexico City. They gave him money and he told them when the raids were coming down so they could avoid them.

After that, Thomas's notes stopped abruptly, of

course, but Eva hadn't needed more to tell her how the story ended. Obviously, Jack had discovered what Thomas knew. To prevent his disclosure, Finely had told *los militares* all about it, and they'd done the rest.

Later that night, she and Daniel had gotten on another bus…and then another. Somewhere in Central America, they'd switched to trains. By the time they'd gotten to South America with false Canadian passports she'd purchased in Mexico and a birth certificate proclaiming "Daniel Cantrell" to be her son, Eva had finally felt comfortable enough to take a flight.

The destination had been in the back of her mind ever since they'd fled Houston, but she hadn't acknowledged it until that point. The summer before, in the small Mexican village where she'd lived for three months, teaching English, there had been another volunteer, a gorgeous woman from Mendoza, Argentina. One night, they'd laughingly argued about the remoteness of the village where they were posted, Eva insisting there was no place on earth less connected to the rest of the planet. The dark-haired beauty had shaken her head vigorously and proclaimed it a metropolis compared to the tiny towns dotting Patagonia. She'd specifically mentioned Comodoro, explaining about the wind and the harsh environment. Calling it "the perfect location for disappearing," she'd told Eva all about the town.

It was the loneliest place on earth.

Crossing the filthy street now, Eva jumped quickly

over a stagnant puddle while behind her a horn blared rudely, a long, single note. She ignored the sound. Argentineans used their horns constantly. It meant nothing.

But the tall, imposing man walking in front of Eva obviously didn't know that. He turned to look. She hadn't noticed him until this very moment, but now, seeing him for the first time, she wondered why. He was unlike anyone she'd seen so far in Comodoro. His appearance—clothing, demeanor, attitude—set him apart from everyone else on the street.

Taller than anyone around him, he seemed prosperous and sleek, his dark clothing expensive and expertly tailored, his hair long over his collar but trimmed and clean. Beneath the clothing, she was sure there were broad shoulders and well-toned muscles. He had a certain air about him, and it took her a moment to realize what it was. He walked with a very particular gait that was both sensual and graceful, his posture enhancing the impression. Straight but fluid, it reminded her of Thomas after he'd done his Treasury training...almost military-like.

He couldn't be anything but an American.

The realization hit her, slamming into her brain with a visceral abruptness, the results immediate. An instantly dry mouth and hands that were suddenly freezing. A stomach that churned and fought against the breakfast she'd eaten hours before. An American? Here? Who was he? What did he want? Was he...looking for her?

She ducked into the nearest *confitería* and walked

quickly to the rear of the little shop, taking cover behind a chest-high shelf of goods, her head down. Fear lodging in her throat with a deadly knot, she pretended to study a row of candy bars for a few seconds, then risked a glance toward the window a moment later. She couldn't see anyone save for five small children, pointing to the various pastries lining the glass and obviously wishing for the unobtainable.

Waiting several more moments and ignoring the shop manager's puzzled stare, Eva finally eased back into the street, looking both ways. She spotted the stranger instantly, on the north side of the street, almost four blocks down. He was heading into the Austral—the only hotel in town that had fewer roaches than guests.

Standing outside the shop, just inside the doorway, Eva watched the man disappear into the lobby of the hotel, the swinging door shutting behind him. Her heart pounding the fast, uneasy rhythm it hadn't sounded since they'd settled in Chubut, Eva told herself he could be anyone. There was a huge oil field in the empty plains outside of town, so he could be here on business. And surely suppliers *had* to come on occasion to restock the pitiful shelves the few stores in town boasted and to take new orders. They weren't *completely* isolated. The local military base probably had new people in and out, too.

But in the past eight months, she'd seen no one who looked like this man. Who looked…American.

Making her way slowly up the street, she chastised herself and tried to calm down. Sooner or later, outsiders were bound to stop briefly in town. If she had a heart attack every time someone different showed up, she wouldn't last long, would she?

A few minutes later, she was almost even with the windows of the hotel. Taking a deep breath, she slowly walked by, her glance seemingly casual as she passed the shimmering plate-glass windows that separated the hotel lobby from the pitiless wind. A catch came into her throat as her heart battered itself against her ribs.

He was waiting patiently beside the counter.

His eyes met hers.

EVA SOLIS, despite her beauty, looked positively ill as she stared at Michael Masters through the hotel window. Her porcelain skin drained completely of color and even her lips grew pale. Her eyes, as they locked on his, were the only point of color in her face. They were two dark orbs of terror, feverish in their intensity. For one long heartbeat, she held his stare, then turned and slowly walked away. She didn't run, she didn't bring attention to herself...she simply walked away.

Quickly, Michael took the stairs to his room. She'd had a bag on her arm—she was probably going to the market located behind the Austral. Looking out his bedroom window a second later, he congratulated himself as he spotted her once more. Eva Solis had not been an easy catch, but he'd found her.

For an amateur, she'd done a damn good job of getting herself and her nephew out of Texas, then out of the country. She'd clearly been prepared with a certain amount of cash and a plan—and that told him a lot. Those kinds of arrangements weren't often made by innocent people. On the other hand, the provisions could have been a precaution of her brother's, not necessarily her own. The facts didn't make absolute sense, but if Michael had learned one thing during the past forty-four years, it was that life didn't make sense. Ever.

Watching Eva scurry into one of the covered stalls ringing the market area, he wondered if the woman knew how vulnerable she really was. He was good, very good, but if he'd found her, others could do so as well.

Knowing she'd volunteered in Mexico every summer, he'd started with the assumption she'd headed there, and using his past experience, he knew she'd probably take a bus. People on the run usually did that if they could—the airlines kept too many records. Besides that, flying was expensive. A quick call had told him her credit cards were maxed out—she was traveling on cash and would want to save as much of it as she could.

None of his regular contacts at the bus station had remembered *her* but one of them had spotted the boy. "Spacey," the guy had recalled. From there, they'd taken a bus to Brownsville, a dismal town on the border between Texas and Mexico. Everything that left Brownsville—bus, plane or train—eventually ended up in Mexico City, so Michael had headed that way, too. Sure enough, he'd picked up their trail in

Mexico City. A jumping-off spot for the rest of Latin America, it was there that Michael had gotten his first solid lead on where her real destination lay.

In a routine sweep of old contacts, he'd called Paco Luna. If you were in Mexico and needed underground help, Paco was your man. Fake papers. Disguises. Convenient families who'd adopt you for traveling. Whatever your requirements, legal or otherwise, Paco could help, and if he couldn't, he'd know someone else who could. Eva had been smart enough to stay away from him, but she'd unwittingly used one of his many nephews for help. The old guy's ethics hadn't changed—if you had more money than the last guy, you got Paco's loyalty. He was eighty, but his hands were still steady and his memory clear. He'd called the eldest son of his sister, and the man had told Michael just what he'd needed to know—that Eva had indeed been there and she'd asked, in passing, if he'd ever been to Argentina. He'd given her fake passports with new names for her and the boy, plus a birth certificate for him.

It'd been easy after that. Another link he'd discovered had been Liliana Concho from Mendoza, Argentina, a woman Eva had volunteered with one summer. After Michael had found her, he'd called and told her he was a long-lost cousin of Eva's who needed to get in touch with her and did she by any chance know where Eva might be? Their conversation had been friendly, and the woman had eagerly recounted a talk she'd had with Eva about remote places, specifically Comodoro Rivadavia. He'd known instantly the place would have sounded too perfect for Eva Solis to resist.

And she hadn't.

So he'd found her—and even though she'd taken precautions, others would do the same. The relatively quick deaths her brother and sister-in-law had suffered were nothing compared to what would be in store for Eva Solis when she was located.

She was a beautiful woman—her death would take a long time. The men doing the killing would make a sport of it.

And her nephew? He'd simply disappear. A seven-year-old life that meant nothing. He'd never grow old, never have children of his own, never live out the dreams his father had probably had for him.

Usually this kind of thinking came to Michael without passion, without emotion. He thought of himself as the keeper of the lost and found. Like books, like umbrellas, like cars in a parking lot— people got lost, and he found them. Since he'd opened Masters Incorporated after leaving his government job, locating people had become his business—and his way of life.

So far, he'd had plenty of business, too…from every side.

He'd never had to hunt down a woman, though, much less a woman with a kid. His targets were usually men, men who didn't want to be found.

She came out of the last stall and looked nervously upward toward the hotel. It didn't really bother him that she'd seen him downstairs. She didn't know him, of course, so she had no idea who he really was, and even if she did, what could she do about it? Getting out of Comodoro was complicated. To try to leave now would be stupid…and Eva Solis was not stupid.

He watched as her gaze swept over the hotel's windows. It swept back and forth once, and then again. Could she tell which window he stood behind? Did she know which room was his? He didn't think so, but if she did, again…what did it matter?

He used the opportunity to study her further and noted her clothing almost approvingly. She wore heavy boots with worn blue jeans that helped her blend into the crowd, a turtleneck sweater topping them. Her dark wool coat, a navy pea jacket, looked secondhand but heavy enough to fight off the Patagonian cold. It was bulky and concealing, but not so much that he couldn't make out the curves beneath it. Rough, practical clothing hadn't been her usual style back home, according to the photos he'd seen. She'd changed her hair, as well, since they'd been taken. It was longer and straighter, darker, too. Had she dyed it or was this her natural color? The wind whipped strands of the black silk into her eyes even as he stared. Lifting one hand to peel it back from her cheeks, she continued to gaze upward, her trim, muscled body leaning into the wind and defying it.

She was more beautiful than the photos had revealed. More beautiful and more sensual. There was a very appealing strength about her, an energy and forcefulness the black-and-white glossies had been unable to capture. He saw it in her body and the elegant way she held herself. He saw it in her tilted face, the planes and valleys of her expression filled with it. Before he could stop himself, he found himself comparing his wife's blond beauty with this woman's shadowy sinuousness. Amy's slight frame opposed to Eva Solis's fit athleticism. The remembered nights of soft appeal against the possibility of a darker sensuality.

The last thought jerked him abruptly back into the moment. What in the hell did he think he was doing? Thoughts like this had no place in his life now. None whatsoever. He'd put all that—emotions, love, softness—behind him. In fact, he'd buried them, buried them in the same grave he'd buried Amy in. A life with feelings no longer existed for him.

And it never would again.

Eva Solis dropped her gaze, pulled her coat around her in a protective gesture and hurried nervously out of the market. Shaken by his thoughts and unnerved by their unexpected appearance in the empty silence of his hotel room, he watched her leave.

DANIEL WAS PLAYING stickball in the alley with a ragtag group of friends when Eva got home—a rough-and-tumble game with a broken piece of wood and a battered tennis ball. Still nervous and upset, Eva put on a smile. She was determined not to alarm him unnecessarily. She called out to him, and he scowled, but he dropped the bat and came toward her.

"How many times have I told you not to play out

there?'' Reaching out, she smoothed back a lock of his hair. "Play in the courtyard. That's the reason we got this house, remember?"

"It's more fun in the street."

Her dark eyes met his light ones, a catch coming into her throat. Looking at him made her remember. Sally. Thomas. Life on a different planet. "I know," she said softly, "and I'm sorry. But I think it'd be better if you played in there." Smiling, she tried to lighten her voice. "Humor an old woman, okay?"

He grinned back, a gleam of mischief in his eyes. "You're not *that* old…yet!"

She acted as if she was going to slap him, and he dodged her open palm, laughing and racing up the stairs and into the house ahead of her, the door creaking shut before she could get there. His ringing amusement was the sweetest sound in the world.

It had taken months for him to brave even a smile after they'd fled, and Eva had understood completely. He'd seen both his parents murdered, and it wasn't like TV. They hadn't gotten up and walked away. He hadn't been killed himself because the shooters hadn't seen him. Huddled in the bushes, he'd managed to escape, his only description of the men too vague to be useful.

Eva had tried, though, pressing him beyond what she should have—asking him about that day time and time again. He'd only been able to say there were "lots" of men with guns and one "bad guy." She'd tried to understand the distinction, but all he could say was that the "bad guy" didn't have a gun. He'd simply directed the others who did. Daniel thought he might have seen this man once before, but he wasn't sure and couldn't remember where. Maybe at the office…maybe not. Eva was still trying to figure out how she could get her hands on a photo of Jack Finely.

Reaching the door, she paused and looked back down the street. It was seven o'clock, and the sidewalks were packed. She'd wanted to stop every few feet and turn around on her way home from the market, but she'd forced herself to keep going, stopping only twice to look behind her and check. Each time, she'd seen no sign of the tall, dark stranger, but his presence was almost palpable. He was there, in town, doing something, and Eva had the horrible feeling that that something involved her. Each time she had the thought, she pushed it away and told herself she was acting silly, but was she?

She went inside with a final nervous glance and slammed the door shut. Throwing the bolts, she listened, brass hitting brass, the sounds echoing against the marble staircase. She'd picked this house because it seemed safe. The garage was on the street level, the living quarters up two flights of stairs. In typical South American style, all the rooms were set around an interior courtyard.

Going upstairs with her groceries, Eva finally made it into the kitchen. Maria hurried to help, her arms outstretched to take the bag, her Spanish so rapid that even Eva caught only snatches…enough to know the woman was fussing at her for not letting *her* pick up the things at the market. Eva just shook her head. She'd tried to explain that Maria, her landlady, was doing too much for them already, but with a generous spirit that matched her dancing brown eyes, she'd said she only wanted to help.

And help she did. Whenever Eva couldn't be there, Maria kept a very close eye on Daniel. The tiny, dark-haired woman had been a godsend. Why sit and do nothing? she'd asked. Constantly scrubbing, mopping or cooking—in her own house or sometimes in Eva's—she'd become part of their routine, an unexpected bonus. She even seemed to understand Eva's determination to keep a low profile and not mingle with the locals. Best of all, she asked no questions. Like most people in Latin American countries, she had a short memory—it hadn't been that long ago when people who asked too many questions disappeared during the night.

Eva handed over the groceries to Maria, then walked quickly into the living room. Up one floor, it looked down onto the main street. Scanning the sidewalks and bumper-to-bumper cars, she saw nothing unusual. The vendors across the street were still hawking their knockoff T-shirts from America. METALLICA! one claimed. DON'T MESS WITH TEXAS, another read. And the Gypsies were at their usual posts, attempting to read palms. Everything seemed normal.

Pulling tight the exterior window shutters, Eva felt slightly better. Closed in somehow, a little safer. With her hand on the lock of the window, she couldn't help but think about home. Back then, her biggest worry had been concern where the safest place to park her car was. How things had changed!

After dinner, Eva found herself again at the window. She opened the shutters a crack. Thankfully, there was nothing unusual going on, but she couldn't shake the anxiety eating at her. Forcing herself away from the window, she glanced toward the stairs and Daniel's bedroom. He was her only family now. She had to do all she could to protect him…and she had to do it on her own.

A huge hole where her heart had been opened a little bit wider. Would there ever be a time when she didn't miss Thomas? When she didn't think of things to tell him, then realize he wasn't there to tell? When she didn't think of things she needed to ask his advice about, then remember he couldn't give it anymore?

And Sally… She'd been the sister Eva had never had. When Thomas had brought her home and introduced them, they'd become friends immediately. Sally's bright smile, her always happy attitude, her silly elephant collection… Eva's heart cramped as she remembered how happy her sister-in-law had been about the pregnancy. Buying an enormous teddy bear, she'd seated the stuffed animal in the empty chair at the breakfast table one morning and that's how she'd told Thomas they were expecting again. After two lost babies, she'd been positive this pregnancy was going to go perfectly.

Her throat closing, Eva got up from her chair and

moved restlessly back to the window. She'd taken a part-time job teaching English and she had papers to grade, plans to make, tasks to finish. But how could she, knowing that somewhere out there was a man? A man who looked too suspicious.

Gazing through the partially open shutters into the now empty street, she wondered again about the stranger. If she let her paranoia run wild, she could imagine a thousand scenarios, from Houston to Washington. Who had sent him? Finely was her first guess, but what about the other possibilities? Could he be from H.P.D. like Thomas had mentioned? What about the guy named Williams in Washington? Thomas hadn't really known him, either. Could he have sent the stranger? The more Eva thought about it, the more the questions brought her straight back to Finely. He'd sent him, she was sure. At night, when she couldn't sleep, she'd often imagine someone coming after her but not who they were. For some reason, that was her biggest fear. If she knew who they were, she could fight them, but a faceless, nameless enemy scared her the most. Now he had a face and she was still scared to death.

If Thomas's killers hadn't been hired by Jack, then they had to have been working directly for the men Thomas had been about to arrest—*los militares*—and that scenario would be even worse than Jack. They were professionals. They weren't about to let a seven-year-old kid and a woman interrupt the process of turning weapons from the Mexican army into money for themselves. Killing her to get to Daniel would be like swatting flies for them.

To reassure herself, as if counting the beads on a rosary, she listed all her precautions. No one could have possibly followed her here from Texas. She'd taken too many safeguards. No one here even knew her real name. Her papers listed "Evita Cantrell" as the mother of "Daniel Cantrell." And finally...the house was like a fortress. If the worst happened and someone actually managed to find out where she lived, he couldn't get in if he wanted to. There was one way in and one way out.

She stared out the window a little longer, then turned and went downstairs. After checking all the doors and windows the way she did every night, she finally assured herself they were locked in for the evening. Returning upstairs, she went into her own suite of rooms.

A long, hot bath eased some of her nervousness and a glass of wine did the rest. By the time she dried off, slipped into her nightgown and brushed her hair, Eva finally began to relax.

But she couldn't go to bed without looking outside one more time.

Gliding through the darkened house, bare feet against polished marble, she headed back to the window of the living room. The wind had picked up again and it sounded even fiercer than usual, beating against the exterior with angry gusts. The house complained, the creaks and moans making her feel as if she were on a ship. Banging against the glass, the shutters added their own rhythmic counterpoint, a clashing of wood against glass that rattled them both.

The first night they'd stayed in the house and the wind had taken hold, Eva had been terrified the windows were going to burst into a thousand pieces at any moment. The glass had held, though...and continued to. She'd almost gotten accustomed to the sound now. Still, tonight, the windows seemed in more danger than usual of shattering, and she understood completely. She felt the same way—brittle and on the point of explosion. She reached the window, pushed open a shutter, then looked down.

And her heart stopped.

He was standing at the end of the street, staring up at the house, his face in shadows, the wind tossing his hair. There was no question in her mind that it was the same man. His outline was unmistakable, his tall, virile body upright and imposing, his aura so strong and powerful it seemed to leap across the street and come straight at her. In another time and place, she would have been attracted, tempted...probably even seduced. Right now, all she felt was terror.

His steady stare was trained on the house.

CHAPTER THREE

SHE STARED BACK for just a second, then with a strangled cry, Eva whirled and ran across the room to the stairwell. She half fell, half ran down the stairs, her bare feet slapping against the marble until she was on the street level, her frantic eyes going to the brass locks, her fingers pressing against the bolts just to make sure they were thrown as far as they would go.

Convincing herself the locks would hold, she turned and ran back up the first flight of stairs and into the hall, her pulse still hammering. Taking the next set of stairs two at a time, she stumbled onto her hands and knees. Grabbing the wooden handrail, she propelled herself upward without fully regaining her balance, her heart now thumping so hard she thought it might escape from her chest. Careering through the upstairs hall, the wooden floors slick under her bare feet, she reached Daniel's room within seconds and threw open the door.

He was sleeping peacefully, one leg thrown outside the covers, a comic book spread across his chest.

She leaned weakly against the door frame, her chest rising and falling with each rasping breath, relief coming over her in a wave. He was safe—they were *both* safe.

But for how long?

Her chest still heaving, she turned and stumbled back down to the living room. Slowing only when she got to the window, she edged closer and closer until she could peer down into the street once more.

It was empty. Completely void of life. The only visible movement was an empty soda can rattling noisily down the pavement. Finally, even it disappeared, a last push of wind sending it around the corner.

Turning away from the window, she collapsed slowly, her back supported by the wall, her knees drawing up to her chest in an empty gesture of defense.

He knew where she lived.

Her mind refused to go past that obvious fact, and the words repeated themselves over and over in her mind like some kind of useless mantra. He knew where she lived. He. Knew. Where. She. Lived.

He knew.

She took several more deep breaths and tried to organize her thoughts. He was unquestionably looking for her. Otherwise, it was too much of a coincidence that he would be standing in front of her house at midnight staring at her windows. Should she grab Daniel and run? Tonight? Pack up what they could and disappear? Again? Closing her eyes, she rested her head against her knees. Where would they go? What should they do?

The questions overwhelmed her, and for the first time since they'd left Houston, Eva was hit with a sense of total helplessness. She couldn't do this on her own. That was all there was to it. She just couldn't do it.

Suddenly, the image of her brother's face filled the empty darkness behind her eyelids. *Stay calm. Don't do anything stupid. Think it through.* Then softer, more reassuring. *You've done great so far. You can handle this, too.* His voice was so real, so vital, her eyes shot open.

But of course the room was empty.

The words remained, though, and their gentle reassurance calmed her heart into a slower rhythm. She *had* protected them so far, and if she thought it through again, she'd be able to continue. She just had to think. Gradually, her mind began to work again, the options coming slowly into focus since there weren't too many to consider.

They could leave or they could stay.

Leaving would be complicated. Comodoro had an airport, but the transports were primarily military. Private planes landed and took off frequently, especially from other Latin American countries, but even if she could arrange something with one of those, departures were often canceled because of the weather. A commercial flight to Buenos Aires was scheduled but only once a week. Six long days stretched between tonight and the next plane out. A lot could happen in six days.

The bus? That was a possibility, she thought, hope

suddenly blooming. But only to get to the next village. No one would venture over the mountains to go farther this time of year. It was just impossible. The roads were horrible in the best of seasons—at this point, they were practically nonexistent.

The same applied even more so to her own vehicle. When they'd first arrived, she'd bought a used four-wheel-drive truck thinking it would have no trouble getting over the mountains. But that had been before the really cold weather had set in. She'd only recently learned how impossible that drive was. Even if they somehow managed to escape the stranger's watchful eyes and leave town, even if the roads were passable, they'd still get nowhere fast. In the pampas, the lonely stretches of desolate brown land outside of Comodoro, there were no Exxon stations with smiling attendants and clean washrooms.

Her shoulders slumped, and she stared up at the ceiling, her eyes filling again with hot, burning tears of frustration and fear. She'd brought the two of them to the ends of the earth to protect them. But that meant something else, too, something she hadn't fully recognized before. They were trapped. One contingency plan wasn't enough; one escape route wouldn't do. There was no way into Comodoro— *and* there was no way out.

"AUNT EVA? AUNT EVA?"

At the sound of Daniel's voice, Eva came to instantly. There was no waking up, no gentle arrival of awareness. One minute she was asleep and the next she was on full alert. Heart thumping, pulse leaping, her eyes shot to the window. She'd slept all night in a chair pulled close to the glass. Every hour or so, she'd blink awake and stare out into the empty darkness. He'd never returned, though.

Now it was light. The street was full of sunshine and busy shoppers. Pushing and hurrying, they packed the buckled sidewalks, children and bundles hanging from their arms. Weaving in and out of the crowd, a black-and-white dog chased a smaller tan one, both of them nipping and barking as they dodged cars and well-aimed kicks. Everything looked normal. Completely safe. There was no sign of the stranger.

For a single moment, Eva wondered if she'd dreamed the incident, but her doubts didn't last. The copper taste of fear still seemed to linger in her mouth, and the edgy nervousness she'd escaped in her sleep was already returning.

"What's wrong?" Daniel stood beside her chair, his hands clutching the upholstered arm. "Why'd you sleep here last night?"

Eva's eyes met Daniel's. Their green depths were full of anxiety. "It's nothing," she said calmly. "Everything's fine. I...I fell asleep reading and never got to bed. Silly, huh?"

He didn't believe her. She could see it in his eyes.

"It's okay," she said softly. "Don't worry."

He looked at her a second longer, then he nodded his head, turned and went into the kitchen. He had more questions, but he didn't really want to know the answers. He wanted her to tell him just what she had—that everything was fine and she was taking care of them both.

She wished she could do the same—pretend that things were all right—but she couldn't. Her job was to find out more, get more information. Lacking all the details, she simply couldn't uproot them again and feel it was the right decision. Walking into the kitchen she realized that sometime in the middle of the night she'd decided what she had to do. Her gaze flicked out the kitchen window toward the other end of town, toward the Austral Hotel.

There would be clues there. In his room.

Daniel's voice broke her concentration. "We're having a party at school today, Aunt Eva. This weekend's gonna be a holiday—*Pasquaz*...uh...*Pascale*...ummm...''

Turning to her nephew, Eva smiled. "It's Easter. *Pascua*.'' She reached out and straightened the collar of his shirt, then brushed his cheek with her hand. He'd had such a horrible past year, but he'd been such a trouper, he'd pulled her along with him. A lot of the time, when she'd thought she was going to lose it, he'd been the one who'd kept her going. Just like his dad would have. No complaints, no whines.

Suddenly, she wanted to reward him, even if it had to be in a trivial way. "Why don't I get us some eggs to decorate?'' she said. "We can hide them in the courtyard and have our own little celebration after Mass. What do you say?''

His eyes dipped to the floor. Obviously hesitating,

he pulled his bottom lip between his teeth. How many times had she seen Thomas do that very thing? Her heart twisted. He didn't answer.

"Daniel? Would you like that?"

"No," he said abruptly, his voice louder than usual. "That's a little-kid thing. I'm not little anymore."

Closing her eyes for just a moment, she remembered his face, his white, white face, beside the bushes that afternoon. It seemed like another lifetime...and it also seemed like yesterday.

"You're right," she said finally. "You aren't a little kid anymore...but it still might be fun, don't you think?"

He shook his head. "I don't want to have fun."

"You don't want to have fun? Why not?"

"I just don't. It wouldn't be right. I...I wish..." His eyes suddenly swam with tears. Angrily, he took a swipe at them and sniffed hard. Turning away from her, he stood at the window, his posture stiff and unyielding.

Her heart aching, she went to stand beside him. "I know what you wish," she said softly, her own voice catching as she put her hands on his rigid shoulders. "I wish the same thing, but they're gone. And it's up to us to go on without them." Kneeling down to his level, she turned Daniel around and looked into his eyes. "We have to do what they'd want us to do. You know that, don't you?"

His eyes darkening, he sniffled and didn't answer.

"Your mom and dad loved you more than anything in the world, and if they were standing here right now, they'd tell you that. They'd also tell you that part of living is having fun. And just because you do that, it doesn't mean you don't still miss them.''

She couldn't help herself. She reached out and pulled him toward her. Stiffening slightly, he offered a token resistance, then melted against her, his sturdy arms going around her neck as though he couldn't control them. They stayed that way for a few moments, then Eva spoke.

"Hiding Easter eggs is a tradition," she said, her voice muffled as she spoke against his sweet-smelling hair. "You know what a tradition is, don't you?"

He pulled back slightly and stared at her, Thomas's eyes in a little boy's face. "It's something you do over and over?"

"That's right. And I bet if you think hard, you can remember a tradition your mom always made sure was done at Easter."

He twisted his mouth again as he thought. "Well…she'd always paint my name on an egg and hide it somewhere easy for me to find. Like in the mailbox in the front yard."

Eva smiled. "Then let's do that. I'll paint one with your name on it and—"

"I'll do one with *your* name," he said seriously.

"It's a deal." Putting her hand out, Eva waited for him to shake it.

He looked down at her outstretched fingers, then

slowly he put his hand in hers. Pumping once, he said, "Deal." He tried to smile, but the expression faltered. "I still wish they were here, though."

"I do, too, sweetie. I do, too." Her heart bursting with love for the boy who was her only family now, Eva stared at him and knew one thing for sure. She'd do whatever it took to protect this child. He'd seen things no little boy should ever have to see, had dealt with things no youngster should be forced to face. He deserved better, and she was going to make sure he got it.

SITTING AT THE CAFÉ on the corner, Michael sipped his scalding coffee and watched the woman before him. She was sweeping the floor, a battle she clearly waged every day and just as clearly lost. The minute she'd get the dust into a pile, someone would open the door and walk in, then the wind would send it swirling. She'd start all over again, her eyes never leaving the floor, her methodical movements almost hypnotic. Her determination was admirable, but it was totally useless. She was fighting a losing battle.

Just like Eva Solis.

The distance, the wind, the darkness, had all separated them last night...but not far enough. He'd still been able to feel her fear as plainly as if it had reached out and grabbed him. She knew he was here. She couldn't help but suspect more, especially after seeing him again, but there was no place for her to run. And if she did, it didn't matter.

He'd found her here. He could find her anywhere.

Picking up his coffee, he took a sip and grimaced, it was as strong as it was hot. Her look of fright had revealed her complete and total shock. She'd thought she was safe, believed she'd hidden her cub in the deepest den possible. It must have been a rude awakening for her, he thought without satisfaction. She'd tried so hard...and this is what it came down to. A strange man stalking her, knowing the chances and fearing the worst.

His mind flicked backward in time, flashed on an image he knew he'd never outrun. His wife, Amy, dying in his arms. Had she experienced that same fear, felt that rising tide of nausea, known she was looking at death?

He gulped the bitter coffee, a penance for his thoughts, and let his eyes return to the school across the street. The little boy had gone in early that morning, standing in line with all the other kids, his schoolbooks in a backpack, his clothing covered by the white smock that passed for a uniform here. The building itself was pitiful. Broken windows, dust-filled doorways, walls that hadn't seen paint in years.

The classrooms were so crowded the kids had to go in shifts—one group in the morning, the other in the afternoon. The lucky ones got private tutoring when they weren't in class. The woman behind the desk at the hotel had explained it all to him last night. Her own son went to the English Institute after school, she'd said proudly. He was learning English so he could have a better life.

They had teachers from everywhere, she'd chattered, cutting her gaze to him and mistaking his interest. Buenos Aires, Córdoba...they even had a new one. *La canadiense,* she'd explained, who lived on Pelligrini Street. *Inteligente y muy linda, también.* A Canadian woman. Smart and very beautiful.

It was exactly what he'd expected. Her stash wouldn't last forever, and she'd had to make money somehow. Teaching English was the perfect answer.

"*¿Señor? ¿Más café?*"

Michael looked up. "*No, gracias.*"

The man standing before him, holding the coffee-pot, was apparently the proprietor. Only the owners handled the money, and he'd been behind the cash register since Michael had walked in. His curiosity had gotten the better of him, though, and he finally approached Michael. Hesitating now, he smiled shyly. "You are here for the shooting?" He made a gun with his finger and thumb, pointing it toward the street. "Bang, bang! You are the hunter, no?"

Looking up, Michael smiled, the irony of the man's question not at all lost. "*Sí, señor.* I am the hunter."

THE PHONE BOOTH outside the Austral was actually working for a change. Eva gripped the filthy receiver and held it up to her ear, as far away as she could keep it and still hear.

"*El americano,*" she said, slurring her Spanish as much as she could to make it sound more Argentinean. "Is he there? I need to speak with him. He's in room..." Security in Argentina wasn't what it was in the United States. Knowing the operator would supply it, Eva hesitated as if she were looking up his number.

"Room 305," the helpful operator answered. "But he's gone out right now, *señora.*"

"And when do you expect him back?"

"He didn't say."

"Thank you."

"De nada."

With a grim smile, Eva hung up the phone, then slung open the door of the telephone booth and sprinted up the block. Turning, she hastened along the street the hotel faced in the rear. Slipping inside from the parking area, she went quickly to the service stairs and took them two at a time. She and Daniel had stayed here when they'd first arrived. She knew the hotel as well as she knew her own house.

Once in the hallway, the rest of it was easy. The maids were chattering down the hall, an open door telling her which room they were cleaning. She eased into the tiny closet off the hall that served as their supply closet, snatched up a smock and thrust her arms through the sleeves. After tying a cotton scarf over her head and perching a pair of reading glasses on her nose, she took a quick look in the cloudy mirror hanging crookedly on the wall. As far as disguises went, it was pretty pitiful, but for now, it was the best she could do. The master key was exactly where it had been when she and Daniel had stayed there—on a battered brass hook by the door. She grabbed it along with an extra cleaning bucket, then with a determined step she headed toward room 305.

THROWING A FEW PESOS on the table, Michael nonchalantly rose from his chair in the café and headed out. Walking slowly, he passed the elementary school, then headed for the English Institute. He wanted to make sure he knew where it was. When things got hot—and they would—she might try to hide there.

He wasn't going to underestimate her.

He pushed his way through the crowded streets and ignored the gritty wind hammering at his back. On Cinco de Mayo Street, he found the institute. Obviously a former residence, it now looked no more prosperous than any other building on the street. Peeling paint, cracked windows, a sidewalk that was missing a large chunk. As he stood outside the metal fence marking the building's boundary, a sudden explosion of barking startled him. He jerked his head this way and that, but saw no dog. Finally, it registered. The sound was coming from overhead.

He lifted his eyes and instantly spotted the huge German shepherd. His paws gripping the upper railing that ran around the perimeter of the flat roof, the animal was peering over the edge of the building and looking down at Michael, snarling and showing his teeth. His canine ferocity held warning, a warning Michael couldn't ignore.

They locked stares for just a minute, then the dog's head disappeared behind the rim of the roof. He was

out of sight for now, but Michael could hear the click
of his nails as he nervously patrolled his airy com-
pound. Shaking his head, Michael started down the
street. It was time to check in with Houston. He
headed toward the Austral.

ROOM 305 WAS a "suite." By Argentinean standards,
that meant two rooms and two bathrooms, each a
tight fit for even one person. The entire setup could
easily have fitted inside a single Holiday Inn room,
with plenty of space left over. Eva was familiar with
the room. It was the hotel's only suite. She and Daniel had had it when they'd been here.

She quickly locked the door behind her and began
her search. Information. That's what she wanted. Papers, a passport, anything that might give a name to
the man and some idea of his purpose in Comodoro.
She went straight to his suitcase.

A half-dozen shirts, neatly folded and pressed, lay
on top of the same number of pants. The labels were
American, just as she'd assumed. The satisfaction she
felt at being right was underscored with a leap in
anxiety. Under the top layer of clothing, she saw
more of the same—pajamas, shoes, socks, under-
wear—everything American and commonplace. He
could have bought them in New York, Los Angeles
or anywhere in between. The only thing they told
her, besides their country of origin, was that he had
money. Everything was of the finest quality. Her fingers lingered on the cuff of one of the shirts. The
fabric was soft and clean, silky to the touch.

She couldn't help herself. She picked the shirt up and brought it to her face, closing her eyes and drawing in a deep breath. It even smelled like home, she thought with a sudden burst of agony. The water in Comodoro was so dirty that clothes never got this soft, this clean. She'd become so used to it, she hadn't realized the difference until now. She breathed in again, and a different scent registered, the scent of a man. It lingered in the folds of the clean shirt like a fingerprint—unique and distinctive, the stranger's alone. Exotic and personal.

Opening her eyes, she dropped the shirt and slammed the suitcase shut. She was losing time, acting nutty like this. Hurrying to the other side of the room where a small desk sat in one corner, she began to open and close the drawers. They were empty—not even a scrap of paper. Beside the desk, she noticed a trash can. Grabbing it, she stared inside, but it was just as barren.

Her frustration began to grow, but she ignored it and headed for the bathrooms. One was untouched, but the larger of the two, the one with a tub filling the entire end of it, had a small black kit sitting on the counter. The case was made of soft, sensual leather, and her fingers trembled as they unzipped it. Feeling awkward at touching such an intimate, personal item, she dumped the contents of the case on the marble countertop, then tossed it to one side.

A razor, soap, toothpaste. A black comb, deodorant, a plastic reel of dental floss. Nothing unusual. Scattering the various items around with her hand,

Eva stared until her eyes picked out something un-expected. A small plastic rectangle about four inches square. Picking it up, she saw immediately what it was—a closed picture frame. With her fingernail, she popped open the latch and the top fell back.

A blond woman stared up at her, a *beautiful* blond woman. Dressed casually in a sleeveless tank and shorts, she was sitting outside on the grass, a bank of candy pink azaleas exploding in riotous color be-hind her. Eva recognized the bushes at once—she'd had a great yard back home. They were Pretty Bells, midseason bloomers unique to Texas. They wouldn't grow anywhere else. The photo had to have been taken there.

Eva's eyes returned to the woman's face. Framed by her long, fair hair, her cheeks were high and sculpted, her lips full and soft. Everything about her seemed gentle and quiet, an air of fragility overlying her image. She was the kind of woman men loved to love. She'd make them feel strong and protec-tive—she'd make them feel like men.

Eva's fingers tightened on the frame, an unbidden sweep of something almost like envy coming over her. She'd known women like this back in college and marveled at their skill. Beautiful Southern belles who could wrap their men around their little fingers as easily as they curled their glossy hair. Eva could easily imagine the woman in this photo smiling up at the tall, dark stranger and bringing him to his knees.

Eva gathered up the scattered toiletries and replaced them in the case, tossing the picture back inside, as well. She knew more now than she had a minute earlier. He had a wife…or a sweetheart. And they lived or had visited Texas some time in the spring. It wasn't much, but it was a beginning.

A beginning that scared her.

She returned to the bedroom, glancing nervously at her watch. She'd been in the room ten minutes. Fifteen was her limit, she'd decided before going in. Any longer was too much of a risk. Her eyes sweeping over the second bedroom, she suddenly spied something she'd missed before. The edge of a black case was peeking out from under the bed skirt. She crossed the room, then dropped quickly to her knees and pulled on the case.

It was heavy, but she kept pulling. A second later, when the box was completely revealed, her heart tripped against her chest. It was almost five feet long and approximately three feet wide, hard-sided with a sturdy handle on top.

Glancing nervously over her shoulder toward the door, Eva reached out, the brass locks cold and hard beneath her shaking fingers. She pressed against them and prayed. A moment later, when the locks released, the sound was piercing, the noise of it echoing in her mind like a cannon shot. She grimaced and looked back over her shoulder—the sound must have reached the hallway. The door stayed closed and the only other thing she heard was her heart thumping away inside her chest.

She took a deep breath and returned to her task.

Slowly lifting the lid, she gasped softly and put her hand over her mouth in shock. Dark foam, custom fitted into the metal interior, held a series of cutout compartments, each filled with the various parts of a gleaming, high-powered rifle. A Remington 700 bolt-action with a laser sight and scope, to be specific. In Washington, where she'd once done some special Treasury training, they'd performed target practice with the .30-06.

The weapon of choice for U.S. Marine snipers.

Eva rocked back on her heels and took a deep, shaky breath. Who in the hell was this guy? *What* in the hell was he doing here?

Seemingly of their own volition, her fingers reached out and traced the hard metal of the barrel. It was cold, and an icy shiver of fear traveled from her hand to her arm, the sensation lodging near her heart, now a frozen lump she couldn't ignore. This man was here to kill. A gun like this wasn't used for anything else.

The metallic taste of anxiety replaced all her other emotions. Staring blankly into the case, she knew she had to do something, but what? A storm of thoughts went through her head, then slowly, it registered that she was looking at more than just a gun. Tucked inside one corner of the case, a small square of white paper, just the corner revealed, beckoned to her.

She reached out and gently tugged the paper out from its hiding place, the raised lettering and shape giving away its purpose before she even read it. A business card. Her pulse accelerated, a racetrack of adrenaline, as she brought the card up to read.

Before her eyes could focus, a sudden noise sounded behind her, out in the hall. She recognized the clicking sound—a key going into a lock. Her heart crashed against her ribs, but she had no time to think. All she could do was react. She slammed the top of the case down, snapped the locks and shoved it back under the bed.

She jumped to her feet and grabbed her bucket.

The door slowly swung open.

The stranger stood before her.

CHAPTER FOUR

MOMENTARY SURPRISE darkened his eyes, but other than that, the man before her didn't react. He said nothing and did nothing, his expression a granite mask she couldn't read. The effect was chilling, and she flinched, a cold wave of fear washing over her. She'd seen this kind of empty look before, and immediately Eva knew she'd made a tragic mistake by coming to the hotel.

This man *was* a professional. He had to be.

If he wasn't, God help them both. Something had put that emptiness in his eyes, and if it hadn't been training, then it had to have been something terrible, something awful, something so bad he'd had to push everything else out of his psyche to get rid of it. There were guys like this at the office, guys who'd lost their partners or their families, or their own ability to say no. Guys who were suffering. For some unexplained reason, the image of the photo in the bathroom flashed into Eva's mind, the picture of the blond woman who'd looked so fragile and beautiful. Was she behind this bleakness?

Her fingers gripping the cleaning bucket, her heart pounding, Eva ducked her head and sputtered an apology in Spanish. She couldn't tell if he understood or not, but she wasn't about to hang around and figure it out. With sweat breaking out across her forehead, she brushed past a chest as hard as the wall and almost as wide. She caught a fleeting impression of the same scent that was on the clothing in his suitcase, and her stomach knotted. A moment later, she was fleeing down the hall.

MICHAEL LISTENED to Eva's footsteps pounding down the carpeted corridor. When he'd been a kid, his father had unintentionally trapped a fox in their garage. Michael had opened the side door, and a blur of red had streaked past his legs, startling him into a heart-ripping fear. Turning, he'd watched it flee, a flash of fur disappearing into the thick underbrush of their Montana farm. The animal had expected death but gotten redemption, and it was running to make sure things stayed that way.

The comparison was obvious—but Eva's reprieve, unlike the fox's, was only going to be temporary.

Entering the room, he had to acknowledge one thing. He admired her courage. Breaking into his room and searching it was pretty gutsy. His unexpected arrival hadn't made things easy, either. She'd kept her head, though, stayed calm and been smart.

He should have taken the opportunity to grab her and do his job, but that wasn't how he wanted this one to go down. He wanted to take his time and draw her out, to see who she might be seeing, to learn what she might know. He felt, for some reason, he wasn't getting the full story from Houston, and he needed more information. For his own protection, if nothing else.

He checked his suitcase and the kit in the bathroom. She'd looked through everything, that much was obvious. A moment's anger tumbled through him when he noticed Amy's picture frame half-open. He picked it up intending to snap it shut, but opened it instead. His dead wife's blue eyes looked up at him. Their open friendliness was the complete opposite of Eva Solis's dark and troubled gaze. The two women couldn't have been more different.

He snapped the picture shut and moved back into the bedroom. He picked up the phone and asked for a long-distance line.

Miraculously, it came through—thirty minutes later.

"I've found her," he said without preamble.

"And the kid?"

"He's with her, no problem."

"Where are you?"

For the first time, Michael hesitated. He didn't like the anxious tone he heard. It made him uneasy. "Let's just say she found a good spot and leave it at that. I'll give you the details when we get there."

"All right." The answer was curt and impatient. "When are you coming back?"

"Next week. That's the earliest flight."

"That's not soon enough. Find another way."

"There is no other way."

"There's got to be another way, dammit. This woman's life depends on it."

"That may be, but the facts stay the same." Michael's voice was flat, unequivocal. "I can't get them out until next week."

"You're sure?"

"I'm doing my job and I'm doing it well. We'll get there as soon as possible."

"You won't lose her?"

Warning bells went off in his head, a jangle he couldn't ignore. "I've never lost anyone yet, have I?"

"There's always a first time."

He turned his head and looked out the hotel window. The wind had picked up again, violent bursts actually flexing the glass within its metal frame. "Not for me," he answered. "Not anymore."

THE ICE IN HER DRINK clinked against the crystal sides of the glass. Eva brought her other hand up to steady the tumbler of Scotch, but it hardly mattered. She continued to shake, her knees actually trembling one against the other.

What in heaven's name had she thought she was doing?

With both hands, she brought the glass to her lips and took a long gulp, the liquor burning a fiery path all the way down to her stomach. She kept one eye on the road and one on the sidewalk, looking out the window of the living room to the street below. She didn't think he'd recognized her, but who knew for sure? Above the rim of her drink, she studied the faces hurrying past her house. None was familiar.

Her question repeated itself. What had she been thinking? She was a translator, for God's sake, not Mata Hari. Had she really assumed she'd find out all about the man? She fished the white business card out of the pocket of her jeans and laid it on the table before her, staring at it once again, the words already memorized.

Michael Masters, Sales Manager
Specialized Oil Field Equipment

Underneath his name there was a phone number. With a 713 area code. Houston, Texas.

She brought the drink up and pressed the glass against her forehead, the cool wetness doing nothing to relieve her fevered brain. Was that his real name? Did he really work in the oil business? What in the hell did he need a gun like that for if he was only an equipment salesman?

Was it just a coincidence he was from Houston?

A queasy feeling of anxiety camped itself in her stomach. She simply didn't know what to think. If he *was* a professional, he should have recognized her, and if he had, then it made no sense for him to let her go. Maybe her disguise had been better than she'd thought.

And maybe he was just a salesman. A salesman who took midnight walks. A salesman who traveled with a .30-06. A salesman with stone-cold eyes who could turn her knees into mush with a single look.

Stranger things had been known to happen.

But she couldn't remember when.

Staring at the card, she felt her resolve flicker. Paranoia wasn't smart. It made you make mistakes and do stupid things. Then you'd create even more problems for yourself by trying to back up and rethink. How many times had Thomas told her this? *Trust your instincts, not your fears.* He'd repeated this time and time again. But she had no instincts on this one—all she had were fears.

She took another gulp from the glass. The simplest thing to do was call Houston. She'd phone the "Specialized Oil Field Equipment" company and just find out if a Michael Masters actually worked for them. She'd be on and off in a matter of seconds; a trace could never be done.

Then she'd know for sure. If it was a bogus office that Jack had rigged up, they'd mix the truth with lies. They'd be vague, probably confirm that Michael Masters was a sales manager, but probably not tell her exactly where he was. Most likely, they'd try to keep her on the line, to get as much information from her as they could, do anything to draw out the conversation. They'd know that she was onto him, but that would be all.

And if he really was a salesman, then she'd find that out as well.

Turning, she looked at the clock on the bookcase. It was too late to make the call tonight, but she'd do it first thing in the morning.

Exhausted and spent, both physically and mentally, she lifted the glass to her lips and drained the contents.

DANIEL STOOD BEFORE HER, his face scrunched up, his eyes narrowed into tiny slits. "I don't care what you say—I'm not some kind of baby. I can go to school by myself."

"Normally, that's absolutely right." Picking up some homemade cookies, Eva wrapped them in plastic and placed them inside Daniel's backpack as she spoke. "But normal is not something in our lives right now. I'm going to walk with you to school and I want you staying there until you see me out front. We'll come home together."

"Why?"

She didn't really want to explain, but she didn't have any other option, did she? It was a fine line she walked between keeping him scared and keeping him alert. She dropped to her knees to be at his level. "I've seen someone in town I don't recognize. I'm figuring out who he is as we speak. I don't want you frightened, but I think it's best if we walk together for a while."

He looked at her sharply, fear rising into his eyes. "Is he here? The bad guy and the killers? Did they find us?"

Keeping her voice low and reassuring, she spoke softly. "I didn't say that—I said there was someone here I didn't recognize, and I want to know more about him before I can feel comfortable about your being alone."

She started to go on, but she stopped. They hadn't talked about the murders for quite a while. At first, it had been their only topic of conversation, but as the months passed and Danny seemed to recover a bit, she'd been more than happy to let the bad memories fade. She had to bring it up now, though. It was too important not to.

She looked down, then raised her face to his. "Danny, that day…that day at the cabin… How much do you remember about the bad guy and the others—the ones who had guns?"

He bit his lip. "What do you mean?"

"Do you think you'd recognize any of them if you saw them again?"

"I…I don't know. It happened so fast, and I was scared. All I remember is that he was really, really tall. Probably as tall as Michael Jordan." He swallowed hard and blinked. "I think he might have had black hair, too, but I'm not sure." His eyes grew huge. "Do you think this is him? Here? Right now?"

"I don't know who this stranger is," she answered in a matter-of-fact voice. "It's been a while since we left, and I was just wondering if you thought you could recognize the man after such a long time, that's all."

His voice began to tremble as he spoke. "Maybe we shouldn't go to school at all. Maybe we should just stay home."

"That isn't necessary." Although she'd actually considered it. "But you need to be careful. Look out for strangers and be aware of where you are. You remember what to do if someone approaches you, don't you?''

''Scream, then run.''

''That's right. Then you call me. Don't—''

''Don't go off with anyone no matter what they say.''

''Exactly.'' She smiled and tried to erase the fear so evident on his face. ''It'll be okay. Really.''

He nodded, then dropped his gaze, his feet shuffling against the floor. Something was still bothering him, but what? She stared at him, a wave of inadequacy threatening to swamp her. She knew nothing about kids, absolutely nothing. Back home, there were resources, psychologists, therapists. Here she had nothing, not even experience. She and her ex had always planned on starting a family, but he'd decided to start an affair instead. She still wanted children of her own, but not without a husband. Suddenly that seemed as if it would never happen. Not in this lifetime.

''What is it?'' she asked softly. ''Are you scared?''

He shook his head, his voice muffled. ''The other kids will laugh at me.'' He looked up. ''Only babies get walked to school.''

She took a deep breath of relief. *This* she could handle. ''They won't even know. If it makes you feel better, I'll stay behind you. No one will even know we're together.''

''How far?''

She looked at him in puzzlement. "How far what?"

"How far back will you stay?"

"How far would make you comfortable?"

His lips came together and twisted. "A mile?"

She shook her head.

"Half a mile?"

"Try five feet."

He looked at her with a hopeful expression. "How about six?"

She waited a moment as if she was considering his last offer, then she spoke. "You drive a hard bargain, but I guess I can live with that. Six feet it is." They shared their customary handshake, then she put a hand on his shoulder, sudden emotion thickening her voice. "I know it's been hard, Danny, but we'll get through this together. I promise you that."

He met her gaze with his Thomas eyes. "It'll be okay," he said with reassurance. "You'll take care of us just fine." Patting her on the back, he gave her a swift hug, then turned and ran upstairs.

Standing up, Eva looked out the window over the sink, a cold knot of worry lodging in her chest. She prayed to God Daniel was right.

THEY WALKED QUICKLY down the street. Just as she'd promised, Eva stayed several feet behind Daniel. It wasn't the promised six, but he'd never know the difference. She had to be closer to him than that—if Michael Masters appeared out of the blue, she had to be close enough to do something. What that "something" was, she didn't quite know.

She pushed ahead, early-morning shoppers crowding the sidewalks. The usual combination of wind, swirling dust and too many bodies made the going difficult, but she managed to keep Daniel in sight. They crossed a busy intersection, the cars whizzing by and honking continuously, the smell of diesel fuel mixing with the standard miasma floating up from the curb. A sudden burst of wind shot dust into Eva's eyes with painful, stinging accuracy. She blinked rapidly, the tears blurring her vision of Daniel only a few feet ahead.

She blinked again.

And screamed.

CHAPTER FIVE

THE CAR, COMING out of nowhere, going against the light, burst into her vision. Its sudden and unexpected appearance stopped her heart as if it had already run her down. Shooting through the intersection on two wheels, turning with a deadly squeal of tires, it rounded the corner...and headed straight for Daniel.

Eva launched herself with a shriek, extending her arm toward him. She caught the edge of his smock—then felt it slip through her grasp. Falling to the sidewalk empty-handed, she felt the sting of the uneven concrete bite into her face. She scrambled sideways on her hands and feet and ignored the painful scrape. Immediately, she stumbled upright and pushed herself toward the curb as brakes squealed and rubber screeched against dusty, slick pavement. A loud, dull crash, then the sudden sickening sound of metal grinding against metal almost brought her to her knees. The instant of silence that followed was almost more horrifying than the previous sounds. Eva's breath stopped, then around her people began to yell, one voice rising above the others—her own.

"Let me through, dammit. Let me through!" She realized she was speaking English. Switching to Spanish, she started over and began to push her way to the front of the crowd, ignoring the grunts she heard as she thrust her elbows and knees ahead of her. She reached the curb a second later, and that's when she saw Daniel.

Standing on the other side of the street.

A buzz sounded faintly in her ears, and things started to go black. Taking a deep, steadying breath, Eva shot a momentary glance toward the wreck, then ran across the street and scooped the little boy into her arms.

Almost hysterical, half with relief, half with residual fear, she wrapped her arms around his body. She couldn't tell who was trembling more—him or her. "Are you all right?" she asked needlessly. "I thought... Oh, God, Danny...I thought that car had hit you!"

He nodded, his eyes two round disks of fear, filling his whole face. "I—I thought it was going to, too! I jumped out of the way—just in the nick of time! It was headed right toward me. Did it hit someone else?"

"I don't know." Keeping her arm around him, she twisted her head to see better.

Steam was pouring from the engine of one of the cars, a dying hiss. From the other came loud moans. She tried to get a closer look at the drivers, but it was impossible with the gathering crowds. They'd witnessed several wrecks since coming to Comodoro—but they'd never had a call as close as this one.

She turned back to the little boy in her arms and

rested her forehead against his. Closing her eyes, she asked, "Do you want to go home?"

She felt him shake his head, and she opened her eyes.

"I'm fine." He met her gaze. "Really."

"You sure?"

He nodded. "I'd like to go to school. It was just a silly wreck, that's all."

Eva stood up, her legs barely supporting her, and within five minutes, they were at his school. Running up the steps as if nothing had happened, Daniel turned and risked a quick wave in her general direction. Smiling, she nodded once, then watched him disappear inside, a stream of white-smocked children quickly closing the space behind him.

Her heart still galloping, she didn't even want to think about what had just happened, but she had to. Ignoring the sweep of nausea threatening to overcome her, she hurriedly began to retrace her steps. She'd wanted to stay and find out more, but not with Daniel by her side. All she could do was return.

Was it just a "silly wreck"…or something else?

She swallowed hard and forced herself to think. The cars had not been familiar, and the momentary glance she'd gotten of the driver had been only a blur. A man…definitely a man. Dark hair…maybe. Sunglasses? She couldn't tell. Young, old, ugly, handsome—no other details had registered.

By the time she reached the scene of the accident, the cars were gone. Disappointment washed over her. Stopping at a few of the nearby shops, she asked a few questions, but no one had seen anything. Typical.

After a while, there was nothing else she could do. She turned and headed in the direction of the English Institute. Daniel would be safe at school, of that much she was sure. She'd told the school officials when she'd registered him that her husband was violent and wanted custody. They had instructions to call her if anyone showed up besides her. She had faith in the system. She had to, even though things weren't quite as structured in this country as they were back home.

But the thought brought her back full circle to Michael Masters. She'd gotten up an hour early to phone Houston, her hand trembling, her mouth so dry she could barely speak. Which, as it turned out, hadn't even been necessary. Her phone line was dead—an every-other-day occurrence in Comodoro. She wondered briefly if someone had cut the lines, then dismissed the notion entirely. Not having a working phone was more normal than the opposite here. She'd have to call from school, if its lines were up.

Still trembling, Eva opened the creaking metal gate in front of the institute and gave a quick glance around her before stepping inside its dim interior. The building wrapped itself around her, dark and creepy. It had been someone's home before becoming a school, and she never failed to wonder how anyone could have lived in such depressing quarters. The few windows that fronted the street were small and always dirty, while the ones that faced the back looked directly onto a brick wall. Her classroom was on the third floor.

Avoiding the elevator, she jogged up the stairs and went directly to the offices. They were on the same floor as her classroom. She pushed open the door, a haze of cigarette smoke coming from the secretary's desk. Before she could even ask, the woman started complaining. The phones were down here, too.

Exasperation came over Eva in a swift, dark tide, but she pushed it away. This kind of thing was to be expected in this part of the world. If you assumed otherwise, frustration would be your constant companion. She'd have to try again later. Still shaky from the accident, she returned to the hall, then made her way to her classroom and stepped inside.

Coat hooks lined one wall. Shedding her own, she hung up the navy pea jacket and crossed the small room to her desk. Her classroom would be full any moment, and even as she had the thought, the first student came in.

Most mornings passed quickly, but today's session seemed to take forever. Despite her intentions not to, Eva continually glanced at her watch and counted the minutes. She even sent a child down to the office once to check the phones. His answer had been just what she expected. *No funciona.* They weren't working.

The morning finally dragged to a close, and she almost beat the children out the door. Daniel's classes finished thirty minutes after hers. If she hurried, she could make it to the *teléfono público* on the corner. The phone company operated a series of phones in a building next door to their offices. Amazingly enough, the lines there *never* went down. The prices were exorbitant, but today that didn't matter.

Dodging the street vendors and urchins playing catch, she ran toward the corner. The wind had momentarily died down, but it had left its daily legacy—ankle-deep trash cluttering the sidewalk. Kicking aside a tattered newspaper and a clump of candy wrappers, she threw open the door to the building a minute before the place closed for the midday break. The attendant was actually standing, keys in hand, beside the window. She frowned violently at Eva, but she ignored the woman and walked up to the first kiosk.

"No funciona." Without interest, the bored young woman behind the desk delivered the words. "Come back after lunch," she advised. "They might be ready then...and they might not."

A catch developed in Eva's throat. "But...but they always work here—"

"No funciona," the girl repeated. She actually looked at her fingernails in a classic parody of apathy.

"But—"

Behind the kiosk, a chime sounded, identifying the hour. Without another glance in Eva's direction, the girl reached out and drew a shade down over the glass. A second later, her heels clicked away.

"Ahem..." The woman at the front door looked

at Eva expectantly, and there was nothing else to do. She turned and went out onto the dusty sidewalk.

After lunch meant two more hours. Two more hours of worry. Two more hours of anxiety.

Two more hours of not knowing who Michael Masters really was.

Daniel was waiting for her just inside the door to his school. As soon as he saw her, he shot outside, a big smile on his face, the early morning's scare already forgotten. Chattering about his lessons, he'd obviously dealt with the situation in his own inimitable way. He continually amazed her with his switches between maturity and little boy insecurities. That's what it was like, she'd finally decided, to be seven years old.

Smiling down at him, she tried to put aside her worries. "Let's eat lunch at Micky D's. What do you say?"

His face lit up. "I say great! Let's go!"

He skipped ahead of her a few feet, his backpack swinging against his shoulders. Micky D's was the name they'd given to the coffee shop near their house. It wasn't anything like the fast-food places back home, but Daniel didn't seem to mind. He'd even told her once that he liked it better than McDonald's—no one here cared when the street dogs wandered in for a handout.

They reached the small café in minutes. The door standing open, Eva walked in, Daniel at her side. He ran up to the counter and started to place his order, but she followed more slowly, her eyes going over the scattered tables and chairs...just to make sure.

And that's when she saw him.

MICHAEL WATCHED EVA freeze, a deer-in-the-headlights look coming over her expression. A gamut of emotions followed, her beautiful eyes and face shifting expressions as she rapidly appeared to be examining and rejecting her options. She had on the same coat, but this time, instead of jeans, she wore a short skirt underneath it, all curves and dips. He felt his gut tighten. She was beautiful *and* smart *and* gutsy. This assignment was turning difficult.

She made her decision quickly. Moving farther into the café as casually as she could, she went up to the boy and spoke to him softly. He began to object. Her eyes slipped over to Michael, then away—fast. She wouldn't make a scene, he realized with approval. Exactly what he would have done.

Smiling pleasantly, she seemed to acquiesce to the child, and they both gave their orders to the owner. A second later, before they could even move away from the counter, a group of giggling schoolchildren ran inside, their white smocks flapping open, their books banging against their sides. Spotting Eva and the boy, they ran directly to her, swarming all over them both. "Señora Cantrell! Daniel!" they cried, laughing and teasing. "How are you? What are you doing?"

They spoke to her in English.

With a stricken expression, she lifted her stunning

black eyes and met his stare, her throat moving convulsively. Tension rose from her like a cloud. She struggled for a minute, then managed to get her fear under control. She answered the children in English, then shooed them away. Laughing, they gathered up Daniel and pulled him toward a video machine in one corner of the restaurant.

Michael made up his mind a moment later.

It wasn't his normal practice to get friendly with his quarry, but this woman was too close to the edge and looking over. One little push, and she was going to run—whether she had a chance for escape or not. He didn't want to make his job harder than it had to be. Michael rose from his table and went directly to hers.

Stopping in front of her, he smiled. "I couldn't help but hear," he said, tilting his head toward the students now at the counter. "You were speaking English."

She hesitated, then smiled. "That's true," she answered. "We speak English."

"And without an accent."

She nodded, then licked her lips. "We're from Canada."

"Is that right?" He made himself friendly, Texas-style friendly. "I travel up there quite a bit. I'm in the oil business. Go to Calgary. Where in Canada you from?"

"Peterborough," she said without hesitation. "You probably wouldn't know it. It's—"

"In Ontario," he answered with an almost apologetic smile. "I'm a geography nut." He held out his hand. "Michael Masters, by the way. And you're…"

"Eva Cantrell." They shook hands, then stared at each other a few more seconds. She tried to stay still, but her eyes gave her away. They shot toward the corner, then came nervously back to Michael. When she spoke, her voice was steady. "What brings you to Comodoro, Mr. Masters?"

"Michael, please." Without answering, he pulled out the extra chair at their table and started to sit down. He stopped halfway. "You don't mind, do you?" he asked. "It's just so nice to hear someone speak English for a change."

There was nothing else she could do. She inclined her head. "Of course…" she said faintly.

"Well, like I said, I'm in the oil business. Work for a firm outta Houston. I've been here before on business, but this time I'm here for something else."

She stared at him. At the base of her throat, her pulse kept up an uneven rhythm. It was a mesmerizing sight, the soft white skin, the faint blue tracery of veins beneath.

"And what might that be?"

"I'm hunting."

She went still, seemed to even stop breathing. "And what do you hunt?"

"I'm looking for something special this time," he answered softly. "Something unique." Before he could go on, he felt a presence at his side. Turning

slowly, he stared directly into Daniel Solis's bright
green eyes.

The boy was a frozen statue. For moments, he said
nothing, then finally the words came out in a painful
stutter. "M-mother?"

She turned to him instantly, her hand going to his
head to smooth back a lock of hair. She smiled easily
at him. "Yes?"

"I—I don't feel so hot. Do you think we could go
home?"

"Don't you want your sandwich?"

"I'm n-not hungry anymore."

She looked up at Michael and raised one eyebrow,
a movement that was meant to seem casual. It said,
"Kids. What can you do?" Her eyes went back to
the little boy. "Are you sure?"

He nodded.

"All right, then." She reached into her purse and
gave him her billfold. "You go up to the counter and
pay Sr. Norberto, then we'll leave."

He shot away from the table, his imaginary illness
clearly confined only to his stomach, as nothing appeared wrong with his legs.

"I'm sorry," she said, rising at the same time.
"I'd like to stay and chat, but…"

"I understand," Michael answered.

"You have children?" she asked.

The question surprised him. Most people would
have wanted to escape quickly, to get away from him
without further ado. But Eva Solis wasn't like most

people. She wanted to use the moment to her advantage.

"No, I don't have kids." What could he say? *I would have had children—my wife was pregnant—but I got both her and the child killed.*

"You seem to understand," she continued, her head nodding toward the child. "Sudden emergencies, I mean."

He shrugged. "We all have them." The idea came to him swiftly as he continued to stare at her. "Look, I'd really like to talk with you some more. Just visit. Would you and Mr. Cantrell consider having dinner with me this evening? If I have to eat one more meal alone, I'm going to go nuts."

She hesitated while she considered lying. He could see it in her eyes. Finally, she answered. "There is no Mr. Cantrell."

He smiled. "Even better, then." She didn't speak, and he started again. "Look, I'm just traveling through and I'd really like to look at a friendly face across the table." He held his hands up in a gesture of innocence. "No strings, I promise."

Her expression seemed to shift again, her mind undoubtedly assessing the risks and coming up with the same solution he would have. It was easier to keep an eye on him if they were sitting two feet apart. She could use the time to find out more about him. He wasn't surprised by her answer.

"I'd be happy to join you."

"Great. I'll pick you up—"

"I'd prefer to meet you at the restaurant. There's

a good seafood place down by the pier called Dos Piratas. It's the only decent place in town.''

"It sounds perfect. See you at nine?"

She smiled smoothly. "See you at nine."

She turned and left, the child at her side. When they got to the door, the little boy shot a look over his shoulder at Michael. He considered himself a hardened man, but the look on the kid's face turned Michael inside out. It was terror, pure and simple.

He couldn't stand seeing the raw emotion. He shifted his own gaze instantly, and that's when he spotted the other man. He was sitting in the back of the café, deep in the shadows. A soft curse escaped Michael's lips. How long had the guy been there? Why hadn't Michael noticed him before? Was he slipping?

He stared at him now, without appearing to do so. The man was well-dressed in dark pants and an expensive sweater, a cashmere overcoat thrown across a nearby chair. A newspaper spread before him, he sipped from a cup of coffee and watched Eva leave, his eyes darting to her disappearing back, then quickly returning to the paper in front of him.

He was good. He'd slipped innocently past Michael coming in, and even his surveillance of Eva would have gone unnoticed if Michael hadn't turned his head to avoid Daniel's look.

But who was he?

A simple man appreciating her figure…or someone else? Someone more interested than he should be?

Michael watched for a few more minutes, then rose casually. After paying his bill, he stepped outside into the wind. It instantly snatched at his coat with greedy fingers and flung sand into his eyes. He pulled out his sunglasses, slipped them on and prepared to wait.

It didn't take long. Two minutes later, Mr. Cashmere came out, his folded newspaper under his arm. From across the street, in a recessed doorway, Michael watched him turn left and head up the sidewalk. He followed, dipping in and out of the stream of foot traffic, crossing the street several times, then going back.

After a few blocks, the man turned left again and headed up a quieter street, forcing Michael to hang back even farther. When he reached a three-story house with black shutters and a wooden gate, he went inside, the wooden latch screeching in the wind as it swung shut behind him, then locked. Michael continued up the street and passed the house. He felt no eyes staring at him from the windows and saw no twitching curtains. Doubling back down another street, he headed toward the Austral.

DURING THE SHORT WALK home, Eva and Daniel couldn't talk. The blustering wind would have snatched their words and made it impossible. The imaginary conversation going on behind her eyes was bad enough, though. It was giving her a major headache.

She could hear Thomas's voice so clearly, it frightened her.

"What in the hell do you think you're doing? Are you crazy? You don't know shit about this guy."

"And I'll never know more if all I do is hide from him. I have to go, Thomas. It's the only way."

"It isn't safe."

Almost nauseous now, she glanced down at the child beside her. *"Life isn't safe."*

They reached their front door. Eva unlocked it quickly, then they slipped inside and shook the dirt from their coats, leaving them in the stairwell so they wouldn't bring it all upstairs.

She turned to Daniel immediately. "You aren't really sick, are you?"

"No, but I got scared—my stomach felt all funny." He sat down heavily on the bottom step as if his legs had suddenly gone out from under him.

"It's okay. My stomach felt funny, too." She sat down beside him, a new fear building in her stomach as it clenched nervously. "Was that him, Danny? The bad guy?"

He looked over at her. In the filtered light of the stairwell, his face seemed almost green. "I...I don't know. He kinda looked like him. I mean, he was tall and he had black hair...but I'm not sure, Aunt Eva. I'm just not sure." His face screwed up and he began to cry.

"It's okay, sweetheart. It's okay." Eva moved closer to him and put her arm around him, snuggling his body close to hers. He was trembling. "That was a terrible day. You were a really big boy to recall as much as you did.''

''But…but I should be able to tell you,'' he said between hiccups. ''Daddy would have remembered better.''

''Oh, sweetheart, your daddy was trained to do things like that. You haven't been.'' She lifted his chin up and brushed at his tearstained cheeks with her fingers. ''I know for a fact he would be very, very proud of you for helping as much as you already have.''

He nodded, his bottom lip trembling. ''Are you really going to dinner with him?''

She'd been waiting for his question. ''I think I need to. Does that bother you?''

''Do you think it's okay?''

''I have to find out more about him. This is the only way.''

''Can I go, too?'' His eyes suddenly glowed with something so fierce it startled her. ''If that's the guy who killed my mom and dad—''

''Then I'll handle it,'' she answered firmly. ''That's what I'm here for.''

He stared at her a moment longer, then finally he nodded. Rising, he turned and headed up the stairs. She watched him disappear, then lowered her head and prayed. Prayed she was doing the right thing.

LATE THAT AFTERNOON, when she picked up the phone for the hundredth time, the line buzzed loudly in her ear, surprising her. It was the sweetest sound she'd heard in days.

Punching out the code to get a long-distance line, Eva waited impatiently for the operator's voice. She came on a few minutes later, and her Southern drawl brought with it an unexpected wave of homesickness for Eva. "AT&T. How may I help you?"

She gave the woman the number on Michael Master's card and waited while it rang. Her hands were sweaty by the time it was answered.

"SOFE. May I direct your call?"

Eva took a deep breath and said the words she'd been rehearsing. "Michael Masters, please. This is Liz Lasser with Bundy Oil Tools."

"I'm sorry, but Mr. Masters isn't in now. Could I take a message?"

"Does he have a secretary?"

"Yes, he does. Her name is Patricia. Would you like to speak with her?"

"Yes."

Eva closed her eyes, canned music pouring into her ear. So far, so good.

"This is Patricia Lindsay. May I help you?"

Her voice was definitely different. Deeper and more resonant with a west Texas twang, it wasn't the receptionist pretending to be another person.

"This is Liz Lasser. I'm calling from Los Angeles and I'm looking for Michael Masters."

"Well, I'm sorry, Ms. Lasser, but he's not here right now. He's on vacation."

"Oh, dear..." She made her voice sound disappointed. "We met a while back at a trade show, and my boss was really impressed with his products. He wanted me to call and discuss a few things with him. Is there any way I can get in touch with him?"

"I'm afraid not. He's hunting in South America. Some Podunk little place I've never heard of." She laughed easily. "I asked him why he had to go so far—he's a god-awful shot, that's for sure. Waste of good money, if you ask me. He ought to be on a cruise ship or something like that."

The woman was rambling, and that alone was enough to make Eva nervous. "Will he be gone long?"

"Well, lemme see…" Eva could hear papers rattling, then the woman came back on the line. "He left about a week ago, so I'd say another three weeks at least. He wasn't too sure how long he was gonna be gone, and frankly, the boss told him to take off as much time as he needed." Her voice dropped on the last few words.

Obviously, the secretary wanted encouragement. Eva glanced nervously at her watch. A few more seconds and anyone with half-decent equipment would know exactly where she was…but she took the bait. "Is there…a problem?"

"The boss just thought he could use some time off. It's personal."

She wasn't going to say more, the tone of her voice said. This little tidbit was all she'd throw out.

"Well, I hope everything's all right." Remembering the photo in his leather kit, Eva couldn't help but wonder. Did the "personal" problem have something to do with the gorgeous blonde? How much of this was for real anyway?

A pair of onyx eyes, cold and fathomless, came into Eva's mind. She closed down the image and looked at her watch again. God, she was over the limit!

She spoke hurriedly. "I—I'll call back later and catch him when he gets back. Thanks again."

"But I'm sure I can get someone else to help you—"

Eva hung up, the secretary's voice sounding tinny just before it disappeared altogether. She leaned heavily against the chair, the wooden slats biting into her back, a drop of nervous sweat rolling between her breasts.

No one in Finely's operation would think up a story like that. They didn't have that much imagination and the personal details would be too difficult to fake if she wanted to check up on them. Finely usually had only one woman on the undercover lines, too. He was too cheap to do more. Ask the caller questions, he always said. *That's* the way to keep them on the line.

Patricia Lindsay hadn't asked Eva a single question.

It wasn't an absolute, of course, but unless Jack had changed his techniques, that really left only two possibilities. Mr. Masters worked for *los militares* or he was exactly what he said he was.

Outside, a burst of wind rattled the shutters and

sent a whirl of dust and trash swirling through the courtyard. The sudden movement caught Eva's eyes and quickened her pulse. She told herself to calm down, to think logically, but could she? It seemed like an impossible task. The glass in the door leading to the courtyard shook in its frame, protesting the beating it was receiving.

If Michael Masters *had* been sent by the killers, they would probably already be dead. Why wait?

That left just one possibility.

The man had to be who he said he was. A salesman—an undeniably attractive, incredibly sexy, definitely appealing salesman. She could go to dinner, have a nice time and pretend for just a little while that things were normal... They were stuck at the end of the world, but here was a chance to act otherwise for an hour or so. It could be fun—how many men in Houston had she ever known who were this good-looking, this attractive?

Ignoring her remaining misgivings, she rose from the chair and went to dress.

CHAPTER SIX

Dos PIRATAS SAT on a strip of rocky land, squeezed between the *guardacostas* offices and the pounding Atlantic waves. When the wind really wound itself up, there was no way to get to the tiny restaurant. The freezing water would cut off the dilapidated building from the street, and the waiters could do nothing but stand on the front porch and look dejected.

At the moment, despite the earlier gusts, things looked relatively calm. The dark water in front of the restaurant was churning as usual, but it was staying on the pebbled beach and not venturing any farther. Eva approached the building from the right-hand side, walking slowly down the dimly lit sidewalk to pause beside the windows. She'd come early to check things out.

Her gaze took in the tiny parking lot. Three ancient cars had been left at various spots, the Argentineans' haphazard approach to parking more than obvious. Beside two of the rusting heaps, a pair of scruffy cats had come to a standoff, part of a fish head lying in the no-man's-land between them. In the freezing water, a bobbing fishing boat rode the waves, cold and lonely. There was no sign of Michael...or of anyone else.

She knew she was being really paranoid, especially after her earlier phone call to his office, but she'd had to satisfy herself that this was dinner and not a setup. Shivering beneath her pea jacket, Eva took a steadying breath and entered the restaurant. She scanned the tables, but as she'd expected, they were all empty, too. Most people didn't eat until ten or later, usually around midnight.

The waiters, clustered in a group around a television blaring a soccer match, seemed surprised by her appearance. She took a table by the window and settled in to wait, her gaze going out to the barely visible waves.

"Buenas tardes." One of the younger servers was standing beside the table. He smiled. "You are waiting for someone, yes?"

She nodded.

"Then let me get you something to drink. Some wine, a beer...what would you like? I can recommend the *vino tinto,* it's excellent."

She looked into the young man's eyes. They were dark and sexy and roved over her with appreciation. Unexpectedly flustered, she nodded again. "That...that would be fine, thank you."

He dazzled her with a brilliant display of white teeth, then turned smartly and headed to the bar. She sat back and took another deep breath. Men in Argentina, especially young men, took every opportunity they could to flirt. Old women, young girls, middle-aged matrons—it didn't matter. If you were female and allowed it, they would charm you incessantly. Until this moment, Eva hadn't had the time or the inclination to pay them any attention. Then suddenly she realized why the situation had changed. She was wearing an ivory silk sweater with a short black skirt and was obviously waiting for a man. Tonight she was dressed nicely and having a date. Something she hadn't done in almost a year.

With a flourish, the waiter reappeared and set her wine before her. Under his watchful eye, she sipped, then nodded once. He smiled again, his gaze dropping to her neckline before he backed away from the table.

She resumed her vigil, looking out the window. She really hadn't dated that much since her divorce. Brian, her former husband, had cured her of wanting a man around. In the worst possible way, he'd cheated on her—if she hadn't been so hurt, the cliché would have made her laugh.

She'd come home after working late…and found him in bed with another woman. Found the two of them in *her* bed. He hadn't even had the decency to go to a motel. Of course, she wouldn't have expected that of Brian anyway. His other fault was that he was tight. Even before this incident had occurred, she'd begun to wonder what she was doing with a man like him.

Part of her had always suspected she'd married him because she'd thought time was passing too fast. At twenty-six, she'd thought she *should* be married and planning a family. Instead, she'd found herself single and still going places with her brother and his wife. So she'd married Brian in hopes of duplicating Thomas and Sally's loving relationship.

Unfortunately, she'd spent the next five years pretending she hadn't made a horrible mistake. When she'd found Brian that night in bed with some girl he worked with, she'd told herself he'd simply made things easier by being as stupid as he had been. Now, she knew who'd been the stupid one. She had—for staying with him that long.

She looked down into her wineglass. She'd probably never remarry—how could she? Not many men would understand her situation and be prepared to run at a moment's notice. And having a family of her own...that was just a dream. She'd be lying to herself if she said it didn't matter. Never to know what it was like to have her own child, to have a husband to grow old with, to sleep beside every night...these were the things she'd given up when she'd fled with Daniel.

She hadn't really understood, in that split second she'd had to decide, what being on the run meant, but it didn't really matter. She'd do the same thing all over again. Daniel was the only important thing here, and she had to keep him safe.

Out in the darkness beyond the window, a dark shadow suddenly moved. Eva's senses went on alert, her ruminations pushed aside. The tall form came closer to the restaurant, the sides of his long coat moving in the wind with eerie, yet graceful flaps.

Like the wings of a predatory bird, each flutter brought him nearer to the light. His face remained in the dark until just before he reached the door. He stopped at that point and looked through the window, meeting Eva's eyes with a directness that took away her breath.

It was Michael.

HE STEPPED INTO the restaurant, his eyes sweeping over the interior of the dining room. Fishing nets hung from the ceiling, the fragile webs holding globes of brightly colored glass, reflections of light shimmering off their iridescent surfaces. Along the walls someone had painted many different kinds of fish. They swam along the wooden slats with graceful curves, their eyes staring out at the patrons. In one corner stood a painted pirate, his elbow cocked to rest on the bar. One of the *dos piratas,* Michael assumed.

Eva twisted in her chair, her dark eyes piercing Michael's as he moved toward her. She wore a V-necked sweater of something soft and sexy, the virginal paleness of the color offset by its deep décolletage. She'd put her hair up, too, loose tendrils of silky black curls escaping to frame her face and emphasize the graceful curve of her neck. Her cheeks looked flushed, her lips full and ripe. Her smoldering sensuality struck him again. She was a banked fire— he had no doubt that the slightest agitation would bring flames and scorching heat.

She rose slightly when he reached the table, and

he bent down and kissed her, his lips brushing first one of her smooth, soft cheeks and then the other, the faintest hint of her perfume filling the air between them. She stiffened but showed no other signs of nervousness at his kiss.

"There's one thing about Argentina I really like," he said, ignoring the chair opposite her own and taking the one closer to her.

Sitting down once more, she pushed a strand of hair back and arched one eyebrow. "And that is?"

"How they say hello," he explained, gazing at her. "Everybody kisses everybody."

She matched his smile, but her expression held reserve. "It took me a while to get used to it. We never did that in Mexico."

The waiter appeared and looked at Michael expectantly.

"I'd recommend the red," Eva said. "It's quite good."

Michael nodded and she spoke in rapid Spanish to the waiter. He disappeared with a flourish.

"You've lived there—in Mexico?" Michael asked.

Shaking her head, she spoke with ease. "We used to travel there a lot in the summers."

"We?"

"I was married then. My husband was a teacher, and we'd go to a different village each summer and do volunteer work."

Lie with the truth. It was a maxim Michael followed, too.

"And now…"

"And now he goes with his new wife," she said dryly. "His new, young wife. We went to Saltillo and taught. They go to Cozumel and dive."

Michael nodded. "How long have you been divorced?"

"Five years—but it should be more. I stuck it out a little too long."

The waiter appeared with a bulbous glass of wine.

"And you?" she asked as soon as he disappeared. Michael watched as her lips pressed against the edge of her goblet. She sipped, the slim column of her throat moving so sensually the sight of it affected him in a way he hadn't expected. "What's your sad tale?"

Her question refocused his attention. He'd called his office earlier to check in, and Patricia had relayed her conversation with "Liz Lasser." He knew exactly what he was supposed to say.

"When are you bringing her in?" Patricia had asked before he could hang up. "They're calling from Houston."

"Let them call," he'd growled. "There's someone else here who's pretty interested in her, too. I'd like to find out who he is before I do anything else. It could complicate things."

"If you wait too long, things are going to get pretty complicated here, as well."

Eva's voice again broke into his thoughts, bringing him back to the moment. "Tell me about yourself. Are you married? Divorced? Single?"

She was testing him, just as he'd known she would. Just as he would do.

"I was married…but my wife is dead." The words were like broken glass. Even though it had been a while, each time he said them, they cut deeper. He didn't have to fake the abruptness in his voice. "She was murdered."

Across the table, Eva stilled, her fingers freezing on the stem of her glass. "I'm very sorry to hear that."

He waited for her to say more, to try to eliminate the awkward tension, but she stayed silent. After a few seconds, he lifted his gaze. She was looking at him with dark, compassionate eyes, their unending depths filled with something he wouldn't have recognized if he hadn't known her history. She blinked, and the expression was gone.

"So you came here to try not to think about her?"

Her candor surprised him. It was an accurate assessment of exactly what his life had become, and the realization jolted him. He took a moment to answer, a moment longer than he would have liked.

"I came here to hunt," he said, leaning back in his chair and trying to dispel some of the tension. "I grew up in Montana, learned to shoot about the same time I learned to walk."

"That sounds like a Texas tale."

He smiled lazily. "And how would you know that? You hear them up in Canada?"

She smiled back, completely unfazed. "I went to

school in the States. At the University of Texas in Austin.''

The waiter reappeared, and after briefly consulting with Michael, Eva ordered for them both. He listened to her Spanish. It was flawless, of course, the beautiful, seductive language sounding even better than usual coming from her full and perfect lips.

He smiled as the waiter left. ''I have no idea what you said, but it all sounded great.''

She laughed. ''I spoke Spanish before I spoke English. My father was from Mexico. I hated being different when I was a kid, but now I appreciate having another language. I speak French, too.''

''Ah…the romance languages are your specialties, then?''

''I guess you could say that.'' She looked at him over the rim of her glass. ''Is it difficult being here and not speaking the language?''

''I get by,'' he answered. ''And most of the people in the oil business speak a little English.''

''Tell me what kind of equipment you sell. They drill for gas here, right?''

He opened his mouth to answer and caught himself at the very last moment, his admiration for her taking a leap as soon as he realized the trap. ''Actually, the wells here drill for crude,'' he answered. ''There is no gas in this part of Argentina. It's farther north.''

As if she didn't already know that fact, she nodded, an interested expression coloring her delicate features. ''I see. And you sell the local companies equipment for their rigs?''

He nodded. "Everything is imported. There are no manufacturing facilities here."

"Must be expensive."

He leaned back and smiled. "Yeah, but it makes for bigger commissions. And I don't have a problem with that."

She asked him a few more questions about his work, probing, skillful questions. If he hadn't been aware of what she was doing, he simply would have thought her interested. She was good. Very good. His answers must have reassured her, however. By the time their dinner arrived, she seemed more relaxed, some of the tension she'd been holding in her shoulders slowly easing out.

"And what about you?" The waiter placed a huge bowl of steaming paella on the table between them. "What brings you here? Surely there are lots of places more hospitable to teach than Comodoro?"

"There was nothing keeping us in Canada." She reached for the spoon and began to serve him from the bowl. "And I wanted my son to know different cultures. To really know them. There are certain things you won't ever understand unless you experience them. Coming here will teach him how to survive anywhere."

"You make it sound serious."

She looked up, her gaze locking on his. "Surviving *is* serious. That's what it's all about."

"The law of the jungle?"

"The strongest do survive." Hesitating just a moment, she seemed to fall into thought, then she roused herself and smiled once more, her casual attitude back in place. "I want him to experience life as it is, not life through video games. Back home, that's all he'd get."

"And does he like it here?"

She picked up her fork. "He misses his friends...but he'll make new ones."

"And your family? What did they think of your coming to the ends of the earth?"

She raised her wineglass to her lips and took a sip. "I have no family," she said, slowly putting the glass back on the table. "It's only me and Daniel."

"No sisters, no brothers? Nothing?"

"I had a brother, but he died." Avoiding Michael's eyes, she turned her head and stared out at the black water near the edge of the parking lot. Her voice was shaky and then remote, as if she knew she had to get a handle on her emotions. "We were very close."

Again, the impression of truthfulness came with her words. Her grief was real; he knew because he recognized it. He saw the same thing in the mirror every day.

"I'm sorry. It must have been hard for you."

"'Hard' doesn't begin to describe it," she answered. She lifted her eyes to his, and he could read the sorrow in their dark depths. It was a raw, naked emotion that made him feel as if he was seeing something he shouldn't.

He could hardly bear to witness her pain, but it told him something important. He understood, in that instant, that Eva Solis had had nothing to do with the two murders, no matter what anyone implied. The idea had never made sense to him anyway. Why would she go to such lengths to protect her nephew if she'd killed his father and mother?

The conversation turned more general after that, and when he glanced down at his watch a little while later, Michael was shocked to see it was long past midnight, the restaurant finally filling up with a rowdy crowd. He looked at his empty coffee cup, then up into Eva's dark eyes. Their intensity reached deep down inside him, and he found himself wanting to somehow connect with her. To be with her on a much different plane than the one they were on right now.

His reaction shocked him. Eva Solis was unlike anyone he'd ever known, but she was a target, pure and simple. He was there to collect her and her nephew and nothing more. He couldn't afford to have any other feelings for her.

Mimicking his movement, she glanced down at her own watch, then raised her eyebrows. "My goodness! I had no idea it was this late. I need to be getting back...."

He nodded toward the waiter, and a few minutes after that, they were standing on the tiny front steps of the restaurant. "Can I give you a ride home?"

She smiled and shook her head. "That's not necessary. I can walk."

"You live nearby?"

She seemed to hesitate, but the moment came and

went so quickly he wasn't sure she had. "Over a few blocks," she said vaguely with a tilt of her head.

"Then I'll walk with you and come back for my car afterward," he said, taking her elbow firmly. "It's the least I can do to pay you back for having dinner with a poor, old, boring oilman."

SHE WANTED TO BELIEVE HIM. She *really* wanted to believe him.

But she couldn't. Life just wasn't that simple.

Eva looked up into Michael's endless black eyes, however, and asked herself what harm could it do to allow him to walk her home. He already knew where she lived, and if he was the cold-blooded killer she'd first suspected, then why hadn't he already done her in? Could she let her guard down? On a public street...with plenty of people all around...what could he do?

Throughout dinner, he'd appeared to be exactly who he said he was. An oilman from Texas, in Argentina to hunt. Everything he'd said and everything he'd done seemed consistent with that being the truth.

But he was just a little too mysterious, she argued with herself. There was something there, something around the edges of his personality that didn't quite fit. Even meeting him back home she would have wondered what his secrets were. He was simply that kind of man.

And it made him more appealing than ever.

She looked into his eyes and shook her head. "It's

really not necessary for you to walk me home. Thank you for the dinner, though. It was a nice evening. I enjoyed it.''

At her answer, his fingers tightened on her elbow, and her heart jumped automatically. He moved his thumb slightly as he spoke, the pad of his finger lightly caressing the inside of her elbow at its most tender point. ''I know it's not necessary, but I think I should. It's dark and—''

''Oh, I walk everywhere in town.'' She smiled, her attitude as casual as she could make it. ''It's very safe.''

''Are you sure?'' His eyes went flat again, cold and stony. She told herself it was a trick of the dim streetlight overhead, but she shivered anyway. ''There aren't too many places *that* safe anymore. I'd be careful if I were you.''

His fingers were generating a kind of electricity in her, a kind of sensual awareness she hadn't experienced in years. She gently extricated herself from his grip. ''I...I'm sure,'' she managed.

He arched one black eyebrow and held his hands up in surrender. ''Okay, then. Whatever you say.''

She held out her hand to shake his. ''Good luck with your hunting. I hope you bag your limit.''

''Oh, I'll be successful.'' He took her fingers in his, the tension leaping between them once more. ''I'd like to see you again when I get back, though. Could we get together? I'm only going to be in the field a couple of days since the guide won't go out on Easter. I'd have the day free.''

She stalled, wanting to say yes, but something held her back. "We might be going to the beach that day. I'm not exactly sure what our plans are. Could you call me when you get back?"

"I'll do that." His voice was deep and erotic. It rolled over her like a length of silk.

He smiled, then before she could say another word, he bent down and kissed her, his broad hands going to her shoulders to grip them lightly but firmly. The touch of his lips against hers was brief, so brief it was over as soon as it registered, but a tingling aftershock lingered, like an earthquake that refused to quit. It rippled over her, sending out a series of delicious, tiny tremors that she knew she'd be remembering for quite a while. The sensation was strange, strange and intriguing and more erotic than anything she'd ever felt. A moment later, he was gone...but his touch stayed with her and refused to leave.

CHAPTER SEVEN

THE PHONE WAS SLIPPERY in her hand, and Eva realized once again how nervous she was. She'd been this way ever since she'd decided to call Houston and talk to Ridley. To ask for his help. It wasn't the first time she'd talked to him since she'd run. Several times she'd called, thinking she would talk to him about Thomas's notes, but each time, she hadn't been able to actually get the words out, to ask him if he'd been the one to tell her brother the truth about Finely. Something always held her back.

She was calling him now for help, though. It seemed like the best way to finally set her mind at ease about Michael Masters. She couldn't get the man out of her mind, and the kiss they'd shared after dinner simply refused to leave her consciousness. At the strangest moments, she'd remember the sensation—the feel of his mouth, the warmth of his hands—and she'd have to remind herself he could be a danger to her. Calling Ridley would settle it once and for all.

She'd explained as much as she could, and Ridley had told her to call back at the end of the day. Her hand shook now as she redialed the number.

He answered instantly. "Ridley here."

"It's me. Have you found out anything?"

"Well, hello to you, too, sweetheart." His Texas drawl filled the line. "Everything's just fine, here, yeah."

In the background, she could hear the raucous sound of men laughing, someone opening and closing a door. It was after five, she realized suddenly, and all the agents were gathering in Ridley's office to decide where to go for drinks. The thought brought forth Thomas, and she closed her eyes. She caught her breath and spoke again.

"You've got people in your office?"

"That's right, baby. I'll pick you up at eight. Is that okay?"

"Just say yes or no. Did you check him out?"

"Yes, that I did."

"Is he who he says he is?"

"As far as I can tell, it's all the God's honest truth, honey. The genuine thing."

Eva closed her eyes. She wanted to feel relief, to simply accept what he said and go from there. Ridley was as reliable as anyone she knew; if he told her Michael Masters was nothing but a salesman, then she should believe him.

The noise in Ridley's office increased, men calling out one to another, a higher female voice sounding in the distance. "You're sure?"

"Absolutely, positively." He waited a moment, then spoke again. "So what are you going to do for me? Turnabout's fair play, you know. Share and share alike—all that stuff."

"I can't tell you where we are. You know that."

"I could help."

"I'm sure you could, but I have to do this on my own. You understand, don't you?"

"Not exactly. Why don't you give me a call later? We could talk about this a little more." Ridley's easy attitude now seemed a bit forced. "I'd really like to hear more about it."

"Do you know anything new…about the situation?"

"'Fraid not, but—"

"Then I've got to go," she said, glancing down at her watch and grimacing. "Watch your back, Ridley."

He waited just a moment, then spoke again. "You watch yours, darlin'."

MICHAEL USED the next day the best way he knew how. He trailed Eva everywhere she went. And right behind her was the well-dressed man Michael had seen in the café.

From the moment she left her house that morning, the man was with her. Stopping at the boy's school while she dropped him off, waiting for her outside the institute, picking her up again after work and following her to the market. Everywhere she went, the man went, too.

Who in the hell was he?

Slipping a fifty-dollar bill to the manager of the grocery store on the other side of the street from Eva's house, Michael settled in to wait and hopefully find out the answer to that question. He watched her house from the upstairs office and sipped a cup of coffee, his gaze going out the window. In the glass of the bank across the street, he could see the reflection of the grocery store underneath him. In one of the doorways, the guy was waiting. Eva had gone inside her own home an hour before.

She was a gorgeous woman, he reflected. Observing her from a distance, he'd been cheated of her full impact. The perfect, honey-hued skin, the lush, full lips, the curve of her neck where it met her shoulders... He hadn't fully appreciated these points until he'd sat across from her at dinner. With her perfume floating over the table to capture him and her dark eyes holding mysteries he found himself wanting to solve, he'd had to tell himself more than once since then that the moment would not be repeated.

She was more than just beautiful, though. She was even smarter than he'd first assumed. No wonder she'd gotten away from the department. They were idiots compared to her. Michael wondered again about his contact there. He was a devious son of a bitch, and Michael wouldn't put it past him to have hired a second gun to find her. He'd done that to Michael once before. He trusted no one...which made perfect sense because he himself was totally untrustworthy.

But no one knew that, of course.

Speaking of which... Michael glanced down at his watch. He'd promised Houston another phone call this evening. But they'd just have to wait. Like he did.

Five minutes later, the guy in the doorway straightened, his eyes trained on a younger man coming closer toward him. The new one stopped, his reflection wavering in the sunlight as Michael checked him out. Young, barely out of his teens. They spoke for a few minutes, then the younger man slipped into the doorway and took the other man's place. He walked away quickly, never looking back.

The vigil continued.

IT WAS EASTER MORNING. They'd gone to Mass, then come straight home. Standing in the kitchen, Eva looked over her shoulder at Daniel. "Have you got everything? Frisbee? Coke? Schoolbooks? We could do some extra studying."

He jerked his head up. "Studying! No way! I thought this was gonna be a picnic—"

"I'm teasing you, silly." She laughed and closed the lid of the egg carton. "Of course it's going to be a picnic. And I'm going to hide all these eggs and you'll never find them. We're going to have fun."

If the weather cooperated, of course. She looked out the window. At the moment, it was an incredible day; the sky was so blue and clear it hurt her eyes just to look at it. That could change within seconds, but maybe the nice weather would hold for once.

Picking up the picnic basket, she glanced toward Daniel again. "Are you ready?"

He nodded, and within minutes they were downstairs and in the pickup. Backing out of the driveway, she headed the truck toward Rada Tilly. The nearby seaside town was the closest thing Comodoro had to a resort. The rocky shoreline offered little in the form of entertainment, but it was, at the least, a change from the dusty streets and dirty sidewalks they were accustomed to. Within twenty minutes, they were there. Eva parked the truck next to the curb on the last street in town. To their right, stretched the Atlantic Ocean.

"It looks cold," Daniel said uncertainly. "Are you sure you want to picnic here?"

She stared out the window of the truck. In either direction, dark brown sand stretched for a hundred yards or more. Beyond the sand, an angry surf rolled back and forth, the lurching swells as tall and wicked-looking as any she'd ever seen. At the north and south ends, terminating the beach, soaring, craggy cliffs rose over a hundred feet into the air. At high tide, their curving sides completely blocked travel to the next stretch of sand. It was a formidable scene.

"We're bundled up," she answered resolutely, pulling on a glove. "It'll be fun. I promise. Besides, we need the change of scenery."

He gave her a look that left no room for doubt—she was crazy, pure and simple—but he opened the truck door anyway and scampered out. Heading for the water, he chased a flock of seagulls into the air with a loud, resounding whoop, then skipped toward the pounding waves. Within minutes, he'd forgotten his reservations and had hooked up with a group of kids clustered around a go-cart someone had dragged onto the hard-packed sand. Bright scarves and wool caps dotted the windy shore, an incongruous sight on a beach but one to which the locals were accustomed.

Eva trudged through the drifts toward a conglomeration of boulders. Offering minimal protection against the wind, the spot seemed like as good a place as any to drop the blanket and basket. In short order, she had the plaid wool spread over the sand and a book open across her knees. Shading her eyes, she checked on Daniel. The group hadn't moved. Reassured, she turned to her novel.

But the words didn't register.

All she could think about was Michael Masters.

And what woman wouldn't? He was strangely compelling with his dark eyes and even darker secrets. Oh, yes, there were plenty of secrets there, of that she was sure. He might not be the killer she'd first assumed, but there *was* something there, something that made her uneasy.

Maybe it had been his reaction to her question about his wife.

Eva had realized immediately how very much he'd loved her. A man couldn't fake that kind of emotion, he just couldn't. But something else had been there, too. Something more intense than merely grief. Eva had stayed awake late last night thinking about it, but she'd come up with no answers, only more questions.

She'd never ask them, though. She respected privacy now more than ever. She didn't want to answer any questions herself, so she asked fewer.

She'd been fairly open with Michael, however. Everything she'd told him had been the truth, more or less. Which felt really strange…and wonderful at the same time. How long had it been since she'd been that honest with anyone? Months, for sure. And she missed that feeling because basically that was the kind of person she was—open and honest and trusting, almost impulsively so before now. Thomas had warned her about it more than once. No, claiming to be someone else and keeping secrets wasn't easy for her, and keeping up the pretense was getting harder every day.

Glancing down the beach again, Eva located Daniel with her eyes, but her mind was far, far away. She'd thought Michael would call, especially after she'd told him they might be picnicking at the beach today. She'd actually planned on asking him to come with them, but the phone had stayed silent. She couldn't acknowledge her disappointment, though. To do so made it real, and making it real would mean she'd have to face the truth. She couldn't afford a relationship, not with Michael, not with anyone. Until Daniel was grown and on his own, Eva couldn't possibly get entangled with anyone—they'd never tolerate her situation.

Suddenly, Daniel began to sprint down the beach, breaking away from the gang of kids to head her way, yelling before she could even hear him. Reaching her side, his breathing hard and fast, he fell down onto the sand beside her and spoke excitedly.

"Can I go with the guys? They're riding the go-cart to the end of the beach and back. It's okay, isn't it? You don't care?"

A protective surge came over her. "Oh, Daniel, honey...I'm not sure that's a good idea. Don't you want to do our Easter eggs?"

"We can do the Easter eggs afterwards. Please lemme go. All the other guys are doing it, and it really sounds like a lot of fun—"

"I thought you didn't want to have fun."

He jerked his eyes to hers, then when he realized she was teasing him, his expression shifted from dismayed to hopeful. Reaching for her hand, he twined his fingers in hers and grinned. "Well, maybe I was wrong."

"Maybe you were."

With her free hand, she reached out and tucked a longer strand of his hair behind his left ear, a move of love and affection. Thomas had hated the haircut, but Eva had thought it cute. She'd sneaked Daniel out just before the trip to the cabin and, with Sally's permission, had financed the new look. If she closed her eyes, she could still hear Thomas yelling....

"Then can I go?" He pumped her hand up and down, swinging it playfully. "Please, can I go?"

She gave in, knowing all along she probably would. "Oh, all right. But stay where I can see you, okay? And don't go too fast. Now be careful—"

He was already gone.

Anxiously, she watched him climb on the back of the little two-seater, an older boy who looked vaguely familiar—maybe from the institute?—behind the wheel. In seconds, with a jaunty wave in her direction, they were off.

Watching the kids head down the beach, she let her mind wander back to the path it had been on before. Perhaps it was just as well Michael Masters hadn't telephoned. With his broad shoulders and dark eyes, he was simply too appealing—too appealing and too secretive. It would be way too easy for her right now to succumb to the release he could provide her. Forgetting her never-ending tension would be heaven, but there would be a price. There always was.

No. She'd stay away from him. At this point in her life, a man with secrets was the last thing she needed.

MICHAEL PARKED his rental car a few feet down from Eva's truck. The wind had picked up a bit and was blowing sand around the tires, pale flecks that almost looked like snow. It had grown a little colder, too. Buttoning his coat, he studied her through his windshield.

She was sitting by some rocks in a partially sheltered spot. A few minutes earlier, the sun had disappeared behind a bank of clouds, but it came out as he watched, a strong streak of light beaming down on her, the rays obviously warming as she lifted her face to meet them.

The scene twisted something in his gut, and he couldn't ignore the feeling that had been building there since their dinner—the feeling *or* the question that came with it.

Just what in the hell did he think he was doing?

The question was a rhetorical one, of course. He knew exactly what he was doing—and if he allowed the situation to continue, allowed his attraction to Eva Solis to build, then he was going to screw up in more ways than he could count.

Professionally. Personally. Emotionally.

He was being paid to find her and her nephew and bring them back to Houston. He wasn't being paid for anything else, and that definitely included falling victim to the dark, knowing eyes he'd stared at across the dinner table, or letting the promising curves he'd noticed beneath her sweater entice him.

He didn't even *want* to be attracted to her, dammit. He had no room in his life for that kind of thing anymore. Not since Amy. He gripped the steering wheel and cursed. Why was he doing this?

Eva turned her head toward the water and a group of kids nearby. Michael followed the movement and located Daniel. Beyond the kids, a few other families were scattered up and down the cold, windswept beach, but mainly it was deserted. Michael continued to look, however, his eyes sweeping over the desolate scene until he found exactly what he'd expected.

A man, sitting alone on the rocks near the water, close to the north-end cliff. A man who definitely wasn't picnicking. Picking up his binoculars from the seat beside him, Michael focused in on the solitary figure. Sure enough, it was Mr. Cashmere, the older guy who'd been following Eva. His teenage companion wasn't with him. As Michael watched, he rose and began to walk toward the cliffs at the end of the beach.

Michael slowly put down the binoculars. He had no idea who this guy was, but one thing was clear. He couldn't be allowed to continue shadowing Eva. Michael couldn't do his own job with him in the picture.

Wishing the other man gone had nothing to do with any kind of twisted need to protect Eva or warn her. None whatsoever. Or at least that's what Michael told himself as he opened the car door and stepped out into the biting wind to head in her direction.

CHAPTER EIGHT

EVA SAW MICHAEL COMING toward her, then heard the kids making more noise than ever. She turned toward the north end of the beach where they'd clustered. Screaming and jumping up and down near the cliffs, they were doing what kids do best. Acting like kids.

She turned back to Michael. He moved with the same fluid grace that had caught her attention the first time she'd seen him. Dressed in a black leather jacket and blue jeans, he raised one hand and waved, his steps bringing him closer and closer. Her pulse jumped into an uneasy rhythm that seemed to match the nearby pounding waves.

"Hello there," she said as he reached her blanket. "How was your hunting?"

"Not as successful as I'd planned, but I'm not finished." He smiled and sank onto the blanket beside her.

Was it paranoia that made her feel his words always had two meanings? Her questions came automatically—she couldn't seem to stop herself. "What were you after? Guanaco? Pheasants? What? You never said exactly."

His expression shifted. It was almost as if he knew

she was testing him, as if he knew that *she* knew about the gun...the gun that wasn't made to shoot birds.

"Oh, a little bit of everything," he said in an off-hand manner. "My guide's pretty loose, and the permit we got covers just about anything." He smiled, his full lips going up in a sensual movement. "We don't plan too far ahead."

"Good thing you don't care—that would be what you got, regardless." She smiled. "It's the Argentinean style. Why plan when you can wing it?"

He started to answer, but his voice was lost in a sudden eruption of screaming children running up to Eva. Converging on the blanket, their Spanish was so rapid and excited, even Eva had a hard time getting it all.

And then she understood.

She leaped to her feet, her pulse racing. "Are you sure? Is anyone with him?" She started to run without thinking, but Michael reached out and grabbed her, forcing her to stop.

"What is it? What's going on?"

"It's Daniel." She pulled away, her mouth dry with fear, her only thoughts of her nephew. "They're saying he got caught on the other side of the cliffs. That he went over there on the go-cart and now he can't return. The tide's come in and he's trapped."

Michael's head jerked up. His gaze briefly searched the end of the beach where the kids had been, then he faced Eva once again. His demeanor was completely different—his expression tight but controlled, his eyes intense but calm. In the space of one second, he'd gone from friendly Texan to dispassionate professional.

"Do you have any rope in your truck? A chain...anything like that?"

Her heart thumping, panic rising in her throat, Eva shook her head. "I don't think so."

"All right. Is there a rescue squad around here? Boats, helicopters? Some way we could go in by water?"

"They barely have a fire department. There's nothing like what you're talking about."

One of the older kids interrupted. His English was accented, but he'd obviously understood enough to reply. "I have the rope, *señor*. In my truck."

Michael turned to him instantly, his attention completely focused as he nodded toward the north end of the beach. "Take your truck to the top of that cliff. To the point right there at the end." He faced one of the other boys. "You go into town and get the police. Understand? *¿La policía, sí?*"

Startled by his clear and perfect Spanish, Eva shot a look in Michael's direction. He'd said he spoke "a little Spanish." Was a Castilian accent and flawless grammar what he considered "a little"?

She shook her head, then forgot about it. She had more important things to worry about right now. They turned in tandem and raced down the beach, Eva's pulse beating so wildly she wasn't sure she'd make it. Within a few minutes, they reached the north end.

Chaotic waves pounded the beachhead. Eva immediately splashed into the water thinking she could swim around, but within seconds her legs were numb. The water was freezing. No one would survive in it more than five minutes. Plunging into the surf, Michael yanked her back to the sandy beach.

"Forget it," he cried over the sound of the waves. "There's no way. You'd die of hypothermia before you knew what was happening."

She tore out of his arms. "But we've got to do something," she screamed. "I can't just stand here."

"We'll go up the cliff." He gestured toward the rocky bluff on their left. "Maybe we can see him from there."

Eva nodded and sprinted off, Michael close behind her. Grabbing clumps of sea grass and twisted roots and branches, she prayed and climbed, Michael pulling ahead of her, his muscular arms making the exercise easier for him than for her. The going was hard, but at least this side of the wind-battered cliff was less steep than the other side, the side Daniel could see. Finally, she reached the top, her hands bleeding and scratched as Michael pulled her the last few yards. They ran to the other side of the small plateau, Eva's throat dry and tight with anxiety, her legs trembling from fear and the effort of the climb.

Michael reached the edge first. He peered over, then lifted his arms and caught Eva as she barreled headlong toward him and the crumbling rim.

"He's there." Michael pointed to a spot in the water, and Eva's heart stopped.

Fifty feet from the base of the cliff, Daniel stood shivering on a sandbar. Water lapped at each end, the cold, unforgiving water of the Atlantic in fall.

He was trapped.

"Oh, my God... How in heaven's name did this happen?" Eva put her hand over her mouth, the bitter taste of disbelief and bile rising in her throat. She turned stricken eyes to Michael. "There's no way we can reach him. The waves are too strong. Even if we throw him a rope, he couldn't get to it."

Michael shook his head and started to remove his coat. "He can if I'm at the end of it."

Her mouth dropped open. "Are you crazy? You can't go down there. You could drown, too."

"And Daniel will for sure unless I give it a try." As he spoke, a cloud of dust rose behind them. The squeal of brakes told her the teenager and his truck had arrived. Michael nodded toward the sound. "I'll tie the rope to the truck bumper and lower myself to the water. I'm a strong swimmer—I think I can grab him, then you have everyone pull us both back up."

"But the water's coming in—"

"And it will only get higher. Have you got a better idea?"

"No," she whispered, "I don't."

"Then let's quit talking and get on with it."

Within moments, he had the rope looped over his chest and shoulders and tied around his waist, the thick hemp biting into his muscular sides. Eva watched helplessly. The wind had picked up. They had a hard time standing upright—what would Mi-

chael do when he was even more exposed on the side
of the bluff?

She stood with him on the collapsing fringe of the
cliff. Peering over, they both looked toward Daniel's
location. He seemed smaller and even more vulnerable, the water coming dangerously closer to him
even in the few seconds it had taken to tie the rope
around Michael.

Michael looked at Eva, his eyes filled with com-
passion. "Don't worry. I'll get him." His voice was
filled with confidence, but she felt only fear. He
reached out, brushed a finger over her cheek, then
stepped to the brink of the cliff.

HE'D DONE SOME RAPPELLING in Vietnam, but nothing like this. The burn of the rope against his thigh,
across his chest and over his shoulder was almost
unbearable. Michael steadied the line with one hand,
steeled himself against the stinging pain and kept going. In the back of his mind, he wondered exactly
how the boy had gotten where he was, then grimly
he accepted the most probable explanation. The man
he'd seen outside Eva's house and then again at the
beach—he'd had something to do with this; Michael
was certain.

A small bush tore at the exposed skin on his back,
and he cursed. With the rope slipping slowly through
his fingers, he fought for a hold against the side of
the cliff with his boots. The leather soles skidded
against the loose dirt and rocks as if they had a mind

of their own, denying him stability. Inch by inch, however, he made his way down the steep side.

The south slope he and Eva had climbed was nothing compared to the side he was on now. That easy incline had been weathered, beaten down by the wind. This side was abrupt and craggy, more rock than dirt, more precipitous than gentle. The rope was his only lifeline. If it broke, he'd join Daniel in the water—but first he'd be beaten by the rocks on his way down the side.

The descent seemed to take forever, but in reality it took only ten minutes. The rope was only long enough to take him to a ledge several feet above the water. He shot a look over his shoulder. Daniel was a good twenty feet away from him, the freezing Atlantic separating them.

Taking a deep breath, Michael loosened the knots at his waist and pulled the rope over his head. Jumping the final three feet, the rope now dangling above him, he splashed into the frigid waters.

The waves were only chest-deep, but it didn't matter. The water immediately permeated his jeans and burned against his skin with astonishing pain. He'd expected cold, but not this kind of fierce assault. He gasped, the freezing water as agonizing as the salt now stinging his cut and bleeding hands. Sloshing through the swells, he made his way to the sandbar as quickly as possible.

The boy was fighting tears and shivering. "I—I saw you coming," he managed to get out. "Can you get me back up there?"

"That's the plan." The wind snatched their voices and stole their words, while the waves, crashing against the sandy strip, greedily took more and more of their refuge away.

"H-how'd you know I was here? D-did Armando come get you?"

Michael stopped. "Who's Armando?"

"He w-was driving the cart when it died. He told me to wait here and that he'd go for h-help." Daniel turned his head toward the edge of the cliff. He started to cry. "I didn't know the water would come up this fast."

"Let's talk about it later, sport. Right now, I think you'd better hop on my back. I'll carry you to the cliff."

"I can swim," the little boy said bravely, a final attempt to show he hadn't just made an almost fatal mistake. "I was going to go to the cliff, and then I saw you coming and decided to wait."

"That was a good decision, but let's try it my way first, okay?"

The youngster's green eyes flicked toward the rocky shore, then resolutely back to Michael's face. "Okay," he said. "Let's go!"

Michael turned around and crouched down, the water lapping at his ankles now. Daniel stepped forward and climbed on Michael's back. There was nothing for him to hold on to except Michael's shoulders, and he dug in with both hands. Michael flinched, then launched himself back into the freezing water.

It had gotten deeper in the minutes they'd spoken. Feeling himself begin to float, Michael took a deep breath and pushed forward, his body straining with the effort of fighting the tide. The waves tugged at him, the brine stinging his eyes and face, but he forged ahead, the boy clinging to his back.

Suddenly, he felt Daniel begin to float away. Reaching back, Michael grabbed him and pulled him closer. Holding Daniel with one hand, Michael stroked the water with the other. He was starting to go numb.

They reached the cliff.

The ledge where the rope still hung was three feet above them. With his fingers digging into the rocky side and Daniel clinging to his back, Michael turned and yelled, his voice hoarse above the waves. "I'm going under the water. You stand on my shoulders and boost yourself up. Can you do that?"

The boy's face was chalk, his teeth chattering from both cold and fear. He nodded.

Michael took a deep breath and slid beneath the paralyzing waves. The boy's tennis shoes scraped over Michael's back and he climbed upward...then slipped.

Popping up to the surface, Michael gasped for air and snatched Daniel back, the outgoing wave breaking angrily against them both. He shook the water from his eyes and blinked. "You okay?"

Daniel tried gamely to move his head up and down, but he was shivering so hard, the gesture was more like a jerk than a nod. "I—I'm okay. Let me try again. I—I can do it!"

"Sure you can! Just go for it, okay?"

Michael took another deep breath and slid beneath the water again. He had no feeling in his legs now. How would he get them up the cliff?

Going slower this time, Daniel's feet found traction, and he hoisted himself upward with a choppy jerk. As soon as the boy's weight was gone, Michael surfaced, panting for air, his lungs about to collapse. He glanced up.

Overhead, Daniel was staring down, his expression triumphant. "I m-made it!" he cried out.

Michael grinned, his hands curling into paralyzed claws because of the cold. He couldn't speak anymore, his own teeth starting to knock against each other. He nodded his encouragement.

He briefly considered sending the boy up alone, but as soon as he had the thought, he dismissed it. Daniel would be dead by the time he reached the top—he had no way to control the rope. He'd be scraped and battered all the way up.

Taking a deep breath, Michael pushed himself up, his fingers tearing at the cliff. He fell once, then fell again. Bleeding, numb and exhausted, he knew he had to make it soon or he wouldn't make it at all.

He launched himself toward the ledge…and caught the crumbling rock with the tips of his fingers.

Shivering so hard his hands could barely function, he finally managed to wrap the main rope around his waist. He held his arms out for the boy. Daniel stepped into his embrace and tucked his legs around Michael, his arms going around his neck. Pulling twice on the rope, Michael felt it go taut, then slowly...very slowly they began to inch upward, Michael's frozen boots stiff against the rocky cliff as he held his legs out to stop them from being dragged over the knifelike projections.

Fifteen minutes later, they were at the top.

EVA REACHED DOWN, her hands slipping over the taut, slick muscles of Michael's biceps to Daniel's thin shoulders. Pulling her nephew from Michael before they even reached the top, she laid him down on the rocky plateau where she'd anxiously watched the rescue. Wrapping a blanket around him, she struggled not to lose it completely.

Her hands went over his body as she spoke. "My God, Daniel, are you all right? Is anything broken? Are you bleeding?"

"I—I'm okay, Aunt—uh, Mom. I—I'm just fine, really." His teeth were clicking against each other, his lips a bluish white. "Are—are you m-mad at me?"

"Mad? Mad doesn't even cover it." Now that he was here and all in one piece, she wanted to punish him. But she wouldn't, of course. She'd hug him and love him and give him hot chocolate. Making her voice stern, she gave none of this away. "We'll talk about it later. You have some explaining to do."

She turned her attention to Michael and flinched when she saw his chest. Where he hadn't scraped it bloody on the rocks, it was bruised and swelling from the rope. Wincing sympathetically, she gingerly wrapped a towel as far as it would go around his shoulders—which wasn't too far.

He followed her gaze with his own and grimaced. "Looks like I had a run-in with a train...and lost."

"I've got bandages and antibiotics back at the house. We'll go there—it'll be better than going to the local hospital." Pulling her bottom lip in, she met his eyes, her emotions kicking in now that everyone was safe. "How can I ever thank you? You saved his life."

Pulling the ends of the towel with both hands, he shook his head, droplets of cold water going everywhere. "You don't have to thank me," he said gruffly. "I did what anyone would've—"

"Oh, no, I don't think so," she interrupted, her voice starting to quiver. Nodding toward a group of men dressed in blue fatigues, she said, "The cops got here just about the time you reached Danny. I didn't see any of them go down that rope to help...and that's their job."

Michael glanced over at the men, then back at Eva. He smiled. "They probably know better. It *was* pretty rough."

She reached out and put her hand on his. "I owe you a debt I'll never be able to repay. This was an accident that could have ended a whole lot differently than it did."

A sudden gust of wind whipped a strand of dark hair into his even darker eyes. Threading his fingers through the still-damp curls, he pushed them back and looked down at her, his expression as fierce as the clouds that had begun to gather overhead. When he spoke, his words sent a shock wave directly toward her.

"This was no accident. It was planned."

through the swinging doors, he peeked inside and looked down at her. His expression was one the doctor had possibly either overlooked. When he spoke, the words came out as if every breath he took hurt.

"This was—

CHAPTER NINE

HER MOUTH FORMED a perfect O, and her fingers fluttered up to her neck uncertainly.

It wasn't surprise he was seeing. It was fear.

"Wh-what do you mean?"

"This isn't the time or the place to explain," he said, his voice dropping as he slanted a look at an approaching policeman. "You stall this guy while I go talk to Danny. Then we'll all go back to your place, and I'll tell you more."

He took a step toward the blanket where Daniel was sitting, but Eva didn't move. She seemed *incapable* of moving, shock and horror freezing her in place. The policeman was almost upon them.

"Go on," Michael said roughly. "I'll explain it all later."

The words seemed to jar her into action. She nodded once, then turned to meet the cop. Michael walked over to Daniel, who was sitting in a circle of his buddies. Undoubtedly fearing punishment, the kids scattered as Michael walked up.

He crouched down and spoke without preamble. "Which one of those guys is Armando?"

Daniel looked around, but the boy was gone, just as Michael had known he would be. He was most likely miles down the road with Mr. Cashmere by now.

"He's not here. I...I guess he went home."

"Did the cart belong to him?"

"No. It was Diego's—he sits next to me at school."

"And where is he? I'd like to talk with him."

Daniel shook his head. "He left. The others told me he's got to figure out what to tell his dad about the cart. His father told him never to take it around the cliff. I guess everyone knew it was bad, except me and Armando, huh?"

Not exactly. "Tell me about Armando. Why did you go with him? And when he left you at the cliff, what did he say?"

"Well, he said he was friends with Diego, and that it was his turn to drive the cart. He asked me if I wanted to go with him, and I said yes. When we got to the other side of the cliff, the motor died. He tried to start it a few times, but it would never go. He jumped off and said he'd go get help. He told me to wait with the cart because if we left it alone, someone might steal it." He stopped speaking and looked over Michael's shoulder at Eva, the green of his eyes changing to a darker shade of jade as suspicion came into his gaze. "Do you think he...was lying?"

"I'm not sure," Michael said evasively. "But for now, let's keep it just between us. Don't say anything to the police about Armando, okay? I promise I'll tell you everything later."

"Does my, uh, mom know about this?"

Michael nodded.

Daniel twisted his bottom lip and chewed on it for a moment. "All right," he said finally, "but if this isn't okay…"

"It's the right thing to do," Michael assured him. "Believe me, you don't want them involved in this. I'm sure if your dad were here, he'd tell you the same thing."

The boy's eyes jerked to Michael's face and grew huge.

Before Michael could say more, Eva walked up, the policeman beside her. He was wearing stiff blue fatigues, the cuffs tucked into polished boots, a heavy leather belt at his waist. His hat, a boxy blue cap with a stiff bill, added to his military air.

"This is *Oficial* Perneau," Eva said. "He's with the *policía provincial.* He heard the call and came right out."

Michael shook the man's extended hand, his eyes going to the brass epaulets and rows of ornate braid chasing their way across his shoulders. Perneau greeted him, then asked Daniel, in Spanish, if he was all right. The boy answered quickly and nodded his head, his eyes shifting uneasily to Michael as he fell silent once more. The lawman's gaze followed Daniel's. Michael met his look, but there was little to read other than mistrust. Perneau spoke again, his eyes never leaving Michael's face.

Eva nodded gravely, then translated for Michael. "He says you're a real hero. No one's ever managed a rescue at this spot before. He wants you to come

down to the station where they can take your photo
for the local paper and interview you like a proper
héroe.''

''I don't think so, but thank him for me anyway.''

She spoke to the man beside her. He raised his
eyebrows and argued briefly, but Eva just shrugged
and smiled. The policeman looked sharply at Michael
again and studied him for another minute, then finally he gave up and turned away, barking orders to
the remaining men. They piled back into the ancient
black Ford Falcons that they'd come in and drove
off.

As soon as they disappeared, Eva tentatively faced
Michael. Her hair had come undone and was hanging
in messy tendrils around her anxious eyes. Two
curved lines of worry had etched themselves on either side of her mouth, another one going all the way
across her forehead. Curiously enough, her frazzled
appearance made her more appealing, giving her an
air of fragility that she'd kept hidden until now. Michael resisted the unexpected urge to wrap his arms
around her and held up a hand instead.

''We need to get everyone home. We'll talk
there.'' Putting a hand on his rib cage, he winced
involuntarily, a spasm of pain rippling across his
chest. He'd bruised a rib. Black dots danced in front
of his eyes.

''You're right. Let's go.'' Eva's gaze locked with
his. ''You can tell me everything there.''

IT TOOK MORE THAN AN HOUR for everyone to get
loaded up and back to town. A young man at the

scene volunteered to drive Michael's car, while Eva and Daniel took their own truck. She glanced toward the dark blue Peugot as she pulled away from the beach. Michael was slumped in the passenger side, his face now gray with fatigue and pain.

This was no accident.

Glancing across the seat of the truck, she peered at Daniel, her brain tumbling in confusion, her psyche still aching from the scare. What did Daniel know about all this? She wanted to ask him exactly what had happened, but she couldn't bring herself to revive him. His eyes were closed, his head resting against the back of the seat. His color had returned a bit, and his lips had lost their bluish tinge, but he looked as exhausted as Michael.

She shook her head and groaned, her hands suddenly trembling against the steering wheel. What on earth would she have done if Michael hadn't been there? What the hell kind of protectress was she, for God's sake?

What was she going to do *now?*

There were no answers to her question. Twenty minutes later, she turned onto their street. It was late in the afternoon and things were quiet for a change, the sidewalks almost empty. She parked along the curb, then roused Daniel. He came awake slowly and shuffled inside, still half-asleep as she got him up the stairs and into his bed. After checking him for hidden bumps and bruises, she finally gave in to his complaints and let him go back to sleep without bothering to bathe him. The dirt behind his ears could wait—he was all right, and that was the main thing.

A few minutes later, Michael's car pulled up. From the living-room window, she watched as Michael gingerly crawled out of the car. She ran downstairs and opened the front door.

He walked in, holding his side.

"Can you make it upstairs?"

He grimaced. "I think so."

She came beside him and wrapped her arm around his waist. Under her fingers she could feel muscles like steel. "Lean on me," she said, her eyes going to his face. "It'll help."

He didn't argue. Without another word, he draped his arm over her shoulder, the warmth of his body making its way up and down her own, his arm heavy against her shoulder as they took the stairs, painful step by painful step. At the top, she got him to the couch and no farther. He closed his eyes and sank into the cushions, his face pale beneath his tan.

"Maybe I should call a doctor," she said. "If those ribs are broken—"

"They aren't broken." He opened his eyes. "I've had worse and done less, believe me."

"A shattered rib can pierce a lung."

"It'll be okay."

"Do you know for sure? Are you a doctor?"

"Yeah, I'm sure, but no, I'm not a doctor."

She stared at him for a long while, the clock behind her ticking loudly in the silence that followed. "You aren't a salesman, either."

He lifted his black gaze to hers. The ripple of apprehension that came with his gaze only intensified her fear, but she couldn't back down. Not now.

"Who are you?"

Silence.

"What are you doing here?"

More silence.

"Why did you save him?" she whispered, her voice finally cracking.

"What was I supposed to do? Let him drown?"

"What *are* you supposed to do? You tell me. And you can start by explaining what you meant about what happened—that it was no accident."

He waited half a heartbeat, then he spoke wearily. "I'll tell you everything...but could we at least tape up my ribs first?"

He didn't think she'd agree, but she finally nodded her head. "Go to my bathroom—it's the first door on the left. I'll get some first-aid supplies and meet you there."

Pulling himself upright, Michael walked slowly in the direction she'd indicated. The small bathroom was spotless, white tile covering the floor and going up the walls, a generous tub and double sink taking up the opposite side, a row of cosmetics and perfume lining its surface. On the other side were the toilet and bidet. He sat down on the latter and waited for her, trying to decide exactly what he was going to say to her.

But he didn't have enough time to decide. She came into the room two seconds later, her hands filled with white bandages and tape, scissors and ointment. After dumping it all on the fluffy white rug at his feet, she began to fill the tub, steam rising as hot water poured out of the tap. She grabbed one of the white towels on a nearby rack and soaked it. A moment later, she handed it to him. "You need to clean up those scrapes, then I'll put on the ointment."

The hot towel burned the shredded skin of his fingers. He made a few quick, inefficient swipes, then handed it back.

"That's not good enough. There's still dirt in the cuts."

"I'll live—just give me the cream."

Frowning, she ignored his outstretched hand and took the towel from him instead, gently pressing it against his skin and cleansing the cuts more thoroughly. Her touch was easy, but it was all he could do to sit still. Looking down at the crown of her head, he concentrated on the sheen of her dark hair and the faint fragrance of lavender that seemed to be coming from the towel. She was done quickly.

Handing him the ointment, she turned away. "Put as much of that on as you can stand. It'll sting, but it'll keep out the infection."

A few minutes later, he asked. "Can you help me?"

She looked up from the bandage she was cutting.

"I can't reach the spots on my back."

Her expression turned uneasy, but she nodded her head. "Uh, sure. Just turn around."

He handed her the tube of cream, then swiveled.

Her fingers smoothed over his skin, easing the cream into the scrapes with slow, sensual strokes. He concentrated on the tiles in front of him. One of them had a flaw in it, a tiny bump. He stared at the raised spot and forced his mind into blankness. The last woman who'd touched him this softly, this intimately, had been his wife. A pair of blue eyes appeared on the white tile, tilted and inquisitive. He pushed the image away. It was replaced by a pair of dark eyes, full of uneasiness. He pushed them away, too.

"I'm finished."

Hearing Eva's voice, Michael realized she'd stopped. He looked down. A white, tight bandage was covering his torso. He raised his eyes to hers.

She rocked back on her heels and spoke softly. "Now you tell me who in the hell you really are...and what you're doing here."

CHAPTER TEN

SHE HAD HER HANDS on her hips, and her black eyes were flashing sparks that told him he could postpone the inevitable no longer. And it was just as well. He was running out of time.

"Michael Masters *is* my real name," he finally said, "but you're right. I'm not a salesman. I work for myself. My company's called Masters Incorporated. It's based in Houston."

The tension in the room went up another notch. Eva said nothing, but continued to stare, her eyes drilling into him. Her words were chilly when she eventually spoke. "And what do you do at Masters Incorporated?"

"I find people," he said wearily. "People who don't want to be found."

There was a sharp intake of breath as her eyes widened and she grew still. Behind her gaze, he could almost see her mind working over his words, turning them, examining them, as she decided what to do. He couldn't help but admire the way she received the news. She wasn't as calm as she appeared, but she was far from panicking.

She phrased her next question carefully. "Are you saying someone hired you to look for me?" She frowned and tilted her head, a perfect imitation of confusion. "Who on earth would care about—"

"Give it up." Despite his appreciation of her efforts, he was weary of the game and too exhausted to carry on anymore. "I know who you are, Eva. I know everything."

She stared at him mutely.

"I know about Thomas and Sally. I know who Daniel really is. I know the two of you were witnesses to their murders." He paused and took a deep, painful breath. "And I know someone tried to kill Daniel today."

She sat down on the edge of the tub. Her heart thumped painfully against her chest, and her pulse roared so loudly in her ears she wasn't sure she'd heard him right. But she had. Her worst nightmare had just come true.

"Who...who...?" She couldn't even get out the words.

"Who hired me or who's trying to kill Daniel?"

"Both," she said hoarsely.

"The man who's trying to kill Daniel is the same man who's been following you ever since I got here. Dark, medium height, looks local, but dresses well. Know anything about him?"

She felt faint. Her fingers gripped the slick edge of the tub. "Someone's been following me?"

He nodded. "Everywhere you go. He was at the beach today with a teenager who is, I'm sure, the same one who was driving the cart when it 'broke down.' They engineered the whole thing and left Daniel out there to be caught by the tide.''

"They…planned it? But how could they know…? I don't understand.''

"They probably didn't have an exact plan, but when you got to the beach, they figured they could wangle something and make it look like an accident. The guy who drove me here said there was a drowning out there just last week. It's called *Punta Peligrosa*—Dangerous Point. Lots of things can happen in a place like that.''

"But why? Why not just kill him? This doesn't make any sense.''

"They obviously want it to look like a mishap. They don't want someone to know they're behind it.'' He shrugged. "Who knows why? Maybe they want to get out of here before anyone can start looking for a murderer. Maybe they don't want you alarmed so they can do you next. Maybe they've been told to make it look that way.''

She stared at him numbly. From the back of her mind came an image, an image of a careering car shooting around a corner and heading for Daniel. Another "accident" that didn't quite materialize. Her throat closed so tautly she couldn't even swallow.

The gunrunners Thomas had been chasing couldn't care less if someone thought it was murder or not. Part of their reputation *was* their ruthlessness. Only one person would really care whether or not it looked like an accident. The one person who could be destroyed if the truth ever came out.

Jack Finely. It had to be. He'd found them, and now he was finishing the job.

But *how* had he found them?

She stared at the man in front of her. "Who sent you to find us?" she whispered. "Who hired you?"

He stared back, a dark stubble shadowing his angular jaw, the look in his eyes hardening. "The Treasury Department. The person in charge is Jack Finely."

She felt the blood drain from her face…actually *felt* the color depart and leave in its place a sickly pallor. Her stomach rolled over, then once again, and she swayed, her ears buzzing loudly.

He reached out to steady her, but she jerked away before his hand made contact. "I'm not here to hurt you," he said softly. "I'm here to help."

"To help me—" She stopped abruptly. "Jack Finely doesn't want to help me. He wants to kill me. Me and Daniel."

"He wants you to testify, then he's going to put you in the witness protection program. You'll be safe. It's the only way."

She was already shaking her head before he even finished. "That program's a joke."

"It's run by the U.S. Marshals. Jack wouldn't be involved after a certain point. He'd turn you over to them, then—"

"I don't care! And it doesn't even matter anyway. That's *not* what Jack has in mind. He set my brother up. He's the one who got Thomas killed. He wants

Daniel and me back so he can take care of us once and for all.''

Michael's face remained expressionless, but something flickered in his eyes. Something that told her she had his attention as she hadn't had before. ''What makes you think that about Jack?'' he asked.

''I know things. I have proof,'' she said evasively. ''Thomas knew. He told me.''

''What are you talking about? What kind of proof?''

She shook her head. ''Oh, no. No way. I'm not telling you anyth—''

He moved so fast she didn't even see how it happened. One second he was sitting across from her; the next moment he had his fingers wrapped around her arm. He was hurt—how had he done that? Her question fled as he spoke.

''I'm your only chance, Eva,'' he said, his breath warm against her face, his eyes drilling into hers. ''I'm the only thing between you and the bad guys. If you don't tell me the whole story, you'll regret it later.''

He wasn't holding her very tight—his fingers were caressing her forearm as much as anything else. She couldn't move, though. She was paralyzed—by his words, by his proximity, by the power radiating from him. He was so close, so intense, that she could feel the tension coming from his body. It seemed to ripple outward, like some kind of net to trap her. It made no sense at all, but for one crazy minute, she thought he was going to kiss her.

Then the moment passed. He eased his grip but didn't release her. "I'm on your side, can't you see that? Yours and Daniel's. How could you think otherwise after what happened today?"

Her mouth was cotton dry. "You aren't protecting us if you take us back. You'll be arranging our murders."

"You don't underst—"

"No. *You* don't understand. Jack Finely will kill us if you take us back. That's how it would work. No other way. He had my brother killed and I know it."

His eyes were two black coals. "Then show me your proof."

"I'm telling you it's the truth—that's your proof."

He waited for a minute, then spoke. "And Houston told me just the opposite."

"Wh-what do you mean?"

He didn't move, but he dropped her arm. Standing so close she could see a light spot near the iris of his right eye, he stayed silent.

It took her a moment to process it all, to completely understand. Then she thought of Jack and how he operated. When she finally caught on, she wanted to throw up. She could hardly get out the words.

"J-Jack told you I had something to do with my own brother's death, didn't he? You think I was behind it?"

"What I think doesn't matter."

"But it's not true," she cried. "I could never kill

Thomas. He was my only family, the only one I cared about. I looked up to him like—''

"All I care about is getting you back to Houston, Eva. Nothing else is important to me.''

Looking up into his gaze, the chilly words of denial ringing between them, she started to speak...then stopped. For just a second, there was something in his gaze, an opening, a window of sorts, that came and went so quickly she couldn't be sure she'd seen it.

He was lying. In that instant, she knew.

The truth *did* matter to him. It mattered so much, in fact, he'd already thought it through and come up with his own conclusion. He didn't believe Jack. He didn't think she really was a killer.

Why he couldn't tell her this, she had no idea, but it was there, in his eyes. He just couldn't admit it to her for some reason.

"I'm not going back there," she said softly. "And I'm sure as hell not letting you take Daniel, either. I'll take us somewhere else.''

"That's not an option.''

"I'll make it one.''

"You can't run. You can't hide.''

"I've gotten this far, haven't I?''

A flicker of something lightened his eyes but only for a moment. "Yeah, you have...but I'll just find you again.''

She fought a sinking sensation. She didn't doubt him for a minute. Looking at his battered body and the sculpted angles of his face, she could easily read the strength behind the words.

"Then I'd run again," she said with false bravado.

"And I'd find you again." He reached out and traced the line of her jaw with his finger, a gentle touch that surprised her so much she couldn't move. "It's my job, Eva, and I do it well. Don't ever think you can beat me at it because you can't."

His voice was low and rugged, so sensual it touched her as surely as his finger.

"I'm not going back," she said quietly. "I promised Thomas I'd protect Daniel, and that's what I'm going to do."

"You can't protect him if you're dead." He paused to let the words sink in. "And that's exactly how you're going to end up if you don't go back with me. Those guys out there—" he pointed with his chin toward the front of the house "—they're just waiting for you. You and Daniel. They failed this once, but next time you won't be so lucky. I don't know who in the hell they are, but I'm sure they learn from their mistakes. By now, they've probably figured out they're going to have to get you first—to get to Daniel."

"We'll leave," she said stubbornly.

"And they'll find you again...just like me." His voice held a hint of anger. "Dammit, Eva, you didn't even know they were here, following you."

Her own anger flared. "That's because I was too busy trying to figure out who *you* were!"

"Well, now you know, okay? And we have to get

the hell out of here before they decide to try again. *That* is the only option—''

The piercing ring of the doorbell suddenly split the tense silence and interrupted his tirade. Eva started, her head turning automatically toward the sound, Michael instinctively stepping in front of her.

Their eyes met. ''Are you expecting anyone?''

She shook her head.

''Do you have a gun?''

She nodded.

''Then go get it and meet me at the door.'' Without another word, he slipped from the bathroom.

Eva followed right behind him, racing down the hall to her bedroom, her legs shaking. She reached under her mattress and pulled out the ancient pistol she'd hidden there, then turned and ran downstairs.

Michael was standing beside the door. Motioning her to one side, he mouthed, ''Ask who's there.''

She licked her lips. ''Who is it?''

There was a moment's silence, and then the answer. *''Soy el Oficial Perneau, señora.* Please open the door. We need to talk to you.''

She stared at Michael, her heart thumping. ''What should I do?''

He thought for a moment, frowning. Finally, he shrugged. ''You'd better let him in.'' He nodded toward her hand. ''You might want to hide that first, though.''

She glanced down at the gun, then nodded. ''Just a minute,'' she called out.

Slipping the weapon in the bag she'd left at the

bottom of the stairs, she squeezed between Michael and the door. The space was tight, and he made no effort to move. As her hand reached for the locks, he stopped her, turning her head with two fingers on her chin. Pulling her closer to him with his other hand, he spoke softly into her ear, his lips moving against her hair.

She knew what he was doing—he wanted to talk to her without the policeman hearing—but her heart thumped uncontrollably against her chest at the closeness they were suddenly sharing. There was nothing between them but his bandage and her thin T-shirt. The heat rising from his skin burned through to hers. Curiously, she shivered.

He whispered. "Don't do anything clever, Eva. I want him to think we're lovers and anxious to get rid of him. Stick to that script, and when he's gone, then you're going upstairs and packing so we can leave."

His touch was electrifying, and his nearness made it almost impossible for her to breathe. She stared up at him, her emotions tumbling with a combination of fear, disbelief, anger and something that felt like—but couldn't be—attraction. She didn't stop to try to figure it all out.

"I'll get rid of him," she said tightly, "but leaving here with you is the last thing I'm going to be doing."

HIS HANDS RESTING on Eva's shoulders, Michael stood behind her as she opened the outer door. The wind had picked up considerably, and the Argentinean policeman standing in front of them had his left hand on his blue cap to keep it from blowing away. His other hand rested on the automatic weapon he had strapped over one shoulder. He stared coldly at Michael before looking at Eva. His quick eyes didn't miss Michael's possessive touch, and that was exactly what he'd been counting on. Michael wanted the man out of here, and fast. As soon as he'd told Eva who he was, the look in her eyes was all he'd needed to know she was going to run. As soon as she could.

"I am sorry to bother you, *señora*. How is your son? Is he recovering well?"

"He's...he's sleeping right now, but I'm sure he's going to be just fine. No serious problems. Thank you for asking."

Michael bent down to her ear and kissed the side of her cheek. "Tell him we were about to go to bed." For good measure, he kissed her again, then straightened back up.

She managed to stifle her startled reaction, turning instead to the man before her. "We...we were just about to retire for the evening, *señor....*"

His watchful eyes had registered their caress, and he inclined his head, a stronger gust of wind howling around the corner, bringing with it a flurry of dust. "Then I won't keep you long. Might I step inside for a moment?"

Shooting a quick glance in Michael's direction, Eva moved out of the way and let the officer inside.

His presence and his weapon filled the tiny alcove with a menacing air.

Michael stepped to one side, his hand sliding slowly down from Eva's shoulder to rest at the curve of her waist. He slipped his hand beneath the edge of her short T-shirt and patted her gently. She glanced up at him, and he smiled, his lips curving upward so convincingly that he fooled even her for just a moment.

And almost fooled himself. The quick kiss had been torture, but this was even worse. Her skin was warm and silky soft, an invitation to his senses, an invitation he hadn't allowed himself to savor for way too long. The level of his distraction startled him, and for a second he wasn't sure he could manage the deception. Then he lifted his eyes to Perneau's and knew he had to. The cop's gaze was dark and hooded, reptilian enough to abruptly remind Michael of where he was, with whom he was dealing and the danger that faced them all.

Argentinean "law enforcement." A real oxymoron. The only laws enforced here were the ones they made up on the spot. Michael's uneasiness grew.

As if sensing Michael's unrest, Perneau looked at Eva and asked about Michael's health. She glanced at him quickly, then told him Michael was fine, although he might have some bruised ribs.

"You should take him to hospital," the policeman said. "They can help."

That's doubtful, Michael wanted to say. He'd

walked past the dilapidated building last week. If Eva had suggested they go there, he would have declined. She'd done a passable job taping him. That's all he needed.

"It's not necessary, but thank you for your concern. I...I've had some medical training, and I took care of it."

"You were a nurse in Canada?" he asked.

"No, but I...I volunteered at a local clinic."

She looked apprehensive, awkward. Michael wondered if the cop detected her disquiet, too. He tightened his fingers against her waist, a move meant to reassure himself as much as her, he realized with a start.

"W-was there something you needed...?" she asked faintly.

The commandant answered slowly, his gaze going to Michael's face before he spoke to Eva. "You will have to translate for me, I believe."

She nodded. "Of course."

He turned to face Michael directly. "Sr. Masters, is it?"

She looked at Michael. "He's confirming your name. Nod yes."

Michael nodded.

"I was wondering if you have a permit for the rifle in your room."

Michael struggled to keep his face blank until she had translated the words, her own startled reaction obvious in the tenseness of her body. Inside Michael's brain, the gears were already beginning to turn.

They'd searched his room.

Why? Probably because they'd been paid to, most likely by the man who'd been following Eva. He had to know by now that Michael was involved with her and he was wondering just who Michael was, what role he had in this complicated game.

Michael looked directly into the cop's eyes, his gaze as cold as the water he'd been in earlier that day. "Of course I have a permit," he said, disdain filling his voice. "It's the law."

Eva blinked at his attitude. When she translated his answer, it held considerably more respect. The cop had already gotten the message, though. Michael's tone had made his feelings more clear than Eva's words ever would.

Perneau spoke again, Eva's English coming right behind it. "Do you have the permit with you?" she asked.

He glanced down at her. "No. It's back in my room. With my gun."

She translated for the cop. He smiled coldly and shook his head. "I don't believe that's true, *señor*. We looked in the case and found nothing besides the weapon. Are you sure?"

Eva started to speak again, but Michael interrupted her. "I got it," he said. "Tell him it's there, but he had no business in my room."

Her eyes shot to his. "I can't do that."

"Just tell him."

She turned reluctantly to the policeman. "My friend assures you the permit is there. He's not questioning your authority, of course, but he thought it was a private suite. Is there a problem?"

Michael's teeth ground against each other at her attitude, but she was playing it perfectly. Better than he'd ever do.

"We were called to the Austral because of another situation," Perneau explained, "and the door to your suite was open. We wanted to make sure everything was in order." He shrugged and smiled in an oily fashion. "To make sure nothing was missing."

"That's very helpful of you," she responded. "We'll go down immediately and check—"

Perneau made a clicking sound with his tongue. "I'm afraid that's not possible. The *señor* will have to come with me now. To the station. We have questions for him."

Eva swallowed, the graceful column of her neck moving nervously. She turned to Michael. "He wants you to come—"

"Ask him why."

She turned. *"Por qué—"*

This time, Perneau interrupted her. "Because there was no permit. We must make sure the weapon is legal."

A slow burn started in Michael's chest. His hands clenched into fists at his side. "I'm not going down there," he said to Eva, his soft voice tense. "Make up an excuse."

She looked up. "An excuse? Are you crazy? What

kind of excuse do I make to a man with a machine gun slung over his shoulder?''

His hand caressed her back, and he smiled tenderly for Perneau's benefit. ''Tell him you're upset and you don't want to be alone right now. Tell him you need me here.''

She frowned in concern, and her voice held a note of warning. ''These guys are serious, Michael. I think you should consider going—''

His stare quickly put a stop to her words. ''I know exactly what you think, Eva, and I know exactly why. It's not going to work, so forget it.''

Her eyes widened, their dark depths unable to hide her flash of consternation at being caught out so easily. Her thinking had been obvious. With him out of the way, she'd be gone. Immediately. But it wasn't going to happen that way.

''You'd never make it,'' he said. ''This is a setup, don't you see?''

''But—''

''Tell him we must go,'' the commandant interrupted impatiently, his voice rough and insistent. ''Right now.''

Michael's fingers squeezed her waist, a note of warning.

She understood even though she didn't agree. ''But I...I really need him here, *señor*. Please...'' she said, her eyes huge. ''Is there no other way we could handle this?''

Perneau looked unexpectedly happy at her answer. ''Oh, *sí, señora*. There's definitely another way.'' He took two steps back and twisted the doorknob, pulling the door open and revealing five other men.

They each held an automatic weapon and the barrels were pointed toward them.

Smiling with satisfaction, Perneau looked directly at Michael. "This is the other way. Do you like it better?"

CHAPTER ELEVEN

EVA'S HEART BEGAN to pound, and behind her, she felt Michael tense.

Perneau spoke in a polite voice. "I can march him down the street like this if he prefers."

"I don't think that will be necessary," she said stiffly. Getting Michael out of her way *had* been her number-one goal, but getting him killed wasn't the way she wanted to do it. She turned to look at him. "There's nothing else you can do," she whispered. "They want you to go now."

His gaze shot over her head toward the armed men, and he studied them for a moment before he faced her again. His expression was grim. "Tell him I'll go, but I want his guarantee he'll release me within the hour."

"Guarantee? He's not going to—"

"Just tell him."

She repeated his words to Perneau, and the cop's gaze swung to Michael. A silent communication seemed to transpire between the two men, then slowly Perneau nodded his head. Michael had nothing to trade, but Eva could have sworn they came to some kind of understanding. Turning to his men, Perneau barked a quick order and they all stepped back.

Perneau stood by, his eyes expectant as he held out a hand toward the street.

Michael turned to Eva, and before she could react, he swept her into his arms. Cradling her head with one hand, his fingers warm beneath the curtain of her hair, he bent his face to hers. Their lips were almost touching. "Put your arms around me."

Like an automated doll, she lifted her arms to his waist and wrapped them around him. His body was steel beneath her fingers, the white bandage smooth and tight.

"I only have one thing to say to you," he whispered, his stare as piercing as the wind whistling around the doorway. "You're in danger. If you try to leave here without me, you're going to get killed. They're taking me so they can get to you." He paused. She could feel the beat of his heart through her shirt. "Do you understand?"

"I understand you have a job to do," she shot back, her voice fierce. "But so do I...and trying to scare me isn't going to keep me from doing it."

He held her gaze for another second, then he lowered his head unexpectedly and began to kiss her, his lips pressing hard against hers, his arms preventing her escape.

She considered struggling but knew she shouldn't. Then, in the space of time it took for the thought to come and go, she found herself responding to him. Sensing her feelings, he pulled her even closer, his hand burning where it lay on her neck, his chest pressing against her breasts. Slowly, sensually, his tongue slipped into her mouth and she felt herself open to him even more, losing—for the moment— any sense of reality that might have lingered.

When Perneau's armed escort began to snicker, Michael raised his lips from hers and loosened his grip. He didn't release her completely, though.

Dazed and confused, still in the circle of his arms, she looked up at him. His eyes were two black stones as he spoke, his voice so low it sent shivers down her body.

"Don't run, Eva. It's pointless. I'll find you no matter where you go."

FROM THE WINDOW ABOVE, she watched them leave. Perneau hadn't handcuffed him, but it was more than clear Michael was going nowhere. Within the cordon of police that surrounded him, he was walking slowly up the street. He glanced back only once. She moved quickly away from the window. When she could no longer see them, Eva turned around to face the empty room, her shoulders suddenly slumping.

She gave herself the luxury of two full minutes to absorb what had happened. Two complete sweeps of the clock's hand to think about Daniel almost being killed, to think about who Michael really was, to think about the other men who were now out to kill both her and Daniel. And at the end of those two minutes, she had two seconds left to think about the way she'd felt when Michael had kissed her. The way her legs had actually gone weak and her heart had acted as though it were about to jump from her chest. A groan of disbelief broke the last and final tick of time. How much crazier could her life become?

She didn't have the answer, but she knew one thing.

She had only an hour to leave.

Gathering herself up, she started toward the bedroom, her brain already whirling with the possibilities. There weren't too many, and suddenly she was glad she'd already started thinking about escape routes after Michael had shown up. With trembling fingers, she grabbed the phone and called the airport. The answer she got was the one she feared the most. "Sorry, *Señora*. Tomorrow's flights have been canceled. Too much wind—"

She hung up before she heard the rest, her fear growing stronger. Now she knew for certain she really had only one alternative. As impossible as it was, she'd have to take a chance and try to drive over the mountains to Chile. The chances were slim to none she'd make it—but what else could she do? Sit in Comodoro and wait for death? Driving out was her only option.

And driving out meant transportation, a vehicle no one would recognize as hers.

She flung some clothes into a suitcase, then grabbed Thomas's briefcase and hurried downstairs. Rummaging in the kitchen, she tossed all the fruit and fresh bread she had into a sack. A moment later, she was running into the courtyard. It connected directly to Maria's house. Eva knocked frantically but softly on her door. After a few minutes that seemed to go on forever, a light came on and the door opened.

A startled Maria stood on the doorstep. *"¡Señora! ¿Qué pasa…?"*

"I need your car, Maria." In her hand, Eva held out an extra set of keys for her truck. She hadn't been able to find her own keys and she'd had to dig these out of the back of a kitchen drawer. "You can have mine."

The trade wasn't fair. Maria drove a ubiquitous Falcon, dark green, a hundred years old. With the roads as bad as they were this time of year, they'd need incredible luck to even get to Sarmiento, the next town heading west, but they'd make it in the Falcon faster than they would in Eva's own recognizable truck. Once there, they could catch a bus or even buy another car.

Maria's eyes were huge as she clasped her nightgown to her body. "Señora Evita—is…is this necessary?"

Eva nodded.

"Will you…come back?"

"Probably not."

"But what about the house? Your things? Your job?"

"Take what you want," Eva answered. "And give the rest away."

The woman stared at Eva a little longer, then she disappeared inside, returning within seconds, her own battered car keys clutched in her hand. "Here," she said, thrusting them toward Eva. "Take it...and take care."

They exchanged a quick hug, then Eva turned and slipped down to the street. Looking in both directions, she saw no one. She ran across the road and jumped into Maria's Falcon, which was always parked there. The engine complained but caught, and after backing the car quickly into the garage, Eva closed the door before even a casual witness appeared. Within minutes, she had the few things she was taking stowed in Maria's Falcon and the briefcase and her pistol lying on the front seat. She roused Daniel enough to get him downstairs and into the car, laying him on the back seat and putting plenty of blankets and pillows around him. With one quick look to assure herself the street was still empty, Eva opened the garage door and eased the car out to the street.

Under the cover of darkness, she turned right, going west. Still, no one was around. Her heart slowed, but only slightly. They drove off into the Patagonian night.

THE MOOD AMONG the armed escort was jovial, almost partylike, as they made their way up the street and headed north toward the police station. With their guns carelessly pointed to the sidewalk and their banter going back and forth, Michael could easily have made a break for it.

But Perneau's steady gaze stopped him. Marching to one side, he kept Michael in his view at all times, his attitude a curious blend of open hostility and braggadocio now that he had him.

They made it to the station within minutes. The three-story building was as pitiful as the rest of Comodoro, but the people he saw were set apart by their obvious anxiety levels and the expressions of dread on their faces—faces that were undoubtedly anticipating certain disasters yet to occur.

Complete and utter silence fell as Michael, Perneau and his men entered.

Perneau seemed oblivious to the sudden, artificial quiet. Striding past the women filling the wooden benches that lined one side of the room, he turned his head toward the rear of the building and spat out some rapid-fire instructions. One of his guards edged Michael in the same direction with the butt of his gun.

An hour later, Michael's earlier suspicions had been confirmed. They'd put him in a cold, empty cell and left him alone. Impatiently pacing from one end to the other the entire time, Michael knew *mordida* must have been exchanged, and for only one purpose. To detain him. Perneau had been bribed to get Michael out of the way for a period of time, an hour being more than adequate.

Eva was probably halfway around the world by now...or dead.

His gut clenched automatically, and his feet dragged to a stop. *Dammit to hell—this wasn't how it was supposed to go down.* Nothing was happening as he'd planned it—not the job, not the circumstances, and certainly not his reactions to Eva herself.

His attention was drawn toward the corridor as footsteps suddenly sounded. They stopped, and Perneau appeared in front of the rusted bars. He held a slip of paper between his fingers. Flipping it back and forth, he smirked at Michael.

He spoke in broken English. "So sorry, *señor*. One of *mis hombres* just found this. It is your permit, no?"

Michael held back an angry retort and reached for the paper.

But Perneau snatched it back.

"You are aware, *señor,* this permit will soon be…um…what do you call it? *Anticuado?*"

Michael supplied the English. "Out-of-date?"

"Ah…you do speak our language, then?"

Michael ignored the comment although it was obvious he could have accused Perneau of the same. "There is plenty of time left on that permit."

"Perhaps…" The man's eyes narrowed. "And perhaps not. There may be some people here in Comodoro who feel it should…expire sooner. Do you understand what I am saying to you?"

"I understand," Michael answered, his voice grim. "But you might want to tell these people I have a job to do here. A job that involves *la señora* Cantrell. If I can't find her…or she has a mishap, it won't matter if the permit has expired. I will eliminate the source of my problems one way or the other."

"These people might not understand."

"I don't really give a damn."

He stared angrily at Perneau through the bars, but all the cop did was shrug carelessly. He'd done *his* job—kept Michael out of the way for an hour. Now he didn't care what happened. He reached forward and unlocked the cell, the noise of the clanging metal loud in the unnatural silence. Impatiently, Michael started to leave. Perneau stopped him with a hand on his arm.

"Go with God, *señor*," he said with a grin. "You are going to need Him."

HE KNEW EXACTLY WHAT he was going to find, but Michael raced to Eva's house anyway, a small prayer burning in the back of his mind that she'd decided to take him seriously.

Banging on the door until his fist was sore, he waited impatiently. When the handle finally turned and the door actually opened, he was shocked. But it wasn't Eva standing in the open doorway.

A short, dark-haired woman glared out at him, her nightgown covered by a thin wrap. He recognized her immediately from his earlier surveillance. She was the *dueña*—the landlady.

She began her denial even before he could speak, her Spanish fast and furious. Michael's matched it.

"Where is the *señora?*" he interrupted. "I need to speak with her."

"I don't know what you're talking about." She pulled her robe closer and peered down the street uneasily before turning back to him. "I'm the only one who lives here."

"She's gone, isn't she? Did she take her truck?"

He peered around the edge of the door toward the courtyard and the windowed garage that lay behind it. The woman tried to shut it in his face, but he managed to catch a glimpse through the glass. Eva's battered black vehicle was a darker shadow inside the already murky space. A measure of hope came over him. He'd grabbed Eva's keys as soon as he'd come into the house after the episode with Daniel. At least he'd prevented her from escaping that way.

Michael stepped closer to the woman, towering over her. "Is she still here? Tell me!"

The frightened woman blinked but refused to back down. She'd taken her stand and wasn't budging. "I...I don't know what you're talking about, *señor*. There's no one here. No one but me." A glint of metal, something she was holding, caught the street-light, the gleam bouncing back to Michael.

He reached out and grabbed her hand, his movement firm but gentle. Opening her fingers, he instantly recognized what she held. An extra set of keys...to Eva's truck. He jerked his head around and saw the empty parking spot across the street. The *dueña*'s own Falcon was gone.

"She took your car, didn't she?"

The poor woman's expression crumpled, immediately confirming his guess. He felt a surge of satisfaction. Eva wouldn't bother to drive to the bus station—it was only a few blocks away. She'd walk it.

And she would have taken a cab to the airport. No, if she'd switched vehicles, that meant she was going to take her chances on the western highway to Chile, the only road that would be open at this time of year. Michael ran all the way back to his hotel.

EVA THOUGHT SHE'D KNOWN dark before, but nothing she'd ever seen compared to the inky blackness she was driving through now. There was no point of reference. No city lights, no friendly houses beside the road, no other cars. Just a vast, empty, black night that had no beginning and no end.

It was inexpressibly frightening.

Glancing in the rearview mirror, she caught a glimpse of Daniel. He was sleeping soundly, his mouth open, a soft snore coming out of it. Michael didn't understand, she told herself, her hands gripping the huge steering wheel until her knuckles gleamed white. He just didn't understand. She would do anything to protect Daniel, and the thought of the danger he'd been in at the beach was more than she could bear. She wasn't going to stay in Comodoro and let those same people have another chance at him. No way.

But even discounting them, she now had Michael to deal with. He acted as though he thought Jack Finely was on the up-and-up, assumed that returning to Houston was the right thing for her and Daniel to do. Was it possible Michael had no knowledge of Jack's real intentions? Was it possible Jack had hired him to find them and sent the second man to kill them?

The more she thought about it, the more she realized that probably was the case. Jack was too clever to reveal his plans to anyone. He would have told Michael just what he did—that he was bringing her and Daniel back to put them into the witness protection program. It was as good an excuse as any, she supposed.

But they'd never end up in the program, or if they did, some "tragedy" would occur and their resulting deaths would be labeled as a "compromised" situation. Unfortunate but sometimes unavoidable. Witnesses could sometimes be found by the bad guys, Jack would explain. The program wasn't infallible.

She glanced over to the seat beside her where Thomas's briefcase and her ancient pistol rested. Inside the case was their money and her brother's laptop computer. The key to everything. Staring at it, she wondered if she should have shown the files to Michael when he'd demanded to see her proof. Part of her had really wanted to—but the other part of her denied the release sharing would have brought. She couldn't trust him. Not now. Maybe never.

Even though he *had* saved Daniel's life.

Groaning with fatigue, both mental and physical, Eva rubbed her gritty eyes and tried to concentrate on the road. What Michael Masters knew or didn't know wasn't really important. Not anymore. She'd never be seeing him again, and despite his warnings, she was fully confident he'd never be able to track them down. He was still in a jail cell, and they were about to disappear again. The road had been tolerable so far. If the weather held, in a few hours they'd be in Sarmiento, and from there, to Chile. Maybe they should even go all the way to Santiago. Maybe it was time to try hiding in the open. Bigger cities offered even more protection in their anonymity than tiny villages did.

She'd just have to be more careful, that's all. More aware of her surroundings. She'd thought she'd been doing a pretty good job, but it rattled her that she hadn't known about the other man following her. She'd obviously managed to escape his eyes as she'd fled town, though. Nothing but blackness continued to swallow their own car lights. She'd be able to see a vehicle approaching or following from miles away.

Michael had been wrong. She'd done it once and she could do it again. Getting lost was not that hard.

The thought brought her back to Michael. He was different from any man she'd ever known before. One moment, he was scaring her to death, and the next, his dark eyes would call out to her. She had the feeling he'd seen too much, done too much, had memories he shouldn't. The body she'd taped up had been battered and bruised. Crisscrossing his back was a series of old scars, white lines that explained he'd gone through worse mishaps, and muscles so hard they told her he felt he had to be prepared for anything. It was a body meant to be a machine. He kept it tuned, repaired and ready for action. That thought scared her as much as anything else had in the past twenty-four hours.

But when he'd kissed her... Something had sparked between the two of them, something that had nothing to do with the danger they were facing. The kiss, his arms, his soft breath against her skin—the combination had been enough to make her want more despite the bizarre circumstances in which it had occurred. And that was a new feeling for sure.

But it would never be repeated. Because she'd never see Michael Masters again.

THE RATTLING SOUND of the car's tires hitting gravel jarred Eva into sudden, painful awareness. Blinking rapidly, she cursed and jerked the wheel to the left, wrestling the car for control and dragging it back to the pavement and away from the shoulder. She must have dozed off. Shocked by the realization, she took a deep breath and rolled down the window beside her, the biting air instantly hitting her face.

Shivering with cold but even more with fright over her lapse, she glanced into the rearview mirror to see that Daniel was all right.

And that's when she saw the car.

It was right behind them, almost on their bumper. An ancient Mercedes with no lights and a single figure behind the wheel.

She told herself he was just another lonely driver sharing the road, but the lie didn't wash. He was too close and going too fast.

Then his bumper roughly tapped hers.

She gasped as the Falcon jumped at the contact, the wheel spinning wildly in her hands, her pistol and the briefcase flying off to disappear somewhere beneath the seat. Cursing soundly, she struggled to regain control of the car. Finally, feeling it respond, she pushed it harder in an effort to escape. Her reward was a little more speed and a lot more noise. The engine seemed to be panting. She jerked a glance toward the floorboard for the gun, but it was nowhere in sight.

From the back seat, Daniel spoke groggily. "Wh- what's going on?"

Another bump, this one more severe.

"Lie down—on the floor!" She had to scream for him to hear her above the wind rushing in from her open window. "Put the pillows all around you."

"Someone's hitting—"

He didn't finish his words before a third bump came. This one wasn't just a bump. It was definitely a hit. She felt the thud of Daniel's body as he rolled off the back seat and lurched sickeningly into the rear of her seat.

"Are you all right?" she yelled.

She heard a muffled "I'm okay" that sounded anxious but convincing.

Gripping the steering wheel as hard as she could, Eva risked another glance into the rearview mirror. All she could make out was a solitary figure behind the wheel. It was too dark to see more, but she thought the driver was a man.

She forced her eyes ahead once more, then wished

she hadn't, her heart jumping into her throat as she saw the route before her. The road was narrowing, twisting more than ever. Hanging on the edge of an incline, it took one torturous turn after another, the unpaved shoulder almost nonexistent. Beyond the edge lay nothing but darkness. Was this the spot he'd been waiting for?

Her heart tumbled in fear as the two cars raced onward. They seemed to be one, he was so close behind her, his brakes screaming a second after hers as she took turn after turn on two wheels. They reached the top of the incline in seconds. She glanced at the rearview mirror and saw with relief that the other car had dropped back.

But as she watched, the old Mercedes surged forward, the wheels plowing against the pavement, the bumper looming frighteningly large in the mirror. Before she could decide what to do, it was too late to do anything.

He hit her. With everything he had—his bumper crashing roughly into hers.

The impact was terrific. The vehicle shrieked. The tires spun. And Eva's heart stopped.

The Falcon sailed off the cliff and into the empty night.

CHAPTER TWELVE

THE SILENCE WAS DEAFENING.

For a moment, Eva thought she really had died. There was no sensation surrounding her but quiet. No feeling, no sounds, no smells, no sight…nothing. Then something wet trickled into her eye. Something wet and stinging. She blinked furiously and raised one hand to her forehead. Her fingers found a gash about three inches long. With a groan, she winced and closed her eyes.

Then remembered. The car behind them, the sickening thud. Daniel.

Her eyes flew open. "Danny? Are you there?"

More silence.

She struggled to gain her bearings, but it was hard in the endless dark. Finally, as her eyes adjusted, the confusing shapes began to take form. She almost wished they hadn't.

The car was tilted on its side, clinging at a desperate angle to the edge of the mountain.

Outside, a shower of pebbles sounded, then a tentative voice broke the quiet. "Aunt Eva? You okay?"

Relief flooded her. "Daniel…I—I'm fine. You all right?"

"I'm okay." His disembodied voice held the same relief as he scrambled closer. "I flew right out the window. I was holding that big ole pillow you stuffed around me. I landed on it, I guess." His legs suddenly came into view, then he bent down and his face appeared. As soon as he saw her, his eyes turned huge and his mouth dropped open in an expression of horror. "You're bleeding! There's blood all over you."

She raised a hand and succeeded in smearing more blood. "It's nothing," she said calmly. "Just a little scratch."

"Can you come out now?"

Her fingers found the edge of the seat belt and followed it to the buckle. "I've got to get the seat belt unstuck, but I'll be right there. Look up...to the edge of the road. Do you see any lights?"

He stood, and she heard him put his hand on the roof of the car as he turned. Another round of rocks pinged against the side of the car, their metallic sound terrifying. The Falcon rocked, almost gently. Her heart leaped into her throat.

"Danny! Don't touch the car! It—it's not stable, okay?"

She heard him move again, his running shoes sliding against the dirt and gravel. "I'm sorry. I didn't know—"

"Don't worry," she answered, her mouth almost too dry to speak as her fingers continued to fumble with the seat belt. "Just don't touch it again, okay?"

"Okay."

The buckle was stuck in the seat. Her fingers dug into the plastic, but the hard cushion refused to budge. Trying not to panic yet, she lifted her eyes and peered out. All she could make out were Daniel's shoes. "Do you see anything?" Continuing to dig, she felt a fingernail rip down to the quick and grimaced. "Look close."

He was silent for just a moment, then he bent back down. She could now see enough in the darkness to tell that his eyes were even bigger than they had been before, and his mouth was twisted with the effort of not crying. "It—it's too dark. And it's scary." His voice cracked on the last word.

"I know, sweetie." She tried to smile with reassurance. The kid had been through hell, and now this! "It *is* scary, but I'm stuck here for just a minute. I want you to find a place and hide till I get out, okay? By a tree, in a ditch—anywhere you can go. Just do it."

"And leave you here?"

She closed her eyes. "I'll be fine. It won't be long before I'm outta here. You go. When you see me crawl out, then call to me so I'll know where you are."

His face disappeared as he stood, and then he shuffled off. She took a deep breath and felt the buckle with the tip of one finger. Digging furiously, she managed to move it an inch, but the car began to tremble again.

She held back a gasp. How far had they rolled already? Could the car drop more? She struggled, her feeling of dread rising another notch as a shower of gravel again sprayed against the car. Daniel, she supposed, digging himself in somewhere in the darkness. She was trapped. He was out there—how could she protect him from here? A scream of frustration and fright built in her throat, then suddenly, Daniel's shoes reappeared.

And beside them stood a beat-up pair of black leather boots.

"I have your 'son,' *señora.* Do you want to kiss him goodbye before I shoot him?"

Eva stopped breathing. The only sound she could hear was the pulse roaring in her ears.

A knee came into view, then it was replaced by a man's face. She'd never seen him before in her life. One of his hands clutched Daniel's shoulder; the other held a gun.

"Who...who are you?" she managed to get out.

"*Su muerte.*"

Your death.

She swallowed, a small cry of fear escaping from deep in her throat. Despite her terror, she realized his Spanish was different, not Castilian. Was he Mexican?

She took a deep breath. "Please...please... You can take me if you want to, but leave the boy."

"My orders are for both—*el pollito* and you."

Again the Mexican pronunciation. The double *l* spoken as a *y.* Argentineans slurred it, made it softer.

Her fingers returned to the buckle. If she could get it free, she might have a chance. She felt faint with fear. "For God's sake, he knows nothing," she said frantically. "I'm the one you want."

"It doesn't matter," he said calmly, almost as if he were talking to himself. "I have my orders. The boy first, then you. Throw the bodies in the car. After I set it on fire, no one will know you were shot."

He stood, and his face disappeared. Struggling against the stubborn seat belt, Eva cried out in panic. *"No!* No! Please..."

The boots moved away. All she could see were Daniel's running shoes dragging against the gravel as he was forced to move, crying and screaming.

"Please..." She tugged uselessly against the cruel strap, her panic reaching new heights, her heart pounding so hard she thought it would explode. *"Wait!"* she screamed frantically.

Then a single shot rang out.

MICHAEL LOWERED THE RIFLE from his shoulder and began to scramble down the side of the mountain. By the time he reached Daniel's side, the boy was sitting on the ground, his legs unable to hold him up a moment longer.

He looked at the dead man beside him, then up to Michael. "You...you shot him."

Michael nodded. "It was you or him, buddy. I didn't have much of a choice."

"That's the second time you saved me."

Michael bent down and looked in the youngster's dazed eyes. "Are you okay?"

Daniel moved his head slowly. "Yeah...I...I guess so. But Aunt Eva—"

"Where is she?" Michael's heart clutched, a painful cramp.

"In the car." He pointed with his chin. "Over there."

"You stay here. I'll check on her."

The little boy looked at the dead man beside him. "Can I move over there? By that tree?"

Michael glanced at the man's body. There was no point in checking for a pulse. His shot had been clean and perfect, guided by the laser sight with deadly accuracy. Right through the heart. There wasn't even any blood...at least from the front.

Michael turned back to Daniel. "That's a good idea. Just stay in sight, okay?" Before he could finish, Daniel had clambered to his feet and was darting toward the scrawny tree.

Michael rose and headed for the battered Falcon. Tipped on its roof, it looked like some kind of upended beetle. He reached the passenger door, and dropping his rifle, he got down on his hands and knees and peered inside.

His breath caught in his chest. Eva was cowering against the door, her legs tucked up, her waist straining against the strap of the seat belt. The ambient light was almost nonexistent, but there was just enough to see more than he wanted to. Blood covered her face, and her eyes were crazed with fear. Then she saw who it was. Her expression went from terror to relief to utter confusion.

"M-Michael?"

He nodded and spoke gently, his heart cracking at the terror in her voice and on her face. "It's me, Eva. Everything's okay." He held out his hand. "You can come out."

She made no effort to move. "Is...is he dead? Daniel?" Her voice was a broken cry of grief.

"Daniel's fine, just shaken up. He's safe. I shot the other guy."

"Daniel's..." She stared at him, her dark eyes two pools of disbelief. "I heard the gun. I thought... You shot the other guy?"

Michael nodded grimly. "Did you know him?"

"No! I never saw him before in my life. He came up behind us in an old Mercedes, then ran us off the road." Her gaze locked on Michael's. She seemed overwhelmed. "You really shot him?"

"I didn't have a choice. He had a Glock to Daniel's head."

"Oh, God." She slumped against the door. "I don't believe this."

He started to reach inside the car. "Come on. Let's get you out of—"

"Don't touch anything," she cried. "The car's not stable!"

He put one hand against the metal door. The ancient vehicle trembled as if it could feel his touch. Rocking back on his heels, Michael paused.

"I can't get out, either," she said faintly, her hand waving over the seat belt. "This thing's stuck. I've tried everything and it just won't give."

He reached into his pocket, pulled out a knife and flicked it open. The blade gleamed in the darkness. "Here," he said, handing it over to her. "Use this. Saw with it. But gently!"

She took the knife gingerly in her blood-soaked fingers, and with slow, careful movements she began to work on the woven belt. Within seconds, it gave way. She looked up, her dark eyes huge. "Now what do I do? If I move, the car will roll."

He glanced down the edge of the incline. It was steeper than he would have liked, but what choice did they have? He looked back at Eva.

"I'll pull, you jump. If the car goes, I'll have you."

"Are you sure?"

"Got a better idea?"

She shook her head slowly. "I...I guess not."

He braced himself against a nearby rock and reached toward her. "All right, then. Give me your hand."

She started forward, then stopped abruptly. "Thomas's briefcase! I've got to get it first."

"Are you crazy? Forget—"

"I can't go without it," she said, her voice brooking no argument as she craned her head this way and that. "Do you see it?"

His eyes searched the darkness, then he saw something dark and rectangular. "Is that it? Over there on the—?"

"Yes! That's it!" Reaching down slowly, she

picked it up and passed it to him. He caught it, then faced her again.

"All right, now will you come?"

Wrapping her fingers around his, she looked into his eyes. He met her trusting gaze, and something turned over inside him, something he hadn't felt in years. The emotion was strange and unwelcome. He pushed it away as fast as he could. He didn't want Eva believing in him. All he wanted was to get her and Daniel back to Houston.

His fingers clasped hers, and he pulled. She came toward him, passing through the window and tumbling into his arms. They collapsed in the dirt, a cascade of pebbles scraping Michael's back, his bruised ribs screaming from the movement.

The car rocked once, twice, then with a long, drawn-out shriek, tumbled down the incline.

Together they watched the vehicle disappear. Trembling violently, Eva turned to him, almost involuntarily. Michael tightened his arms around her, one hand going to cradle her head, the other patting her back. "It's okay," he murmured against her hair. "It's okay. I've got you."

She shuddered a minute more, then finally raised her head and looked directly into his eyes. Her voice was a husky whisper. "I know...and now I'm more scared than ever."

THEY MADE THEIR WAY slowly back up the side of the mountain to Michael's truck, a shiny black Range Rover. Eva didn't bother to ask where he'd gotten the impossible vehicle—or how. She didn't want to know. The man seemed capable of performing miracles—good ones *and* bad. Leaning against the back bumper, she concentrated instead on steadying herself against the chrome fender and fighting off the waves of dizziness now starting to overtake her.

"Aunt Eva! Are you okay?"

Daniel didn't even bother to keep up the pretense anymore. Somehow he'd sensed that Michael knew all about them.

She put a hand on her head and grimaced at the sticky mess she felt. "I'm a little shaken up, but that's all. I—I'm fine."

"You're not fine," Michael pronounced, coming around from the front of the truck and holding out a green water bottle to her. "You've got a nasty cut on your forehead, you're probably dehydrated, and you look like you just rolled down a mountain."

She took the bottle he proffered and looked up at him. "You really know how to compliment a girl."

For a second, he looked startled at her gibe, then he smiled, his full lips turning upward and reminding her of the kiss they'd shared just before she'd left. "I *could* do better," he said slowly, "under different circumstances, of course."

She wasn't sure how to respond at first and tried to stay remote. There weren't going to be "different circumstances" for them. Not now. Not ever. All she wanted was to figure out how to get away from him—and therefore Jack Finely—as soon as possible.

"I'm sure that may be the case," she said coolly. "But we'll never know, will we?"

He read her expression perfectly. Turning to Daniel, he nodded toward a nearby shrine, which was a common sight along the roads in rural Argentina. Fashioned like a small house, it contained dozens of green plastic bottles filled with water—offerings to travelers who might need it. "Why don't you go get one of the bottles and bring it over here?"

Daniel ran off eagerly and returned a second later with a battered cola bottle, which he gave to Eva.

"Wait in the truck. Okay, Danny?"

Pulling a handkerchief from his pocket, Michael turned to Eva and held his hand out for the bottle of water. She gave it to him and watched as he dampened the cloth. Stepping closer to her, he began to gently clean her face, his touch light but firm.

"You shouldn't have run." His eyes flicked to hers, then back to her forehead. "You're lucky it's not you lying down there."

He was right. "I—I do appreciate your rescue," she said. "A simple thank-you doesn't seem good enough—"

"Forget it."

He continued to dab at her face. She tried not to look directly at him, concentrating instead on the hollow at the base of his throat, the point where his pulse beat a slow, steady rhythm. That was an even bigger mistake. Her restless gaze went over his shoulder to the ravine below. She could just see the edge of Maria's car and a dark shadow beneath a nearby tree.

"Wh-what are you going to do about him?" She nodded toward the dead man.

"I'll bring the body back up here and put it in his car. We'll call *Oficial* Perneau from the next town. I have a feeling they know each other. He can take care of it."

She winced as he touched a tender spot. "How did you get him to let you go?"

"He 'found' my permit and released me after an hour or so...just enough time for you to get a head start to here." She raised her eyes to his. They flashed with anger as he held up the square of cotton, dark with her blood. His voice was harsh. "Do you believe me now, Eva? Do you understand how much danger you're in?"

"I never doubted you before," she said quietly. "But I had to take the chance."

"Well, you did—and this is what happened." He thrust his chin toward the incline. "You're damned lucky I figured out you came this way. He had that Glock pointed right at Daniel's head. If I hadn't been able to find you..."

She swallowed hard, past the knot in her throat, and pushed away the guilt that threatened to sweep over her. "I had to try."

"Why?"

"You've got to ask?"

"Yes, dammit, I've got to ask! It was a stupid

thing to do and you're not a stupid woman. Not by a long shot. To run like that made no sense.''

"I didn't have any other choice." She licked her dry lips and stared up at him. "I'll try it again, too, the minute I can. I will not allow you to take us back to Houston, Michael. It just can't happen."

He held her gaze a moment longer, then making a sound of disgust, he held out his arms. "Then what in the hell are you going to do? Walk back? You're injured. Sit here till someone else comes? You'll freeze. Wait here with him?" He gestured toward the sprawled body below. His voice turned sarcastic. "That might be a good option. I'm sure once his friends find out he's dead, they're going to be anxious to talk to you, too."

Her head throbbed, the cut above her eye stinging and burning. Every bone in her body was bruised and aching. She waited until he finished his outburst, then she spoke with a calm assurance she definitely didn't feel.

"I don't know what I'm going to do," she said. "But I'll figure it out. In the meantime—" she paused and looked into his dark, fathomless eyes "—I don't think you'd actually leave us here, regardless."

"I should," he growled.

The wind suddenly picked up and whistled around them. She felt as if they were the last two people on earth. For miles, there was nothing but vast stretches of land, covered only with scrub and grass.

"But you won't," she countered. "You're not that kind of man."

He waited a moment, then moved closer to her and spoke, his voice as harsh and grating as the currents beginning to buffet them. "You don't know what kind of man I am, Eva. You don't know anything about me. I just killed someone without a second thought. For all you know, I enjoyed it."

Her pulse jumped, sudden tension rising between the two of them like steam from an unchecked engine. She took a deep, steadying breath to calm herself. "But you didn't."

He moved even closer and brought a hand to her face, cupping her chin between his thumb and forefinger. Just in front of her eyes, his own chin looked hard, angular, the shadow of his beard somehow sinister. "How do you know?"

"I can tell."

He dropped the tone of his voice until it was silky and low. Mocking her, he repeated, "You can tell." He rubbed a finger over her lips and stared at her mouth before raising his eyes to hers again. "How? By the way I look? By the way I talk?" He dipped his head down to hers, angled it until his breath softly brushed her face. "By the way I kiss?"

She started to speak, but his lips cut off her words. They pressed against her mouth with determined deliberation, their hard edges pushing away any defenses she might have had left. Dragging her closer to him, he forced the length of his body against hers. At every point where their forms touched, she felt hardness, strength and a coiled energy that both appealed and frightened.

But she couldn't stop.

Because, unlike their first kiss, in front of Perneau's men, she felt no confusion this time. She responded to him without reserve, kissing him back, her own lips yielding to his, softening under his touch, relinquishing what little control she had left. She knew deep down what a mistake she was making, but suddenly she didn't care. It was almost as if she needed to feel his kiss, needed to feel his caress—just to make sure she was still alive.

And she definitely was. If she hadn't been, though, this kiss would have brought her back from the dead.

His hands moved over her back and shoulders, then dipped lower to cradle the curve of her buttocks. Bringing her hips even closer to him, she realized how alive he was, as well. If she'd needed extra proof—which she didn't—she had it now in the stiff hardness thrusting against her.

Tearing his mouth from hers, he finally lifted his head but kept his arms around her. He seemed almost incapable of letting her go as he continued to press her close, his eyes as dark and unreadable as ever. His look made her catch her breath, her breasts rising and falling against his chest.

"You know nothing about me, Eva. Nothing at all." His hands clutched at her back, two spots of heat and intensity as he held her to him. "Don't ever make the mistake of thinking you do because you'll come to regret it...and that's a guarantee."

MICHAEL PUSHED THE ROVER faster than he should. The road was almost nonexistent, with potholes huge enough to disappear into and no shoulder at all. The big truck was capable of taking it on, though, the wide tires easily gripping the crumbling pavement and carrying them through the early-morning hours quietly and efficiently.

In the back seat, Daniel slept. He. was wrung out and obviously exhausted. In the front, beside Michael, Eva dozed restlessly. Unable to fully let go and sleep, she moved continually, turning every so often toward the window, then away, her eyelids fluttering open, then slipping back down again as she moved. She was always on alert, he realized, always watching. His eyes flicked back to the little boy stretched out behind them on the rear seat. Did he appreciate the guardian angel he had?

While the Rover ate the miles, Michael blanked his mind. It was a trick he'd learned to pass the time during stakeouts and one he'd come to use even more frequently since Amy's death. As if he'd thrown a switch, a white nothingness filled his thoughts.

But not for long. For the first time in years, he found himself losing the calmness, his turbulent thoughts winning the battle and invading the peace he craved but couldn't achieve.

His gaze returned to Eva. She'd finally given in— her eyes were shut tight, her face relaxed and vulnerable in the green glow of the dashboard lights, her body loose and defenseless. Even in sleep, she radiated strength and courage. She was stronger and more beautiful, inside and out, than any woman he'd ever met, including, he realized with a start, Amy. No one he knew would be willing to simply give up their life as they knew it and disappear—even for the sake of a child.

Her strength only added to her femininity, too. The kiss they'd shared had definitely confirmed that, and his body had responded in kind. It had been stupid on his part, he knew, but he hadn't been able to resist. He told himself it meant nothing, a simple release of tension between them, but deep down he knew better. In his own particular way, he'd wanted to warn her away. To scare her off.

Or was it himself he was really warning?

As he did with anything that got too close, he pushed the thought aside, his eyes going instead to the case resting at Eva's feet. She must think she had powerful proof in that briefcase. What could it be? Her wild accusations about Jack had sounded crazy, but Michael had heard worse and found it later to be true. He was going to have to take a look at that case before long, and that would certainly be an interesting task. How was he going to manage it?

Maybe in the plane, he thought. Before leaving Comodoro, he'd called Houston and talked to his contact. Eva didn't know it, of course, but they weren't heading to Sarmiento. They were going to a small airstrip and boarding a waiting jet Houston had engaged. The plane's range wasn't huge and a lot depended on the weather. With luck, though, it could get them to Buenos Aires. They'd catch the next flight out to the States after that. An overnight haul to Miami, then Houston two and a half hours later. His job would then be over.

And he'd never see Eva again.

Michael would be out of their lives and they would be out of his. Forever. She and the boy would go into the program and disappear.

If they didn't, they'd die. Sooner or later, something would happen—someone would slip up, a bullet would find its target, a knife its mark. Even if he *wanted* to stick around and protect them the rest of his life, something would eventually happen.

It always did.

A light sheen of sweat broke out along his forehead as he realized where his train of thought was taking him. His fingers curled tightly around the steering wheel, his knuckles gleaming in the faint pink dawn lining the horizon. A voice from the past sneaked into his mind.

"Have you ever heard of the savior complex, Mr. Masters? People involved in unsuccessful rescue attempts often experience it." The shrink's attitude had been smug, knowing. *"Because you couldn't save your wife, you may find yourself trying to replay the incident with others and have it end differently, have it end* successfully. *It's not a good way to live your life, Mr. Masters. I'd watch out for it if I were you."*

CHAPTER THIRTEEN

"THIS ISN'T SARMIENTO."

Eva stared out the window of the Rover. When the vehicle had stopped, she'd woken up. Groggy and disoriented, she cursed herself for surrendering to sleep, then turned to Michael, suspicious tension tightening every muscle in her body.

"Where have you brought us? What town are we in?"

He cut off the engine. Raising his hands, he scrubbed his face, the heavy stubble of his beard rasping in the wary silence between them. "This is Bahía Rojo. We're in Chile now."

From the back seat, Daniel spoke up excitedly. "This is Chile? Cool! Can I get out? I gotta find a bath—"

"Go," Eva said, her eyes never leaving Michael's face. "But only to the café right in front of us." She turned around. "Nowhere else. Understand?" Her voice was harsh.

Daniel's eyes widened at her tone, and he nodded, suddenly subdued. Leaving the truck, he looked warily around, then crossed the street, empty this early in the morning.

"You said you were taking us to Sarmiento," she

said tightly, her anger barely in control. "What changed your mind?"

"Nothing changed my mind. I was coming here all along."

"You lied."

"Yes. I lied."

"Dammit, Michael! You can't just—"

He held up a hand and stopped her words. His eyes were narrowed slits, his mouth a displeased slash. "I can do anything that pleases me, Eva. *Anything*. I'm in charge now, so accept it. It'll make life easier for us all."

Anger sparked between them, the tension rising, then flickering into a smoldering flare. "And just what are we doing here?"

He shrugged casually, but she wasn't fooled. Michael did nothing without thinking it through. "This is Chile. Anyone following us would have to go through the same checkpoints we did while you were asleep. They might not have the papers to get past the border."

His answer made sense, she admitted grudgingly, but she didn't want to accept it. "And after here?"

"You know where." He paused. "Houston."

She turned her head and looked stonily out the windshield. Daniel was crossing the street, coming back.

"We've got to get that cut of yours looked at and we've got to get something to eat." Michael's voice was flat. She heard the keys rattle as he pocketed them. "What do you want? Anything in particular?"

"I don't care," she said.

"Are you coming with me?"

"Do I have a choice?"

He didn't answer. He simply climbed from the vehicle and started across the street, meeting Daniel on
the sidewalk. Putting a hand on the boy's shoulder,
Michael spoke to him briefly. Daniel nodded, a smile
on his face, then to Eva's chagrin, they both turned
and started toward the café. Michael shot a look over
his shoulder at her. "Did you really think I'd let you
have him?" his expression said.

She sighed and briefly closed her eyes. Until she
got Daniel alone and explained the situation to him,
their chances of escaping Michael were slim to none.

Opening the truck door, she, too, headed toward
the small café. There was nothing else she could do
for the moment.

Michael was standing at an angle to the door so
he could see when it opened and who was coming
in. When she walked inside, he saw her immediately.
He didn't look surprised when she jerked her head
toward the back of the café, but just nodded.

The first thing she noticed—with disappointment—about the tiny, filthy bathroom was that it had
no window and therefore no avenue of escape. A
single bare bulb hung overhead, the wire strung from
the next room and snaking in over the doorway. The
mirror was cracked and cloudy, and for once, she
was grateful. She didn't want to see more of her face
than she had to. She took one of the rough paper
towels lying on the countertop and wet it. Dabbing

gingerly at her cut, she cleaned it up slightly, then got another towel and washed the rest of her face as best she could. Running her fingers through her matted, dirty hair completed her efforts. The gestures were pointless, but the normalcy of it all was surprisingly reassuring.

Once white, but no longer, the toilet hung on the wall at a precarious angle. She used it, touching as little of the surface as she could and finishing fast, lifting the old-fashioned handle on top of the lid to flush the facility. After quickly washing her hands, she flung open the door to escape the room.

Michael was standing just outside, and she felt her eyes widen in surprise. "Wh-what are you doing here?"

"I was coming to check on you."

"That wasn't necessary—there's no window." Her voice held anger. It was directed at him, but part of her irritation was at herself. Every time she turned around, she found his close presence distracting, making her think of things that shouldn't matter right now. His wide shoulders and dark eyes were doing things to her nerves, unexpected things. Pulling herself back together and focusing once more, she glanced around his towering form. Daniel was sitting at a table, dangling his feet and playing with the sugar packets. "And besides, I wouldn't leave without Daniel. You know that."

"Of course, I know," he answered calmly. "I wasn't worried about your escaping. I was afraid you might have passed out."

"Oh."

He looked down at her closely, his eyes changing as they took in the cut above her eye. She could imagine what the injury really looked like—even in the dull bathroom mirror, it had looked hideous—a knot the size of a radish with a jagged purple line going through it. Self-consciously, she lifted her fingers toward her head, but he reached out and stopped her. Holding her hand with one of his, he raised his other toward her face.

She tensed, but his touch was a feathered brush against her cheek, coming nowhere near the injury itself. The back of his hand grazed over her skin with a whisper, and she caught her breath, her stomach contracting as her awareness of him grew even more.

"We've got to get that looked at," he said. "As soon as we finish eating, I'll find someone who can—"

Abruptly stepping back, she shook her head. "I—I cleaned it up a little more. I don't want anyone here messing with it."

"Don't be ridiculous. You'll have a scar."

She shrugged. "It's no big deal."

"Maybe not right now, but later you'll look in the mirror every morning and be reminded of when it happened."

She remembered his back and the various marks marring his tanned, taut skin. She nodded, finding herself reluctantly touched.

"*Señor—su comida.*" Interrupting them, the woman behind the counter held up two plates and looked at Michael expectantly. Daniel dashed to the counter and took them from her. Two more quickly followed.

They sat down then and ate quickly, Michael with his back to the wall and facing the door. Eva sat beside him, her own gaze continually going to the street and beyond. The food was standard local fare—*Milanesas*—small panfried steaks between buns, an egg added for good measure in between. Eva choked down a bite or two, but concentrated mainly on the pasta Michael had ordered, as well. It would give her more energy anyway.

Daniel chattered cheerfully, totally unaware of the silent tension between Eva and Michael. Michael encouraged the conversation, obviously one they'd started in the truck while she was asleep, laughing and teasing Daniel with a lively debate over which computer games were the best. When he told Daniel a new, improved version of his favorite was out, Daniel's green eyes glowed with interest. He hadn't been able to get anything like that in months, and it was clear his fingers were itching with the wish he could play it.

Eva marveled at Michael's ability to draw Daniel out. She hadn't seen her nephew this animated in months. He was clearly relating to Michael in a very special way.

In twenty minutes, they were finished eating. Michael paid the bill, Daniel at his side, still talking and developing a closer connection to the man minute by minute. Half of her was furious, and the other half wanted to cry. She hadn't understood completely how much Daniel missed his father, missed male companionship. Michael had—and now he was using that knowledge against her.

Oh, God in heaven! How much more complicated could life get? If, by some miracle, she was able to separate the two of them and really explain things to Daniel, it wouldn't matter now. He wouldn't believe her anyway!

They headed back to the Range Rover, Daniel skipping ahead of them. Eva waited until he was well out of range, then she put a hand on Michael's arm and stopped him. "You're not playing fair."

"I don't know what you're talking about."

"You know damned good and well what I'm talking about," she shot back. "You're getting him on your side! I can't leave without him and you're making sure *he* won't leave you! That's not fair."

"You must have noticed I don't play—"

"You don't play fair," she finished. "I know, I know. But this is a little boy we're talking about, Michael. He's just a kid. He misses his dad. How can you do this? How can you play with him this way?"

Michael's face stayed stony a minute longer, then suddenly it twisted with emotion, emotion he apparently couldn't hold in anymore. "Because we're talking about his life, dammit to hell! I'm trying to save it in case you haven't noticed, and the only way I'm going to be able to do that is to get both of you out

of here. What in God's name has to happen before
you get that through your head?''

''That's *not* what you're doing! Not if you take us
back to Houston. What do *I* have to do to get that
through *your* head?''

''You can prove it to me,'' he shot back. He put
his hands on his hips and stared at her with a chal-
lenging look. ''Share your precious information. If I
believe it, I'll leave you alone. I'll tell them you got
away and I'm giving up the case.''

''All right,'' she agreed impulsively, sticking out
her hand as she did when she and Daniel had just
made a deal. ''I'll share. Then you'll understand.''

He paused, then took her hand in his, engulfing
her fingers with the span of his palm. It wasn't a
handshake but a promise, the clasp warm, sensual,
full of implications. ''But if you don't convince
me—''

''I will.''

''If I'm not convinced,'' he persisted, ''then you'll
have to come with me. You have to go into the program, and let them protect you. That's the deal.'' He
looked at her expectantly, then his expression shifted
and his voice dropped. ''You have to promise, Eva.
Promise.''

Something inside her melted at this final word. She
could see what it meant to him and understood—that
this went beyond the two of them. But how or why,
she didn't know.

''All right,'' she said softly, ''I promise.''

''I want more than a handshake on that.''

His meaning was clear, and her heart flipped over as the words sank in. She met his piercing gaze, then took one step closer. Putting her hands at his waist, she stretched up and kissed him fully on the mouth, her body straining to get closer, but her mind remembering that Daniel was most likely watching from the truck.

Even without full contact—maybe even *because* they were touching nowhere else—the kiss was a burning one, the erotic tension of it sizzling between them in the deserted street. Her lips seemed hypersensitive; she could sense both the softness of his and the hardness, as well. The moment stretched on longer than she'd intended, then she finally pulled back—because if she didn't, the situation was going to end up differently than she planned.

"That's my promise," she said breathlessly, her chest rising and falling rapidly, her pulse throbbing at her throat. "Is that good enough for you?"

"It's a start," he said, his eyes darker than ever. He stared at her a second longer, then turned and headed for the truck.

She watched him walk away, her legs trembling, her mouth swollen. The kiss had rattled her, and in a way she didn't want...an emotional way. It had made everything harder instead of easier, and she cursed herself for thinking it might have helped. It strengthened her resolve, however. She knew what she had to do. As he strode across the street and reached the truck, she hardened herself to reality.

If I'm not convinced, then you have to come with

*me. You have to go into the program and let them
protect you.*

All right, I promise.

The words echoed painfully in her head, but she
ignored them and started toward the truck herself.
She had to do what she had to do. She could lie as
well as Michael.

HE ALMOST MISSED the turnoff, but at the last minute,
Michael spied the well-camouflaged road and
wheeled the Range Rover into it. Eva sat beside him,
silently fuming. Since he'd explained about the plane
and the trip to Buenos Aires, she'd said nothing, absolutely nothing. She'd thought he was going to look
at her "proof" there in Bahia Rojo. Not likely, he'd
explained. Too dangerous. They'd be safest in
Buenos Aires—if she won the bet, she could take off
from there.

But she wouldn't win, so it didn't really matter.

A small frame house came into view as they rattled up to the end of the road. The stucco had been
repaired once too often and the tiled roof was missing several key pieces, but the yard was neat and
clean, a border of ivy decorating one wall. A ragged
mongrel rose languorously to greet them as they
pulled in and parked. The Citation jet sitting nearby
looked totally incongruous, especially since there
was no sign of a landing field anywhere in sight.

It wasn't O'Hare, but it was their only choice.

Michael climbed from the truck, the dog trotting

toward him. A second later, a man appeared at the door, pulling on a coat.

The conversation was short. Money had already been exchanged, the plane fueled and readied for takeoff. Michael didn't bother to ask who'd taken care of the actual arrangements—it didn't matter. The U.S. government was everywhere.

Within ten minutes, the four of them were strapped into the jet. It was brand-new, the instruments gleaming, the leather seats spotless, the latest radios onboard, including a sophisticated dual G.P.S. tracking system that provided, through the use of a complicated network of satellites, their exact position at any point in time. With plenty of range, they'd make it to BA without having to refuel. Michael took it all in with an appreciative eye. He was a licensed pilot and, like any pilot, he relished the multimillion-dollar aircraft.

They taxied into the field behind the house, and at that point, Michael realized it wasn't just an ordinary field. The even rows of plants concealed an open center, wide enough for the jet's thirty-five-foot wingspan or an even bigger plane and plenty long for landings and takeoffs. From the highway, the airstrip was completely invisible. With smooth, practiced movements, the man behind the controls examined his instruments one by one, touching their dials and murmuring to himself as his finger traced over a printed checklist he'd removed from the visor above his head. Finally satisfied, he looked up and spoke rapid Spanish into the small microphone attached to his earphones. Nodding as he apparently got his answer, he eased the throttle forward and the Citation responded smoothly. Within minutes, they were racing down the runway. When the plane was airborne, Michael turned and looked in the rear seat.

Clearly fascinated, Daniel's face was glued to the window, his gaze growing wide as their lift increased. Eva was a different story. Her dark eyes locked on Michael's, sending daggers all the way.

He turned around and faced the cockpit, the hot censure of her stare burning on the back on his neck. It didn't matter, he told himself. His job was to keep her safe and see her delivered whether she liked it or not. He closed his eyes and pretended to go to sleep.

BUENOS AIRES WAS GLOOMY when they landed many hours later. Thick black clouds hung over the city as they approached, and Eva didn't realize, until the small jet slipped under them, that it was raining. Even the wild parrots who lived in the trees near the airport seemed subdued, their normally brilliant green plumage dull and sad instead of iridescent and glowing.

Jorge Newberry, the regional airport, was even gloomier. A square, squat building with dirty windows and no personality, it welcomed no one. The guards standing inside reflected the same attitude, their automatic weapons slung over their shoulders, their gazes cold and detached as Michael, Eva and

Daniel came inside and passed under their watchful eyes.

Eva gripped Thomas's briefcase to her chest. It was their only luggage. Everything else they'd fled with had been lost in the car wreck. Michael was traveling even lighter. He carried nothing but his coat as they made their way through the crowded public space. Where his rifle was, she had no idea. She didn't want to know, either.

The cacophony made by the collection of taxis, *remises* and buses was startling as they stepped outside. Everyone seemed to be screaming and waving their hands in the air. The ones who weren't doing that were honking their horns, adding to the confusion. Eva instantly felt overwhelmed, but Michael made sense of it all and, pointing to one of the cars, he managed to get them a ride with impressive speed. She climbed wearily into the vehicle. As much as she hated the situation, she had only one thought; thank God he was with them. Her head was throbbing, she'd been wearing the same clothes for almost forty-eight hours, and she had no energy left. None whatsoever. She would not have been able to marshal the necessary effort if she'd been trying to do this on her own.

Then again—if she and Daniel were on their own, they wouldn't even be here, now would they?

She shot a glance toward Michael. He was sitting beside her, while Daniel was in the front seat next to the driver. The stubble on his face had left the shadow stage hours ago. Now it was definitely in the beard category. It made him look more dangerous than ever.

She'd been angry when he'd explained his arrangements, but somewhere between Chile and BA, she'd decided the trip wasn't that bad an idea. She knew BA—had been there several times on business and once for pleasure, a tourist trip. It was an enormous city—there were thousands of places to hide. She'd need them, too. Once he saw Thomas's notes, Michael would realize she couldn't go back to Houston. And if he didn't believe her? Well, then she'd just have to deal with that the best way she knew how. She closed her eyes and leaned her head against the seat.

Half an hour later, with the clouds clearing, the taxi stopped. Eva opened her eyes and was startled to see they were in La Recolata, an exclusive residential section of town. She'd expected to go to one of the larger downtown hotels—the Aspen Towers or maybe the Park Marriott. Only the most exclusive residences were in La Recolata—it was the land of embassies and movie stars.

Not surprisingly, it was the most beautiful part of the city. Enormous trees shadowed the narrow streets, and each house was exquisite. Even the residents were beautiful. Eva lifted her head in time to see a thin, well-dressed woman exit one of the homes with a small terrier in her arms. Both woman and dog looked expensively groomed. Just down from them, a row of little girls was jumping rope, their

voices musical in the early-evening air, their perfectly ironed school dresses flipping as they skipped.

On the other side of the street, away from the children, waited a jewel box of a park, its emerald trees
echoing with the raucous calls of more brightly colored parrots. Eva let her senses fill with the beauty
of the trees and flowers—an incredible sight after
months in Patagonia—then turned to look at the
house in front of which they'd parked. It, too, was
beautiful. Small but perfect, its pristine white stucco
gleamed in the evening light. Graceful stone arches
covered a beckoning doorway while mullioned windows embraced the dying light. Window boxes were
filled with roses, their blooms bobbing in the cool
evening breeze. The house seemed to be waiting for
them, waiting and watching.

Michael threw a wad of pesos at the driver, then
reached across Eva and opened her door. "This is
it," he said. "Our home for the next twenty-four
hours."

She followed him up the sidewalk to the front
door, Daniel sandwiched between them. When Michael reached out and opened the door just as if they
really did live there and had just gone out for a bite
to eat, Eva wasn't even shocked. Nothing the man
did surprised her anymore.

They stepped inside and she felt her eyes widen.
It was as perfect inside as out. Every piece of fur-
niture, every painting on the wall, even the gleaming
parquet floors, looked exquisite. Through the hallway, in the back, she caught a glimpse of a court-

yard, a lush oasis of peace and flowers. Unable to stop herself, she turned to Michael. "My God! This is incredible! It's gorgeous. Who does it belong to?"

"Don't ask." Seeing her expression change, he softened his tone. "The less you know, the better, Eva. Let's just say a friend of mine is lending it to me, okay?"

She nodded, subdued.

"There are bedrooms and baths upstairs. Take your pick and settle Daniel in whichever one you like. I'll be in the kitchen."

He was going to leave them alone? Her heartbeat surged, but her hopes were soon dashed as she watched him return to the front door and tap out a code on a nearby panel she hadn't noticed until now. He turned around and met her gaze baldly.

"We're all tucked in," he said. "Safe and sound. No one can get in without me knowing."

He didn't need to say the rest. She understood. *And no one can get out.*

CHAPTER FOURTEEN

"IT'S CLEAR HE'S TALKING about Jack Finely and no one else! Thomas says it all right here." Her expression frustrated, Eva pointed toward the screen of her brother's laptop.

Michael met Eva's gaze and tried to concentrate. Since the rain had stopped, they were able to sit outside in the courtyard. It was chilly, but he'd lit the outdoor fireplace, and the logs were glowing brightly, their welcome warmth reaching out to touch them both. In the park across the street, the birds were calling to each other. Eva waited expectantly, the luminous sheen of her skin heightened by the ivory silk negligee she'd selected from the others upstairs. The robe had shocked him at first, but she looked too incredible in it for him to object. Besides, it matched the scene. They sat in what looked like a lovers' tryst, and even though he knew he shouldn't, Michael's thoughts turned to the bedroom. Eva's voice brought him back.

"Don't you see, Michael?" Her eyes gleamed as brilliantly as the fire and with just as much fervor. "Jack Finely engineered Thomas's death because he was about to disclose Jack's association with the gunrunners in Mexico. Finely knew he had to kill

Thomas or his whole scheme would come unraveled.''

Michael forced himself to look at the screen where she was pointing. To his eyes, the notes were cryptic. He tapped the screen with his finger. "But you're guessing at what this really means, Eva. His shorthand is—"

"Clear as a bell! Look…look at this." She translated the abbreviated letters and dashes. "'Am going to confront him next week. JF has to acknowledge the truth. Source says there's no way he can deny it. Will have to do something.'" She looked up at him, her eyes huge and frustrated. "How can you think that means anything else?"

"Thomas could have been talking about anyone! It could mean he was going to take the proof to Jack and was expecting him to do something about it." His finger jabbed at the screen. "And who's this source he mentions?"

"I'm not sure, but I think it's got to be Ridley— Ridley Holt. He's another agent in the Houston office. Ridley was always tuned in. He knew the latest gossip and he would have wanted to help Thomas."

Michael hid his surprise. Ridley Holt helping someone? As far as Michael knew, Holt helped no one but himself. "I'm not so sure…."

Eva shook her head, her hair shining in the light from the fire, too excited to listen to him. "It was Jack, I'm telling you. Thomas was going to confront *him*. Not anyone else…because no one else was guilty."

"There are other guys at that office I trust a helluva lot less. I've known Jack too long, seen him in action. He's not the kind of guy who would rat out an agent. I'd be willing to bet money it's some-one else."

Eva jumped to her feet. "Well, you're not betting money! If you take us back, you're betting with our lives. I'm telling you—"

"Aunt Eevva...Eevva..." Daniel's panicked voice floated out to them on the humid night air. "Where are you?"

Fright instantly rounded her eyes, and Eva turned. Michael beat her to the door leading inside, his hand on his Charter pistol. "Stay here," he said. "I'll check on him."

She pushed past him and bounded inside.

Exasperated, he followed her. They ran into the boy's bedroom at the very same time, Michael draw-ing a deep sigh of relief as soon as he spied Daniel tossing back and forth in the jumbled sheets. Eva dropped to his side and cradled him in her arms, soothing him with soft words and gentle touches.

"It's all right," she whispered to Michael. "Just a bad dream."

Michael nodded but made no move to leave. He couldn't. He was transfixed by the sight of her com-forting the child. How could one woman be so tough and so tender all at the same time?

After a few moments, she rose from the bed. Dan-iel was already sleeping deeply again. Easing out the door, she closed it quietly behind her and looked at

Michael with determination. "I want to finish our conversation," she said in a fierce whisper. "It's important—"

"It is important," he agreed, obviously surprising her, "but so is your health." He reached up and touched the bandage he'd put on her forehead earlier. "You've been through hell the past twenty-four hours, Eva. Let's give it a rest right now and start again in the morning."

She looked as if she wanted to argue, but after a minute her shoulders slumped and she nodded. "I…I guess you're right. I am a little tired."

He tucked a black curl of her silk hair behind her ear. "A little tired?" he asked, chuckling.

She looked up and smiled. "A *lot* tired."

He stared into her dark eyes for a few seconds, and his amusement slowly evaporated. It was replaced by another feeling, a feeling he didn't want but had to acknowledge. "You're one helluva woman, Eva. In spite of everything, I admire you."

Her breath quickened as he continued gazing at her.

"You're beautiful, you're smart, you're brave. You've protected that kid in there—" he tilted his head "—like no one else I've ever known could have."

"I didn't have a choice," she said quietly.

"We always have choices. The brave ones make them, the cowards ignore them."

"But sometimes they're made for us."

Michael shook his head, a pair of blue eyes haunting him. "I used to think that, but not anymore. We're all responsible for our actions. Things don't just happen on their own."

"Never?" she asked. "You don't think there are some things outside our control, things that are destined to be whether we want them or not?"

"I control my life," he said tersely. "I plan it. It wasn't always that way, but it is now. Nothing happens to me that I haven't thought about beforehand."

The air between them shifted, turned warmer.

"Nothing?" she whispered.

"Nothing," he answered. "Including this." Angling his head, he bent lower, and then his lips met hers.

She resisted, but only for a moment, her body swaying closer to his a second later and pressing tightly against his own. He flattened his hands against her back, the silk gliding under his fingers, the flesh beneath calling to him. He gave in and groaned, then dropped his hands from her spine to her buttocks, cupping the curve of their sweetness.

They moved together as their mouths continued to press, one against the other. Her lips were soft and generous, just like the rest of her, and Michael found himself drifting farther and farther into the siren call of her arms. In another moment, he'd be lost.

And he didn't even care.

He pulled her closer still, then bent down and swept her into his arms.

HIS EYES NEVER LEFT HERS as Michael carried Eva to the bedroom. In the back of her mind, she knew she should resist, knew this was going to end up being disastrous, but she didn't care. His arms felt too good, his kiss too enticing, his skin too warm against her own. How long had it been since she'd surrendered to her feelings, given in to her emotions? She couldn't even remember, and now, as she was flooded with sensual possibilities and her body was infused with heat, she knew she could no longer resist. She didn't want to. From the moment they'd met, she'd known it would end up this way. She'd been too aware of him for it to happen any other way.

And why not? She was only human, and for just a little while, she wanted to forget. She wanted a man's arms around her, holding her tight. She wanted him to tell her everything would be fine when the sun came up. She wanted to hear the words, wanted to believe them.

She wanted to feel them.

Michael was more than prepared to grant all of those wishes.

Still kissing her, he dropped his hands to the belt of her negligee and quickly untied the knot. The ivory silk slithered with a whisper from her shoulders to reveal the ivory-and-black lace gown she'd uncovered in the back of the closet. She'd wondered whose it was, but suddenly that no longer mattered as Michael's hands went to the thin silk cords holding it to Eva's shoulders and slipped them away, the gown sliding down into an expensive pool at their feet.

She stood in his arms wearing nothing.

Motionless, he stared at her, his dark eyes tracing her body from top to bottom, their erotic hunger almost more than she could stand. After a moment, he reached for her and pulled her to him with a groan, his mouth nibbling down the edge of her neck and shoulders, stopping only to pull on her earlobe and to whisper words of encouragement when her own hands went to the buttons of his shirt. In short order, it joined her gown, and his pants quickly followed. They tumbled to the bed behind them.

Michael's hands danced over her shoulders and arms and took away the last of any resistance she might have had left. His mouth followed with quick, sharp kisses that landed on her bare skin and took away her breath. Her hands seared his chest, her fingers moving over the broad muscles and tanned skin with an almost uncanny knowledge of what he wanted, of what he *needed* from her. His moans confirmed her feelings as he urged her on wordlessly. She didn't stop to think of what this understanding meant. If she had, she would have jumped up and fled.

They came together like lovers who'd known each other forever. Michael touched her with brief, quick moves, then switched to long, slow caresses. Without her saying a word, he sensed what she wanted, as well, her back arching as his fingers dipped lower and reached her stomach now taut with the kind of desire she'd never before experienced.

She moaned, a deep sound of longing that came from the back of her throat, and he responded instantly, his hands going even lower, his mouth trailing behind. With the kind of touch women dream of, he caressed her, each stroke of his fingers, each lap of his tongue, movements that stopped her heart. The pleasure was so intense it was almost painful. For several endless seconds, she literally could not breathe, then her body shuddered with release, and she pulled air into her lungs as if she were drowning.

But he didn't stop.

Taking her into his arms, he easily rolled her body on top of his, their legs tangling together in a dance of sensual desire. His mouth found hers again, and she tasted the hunger they both felt, the hunger only one thing would satisfy. The contours of his hardened body melted against her own, and still aching for more, she threaded her hands through his thick black hair, her breasts pressing into his chest. She wanted all of him, more than he could probably give, and she pulled at him frantically.

His hands grasped her waist, two points of contact that seemed to burn their way into her heart and soul. Mimicking her own movements, he drew her body even closer and gripped her with his fingers. A second later, he plunged inside her.

She gasped and cried out, the sound of her need muffled against his shoulder as his full length entered her in an exquisite burst of pleasure. She groaned and tried to speak, but her words found no voice. Finally, she called out his name, her fingers clutching the sheets.

His hands pressed against her back as he increased the pace of his thrusting hips. Matching his urgency to her needs, he seemed incapable of stopping, his intensity almost frightening. She grabbed his shoulders and lost herself in the pulsing rhythmic movements.

And a moment later, they cried out together.

Collapsing against his chest, Eva felt the unsteady pounding of his heart. It matched her own. For a few seconds longer, they stayed that way, trapped by desire, shocked by the force of what they'd just shared.

Her body soaked, her pulse still thundering, Eva lifted her head a moment later and looked directly into Michael's eyes, mere inches from her own. They were two flames of desire and passion. Never had she seen him look so open, so vulnerable, and it sent her heart into a spiral of confused sensations. Emotions she hadn't counted on suddenly flooded her, one thought rising above all others....

What on earth had they done?

THE ROLLING THUNDER brought Eva instantly awake. Her heart clamoring almost as loudly as the storm outside, she sat up in bed and pushed the hair from her eyes. In the months she had lived in Comodoro, it had rained only once—the sound of thunder seemed strange to her now. She climbed from the bed to go to the window, but her eyes turned to Mi-

chael first. He was still asleep, the sheets tangled
around his powerful, long legs, his head a carved
profile silhouetted against the pristine pillow.

She reached out to smooth a curl of his hair, then
stopped, her fingers poised just above his forehead.

What had they done?

They'd started out as opponents, then become un-
willing allies against a common enemy. Now—on
the eve of turning against each other once again—
now they were lovers.

Her hand fell back to her side and she left the bed,
moving slowly and silently, her thoughts as confused
as they'd ever been. She'd never known anyone like
Michael before. He was a total contradiction—and
everything about him called out to her.

She picked up her robe, slipped it on and glided
to the open window on the other side of the room.
Thunder continued to boom while flashes of lightning lit the park across the street into day-like bril-
liance. Automatically, her eyes searched the block-
size square of grass and flowers and trees. Slowly,
as she saw nothing, she let herself relax. They truly
were safe here with Michael. The feeling was so unusual she didn't quite know how to handle it.

She eased down into the tapestried chair beside the
window, pulling her feet underneath her and resting
her head against her knees to stare out the glass. This
feeling of being safe—it was one she could get used
to. She hadn't realized what a strain she'd been living
under. Oh, she'd known—on a theoretical level, of
course—that she was always wired, always on alert,

but she'd thought she could handle it. That had been before Michael had arrived, before the situation had turned so terrible. Now her eyes were open. How had she ever thought they could do this for the rest of their lives? Had she really believed she could raise Daniel all by herself—on the run? Had she really believed she could give up her own life? Never have a family or husband? Her eyes flicked to the bed. Never have a lover?

She sighed and shook her head. Being near Michael, letting herself embrace him—what a mistake! How foolish she'd been!

The dark outline of the trees in the park came to life in another flash of lightning. She blinked, and in her mind's eye, saw Daniel walking beside Michael. The boy needed more than she could give him, and she'd been blind to think they didn't need the world around them. She'd told Michael the truth, though. She hadn't had a choice.

Her eyes went back to the bed and the man who'd brought her so much pleasure…and so much confusion. She still didn't have a choice—but she had to do something.

She had to do something…but what?

THE FOLLOWING MORNING, Michael stared at Eva from across the breakfast table as she sipped her coffee. She had dark shadows under her eyes, and her skin was pale next to the white bandage still on her forehead. Glancing up, she met his stare, held it for a moment, then glanced away. She looked rattled—

as rattled as he felt. He'd been glad she'd been gone from his bed when he'd awakened. He didn't know what to say to her.

He didn't know what to say to himself.

Their lovemaking had left him shaken. Before, during and since his marriage to Amy, he'd felt nothing like the passion that had possessed him last night with Eva. She was lit from within, and the fires that burned inside her had started a conflagration inside him, as well. He hadn't understood his reaction—all he'd seemed capable of doing was feeding the flames. And all he wanted to do now was repeat the moment. Looking into his coffee, he groaned, then quickly tried to cover up the sound with a cough.

Daniel glanced up from the cartoons playing quietly on the television resting on the kitchen counter. "We're leaving today, right?" He glanced anxiously at Eva.

"That's right." Michael spoke before Eva could say a thing. "Our flight's at midnight. We'll arrive in Miami around six."

At Michael's words, the boy's expression hovered between ecstasy and anxiousness. He glanced at Eva for confirmation.

"Everything will be fine, Daniel," she reassured him quietly. "Don't worry, okay?"

He pulled in his bottom lip and chewed on it for just a moment, then he nodded and returned to the television. Michael looked at Eva. Her words were unexpected. Was it some kind of trick?

She caught his glance, then tilted her head toward

the courtyard. Nodding, he left the table and went to the open door. She followed. He stepped aside to let her pass, then closed his eyes as the floral scent of her perfume rose up to meet him. He'd never smell freesias again without thinking of her.

She waited to speak until after he closed the door behind him.

"You didn't believe what I showed you in the computer." Her dark eyes were accusing, but her tone was resigned.

He crossed the space between them and reached for her. She stepped back…and his heart broke.

"No. I didn't." He pulled himself together before speaking. "I don't think your evidence is solid." He dropped his voice. "But even if you had convinced me, I wouldn't just leave the two of you here, Eva."

"So you lied to me…again."

They stared at each other for long seconds, a world of communication passing between them that required no words.

"It's just not safe," he said finally, breaking the silence.

"Neither is Houston."

"Say you're right—would you be content to let Finely do the same thing again to the next agent who takes that case? Doesn't that possibility bother you?"

"Of course it does," she said, anguish deepening her voice. "But I have to protect Daniel."

"And you still think that staying down here would do that?" He held out his hands. "You can't deny how dangerous it's been so far."

She dropped her gaze. "I know," she said softly. "That's what I started thinking about last night after we…" She looked up. "Afterward…" She waited a moment, then spoke again. "I had thought we could just disappear—here in BA—but after I gave it some more thought, after I saw the two of you together, I began to wonder if I was really doing the right thing for Daniel. He needs…" She stopped and licked her lips. "He needs more than I can give him. He needs a normal life, too. A father and friends and all the latest computer games. I may be keeping him alive— but at what cost?"

She moved into the center of the courtyard, where the fountain was bubbling softly. Michael watched her, his emotions more confused than ever. He didn't want to care for this woman, but he'd lost his distance when he'd gotten to know her and to see how much she cared for Daniel. Last night, he'd lost even more. That didn't mean he had to lose his head, though.

He moved closer to her and put one hand on her shoulder. This time, she didn't step away. "You can't hide forever," he said softly. "You have to deal with this, one way or the other."

"How?" Her eyes glimmered as she looked up at him. "How do I fix it?"

He swallowed hard and closed his eyes. He didn't want to see the need in her look, but he couldn't deny the truth. If he took her to Houston, she'd go into the witness protection program and he'd never see her or Daniel again. And if he didn't take her back, she'd die. Whoever was chasing her would eventually be successful and they'd get both her and Daniel.

"What am I going to do?" She reached up and circled his wrists with her fingers, her grip as tight as her expression. "Help me."

The last two words broke down anything he'd had left in the way of resistance. She wasn't the kind of person who asked for help, and now she was asking him.

He wrapped his arms around her and pressed her head against his chest. "We'll work it out."

"But how?" Her voice was muffled.

"I don't know," he answered honestly. "We'll be better off in Houston, though. We should go ahead and take that midnight flight. Once we're back in the States, we can think of something. We'll never be able to resolve it all from here."

Her eyes turned huge and she pulled back. "But Finely will—"

"Finely will do nothing," Michael said, his voice sure and calm. "I'll make certain of that."

She didn't look convinced. "But what if—"

"There's a million what-ifs, Eva. You'll drive yourself crazy if you try to think of all of them."

"But you don't even believe Finely's behind this, and I do. We'll never get anything accomplished if—"

He stopped her with a single finger across her full red lips. "If Finely's responsible, we'll find out…and if he's not, we'll uncover that, as well. Whoever killed your brother will pay for it, Eva. One way or the other. I promise.''

Her eyes studied his for a moment, then she moved closer to him again, putting her hand on his arm. It almost seemed as if she *needed* to touch him to gauge whether or not he was telling the truth. Her fingers burned through the sleeve of his shirt, her breath soft against his cheek. ''Do you mean it, Michael? Or is this another lie of yours?''

''I promise,'' he said quietly. ''I'll help you...but after that—I can't do any more.''

It was the last thing he wanted to say, but nothing else would do. He didn't deserve another chance. Not with a woman like Eva.

She stared at him, then she nodded once, and their lips met in a kiss Michael knew he would never forget.

CHAPTER FIFTEEN

AT TEN THAT NIGHT, they took a *remise* to Ezizia, the international airport. It was as crazy and crowded as Newberry, where they'd landed just twenty-four hours before, only the scale was larger. More people, more blaring horns, more jostling. Michael fought his way through the crowds using his shoulders and his voice, Eva and Daniel behind him, all three holding hands. By the time they reached the ticket area, Eva felt bruised and exhausted.

A line of security agents guarded the next step, their airline's ticket counter. Extra security was in place because of recent bombings. Eva took a deep breath and pulled their fake papers from Thomas's briefcase. She shoved them into Michael's waiting hands.

He glanced down at them, his thumb flicking to the last page. Multicolored stamps chronicled their progress from Mexico, through Central America to Argentina. After that, the pages were empty, save for the stamps from Chile. "You haven't used them to leave before now?"

She shook her head. "We never left after we got here."

He glanced up at the row of agents. There were

three men and one young woman, her short navy skirt riding up her hips, her long hair flung over one shoulder as she smoked and flirted with the men. She laughed at something one of them said, but her overall attitude was one of boredom. A row of equally indifferent passengers waited in line, boxes and suitcases cluttering the worn marble beneath their feet. No one was moving. The line hadn't opened yet. Oblivious to the travelers, the agents were apparently on break.

Michael reached into his pocket and pulled out a roll of pesos. Peeling off four, he handed them to Daniel, nodding toward a counter a few feet away. "Go over there and get us something to drink. Don't go anywhere else, okay, buddy?"

Daniel nodded, his eyes serious as he took in the tone of Michael's words. "The bad guys could be here, right?"

"That's right. So you and I have to keep an eye on Eva, okay?"

The little boy nodded. "Gotcha." He turned and hurried off, throwing repeated looks over his shoulder.

"But I'm not thirsty," Eva started to say.

"Neither am I, but we're going to time our approach to the line. We'll sip the drinks while we wait. I don't want to look too obvious about it."

She took a hasty look at the agents. They made her nervous with their uniforms and attitudes, but at least they weren't wearing guns. "Time our approach? What do you mean?"

"I want to hit the girl," he said, his gaze on Daniel at the refreshment counter, his back to the agents. "The men might give us trouble, but she won't."

He told her this with such an air of confidence that Eva had to respond. "How do you know that? Just because she's a woman, you think you can pull the wool over her eyes?"

"I didn't say that. You're making assumptions again."

Eva crossed her arms. "Then explain it."

"She's younger than the men, so she's less experienced." He spoke patiently. "She's also bored. She'll want the line to move as fast as she can get it to because she wants to leave. Her uniform is sloppy, so her work will be, too. She won't look too closely at those passports of yours." His gaze flicked down to hers, then back to Daniel. "Make sense to you?"

Chastised, Eva nodded. He knew what he was doing. Really knew.

Daniel arrived a moment later, three paper cups balanced precariously in his hands. They were filled to the rim with bubbling cola. "Is this okay?" He looked to Michael for approval, not Eva.

Michael grinned. "It's perfect. Thanks."

Daniel's chest puffed out. He sipped his drink and looked around importantly. Michael and Eva made small talk, all the time his watchful eyes darting around the terminal and back to the security agents. When their drinks were almost gone, a large family of Oriental people moved into the line and filled the area behind the ropes. They milled about anxiously, the noise level going up another notch.

"Now." Michael wrapped his fingers around Eva's elbow and urged her forward with a gentle push. "Let's go get in line. There'll be some confusion—we can arrange it so we can get her when she's free."

His fingers burned against the tender skin inside her elbow, and as they moved toward the ticket counter, his hand brushed against her breast, distracting her even more. She glanced up, but his eyes were facing straight ahead and didn't meet hers. They surged through to the front of the line, hidden within the family group. Just as Michael planned, his timing was perfect. Their forward movement slowed, and then they stopped—right in front of the young woman. He smiled and handed her the three passports—his own with the eagle on front, then Eva's and Daniel's.

The girl flipped all three open at once and spoke in Spanish to Michael, the questions so rapidly fired that the words all ran together. "Have-you-packed-your-bags-yourself? Did-you-accept-any-packages-to-carry-from-anyone-else? Have-you-left-your-bags-unattended-at-any-time?"

He answered her in a casual voice, but tensed a little when she closed Eva's and Daniel's passports and focused on his own. Her head came up and she stared at him with more interest, her long red nails tapping an open page. Reading it upside down, all Eva could make out were a series of scrawls and looping swirls. The writing looked Arabic, but she wasn't sure.

"When were you in the Middle East last?"

The date was printed right below her nail, but Michael smiled and answered.

"And your business there?"

He told her he sold oil-field equipment. Eva marveled at his coolness while in the back of her mind, she wondered herself. The Emirates? What had he *really* been doing there? She decided she didn't want to know.

He calmly answered a few more of the girl's questions, then she waved them through. It was over almost before it began. Michael guided Eva toward the long counter against the back wall, his hand again tucked against the side of her breast, his fingers again pressing into the softness of her curves.

He bought their tickets using pesos. Moments later, they stepped away from the counter to head for the boarding area. One last hurdle, Eva thought with trepidation. Passport control.

Passing another guard who checked their tickets, they took the escalator upstairs. The Duty Free store was open and doing a booming business. They went past the brightly lit shop and headed straight to the dual line of passengers clutching their passports and waiting. Michael took a quick look at the two uniformed agents seated behind their glass enclosures, then led Eva and Daniel to the one on the right.

A woman again.

Eva didn't question him this time. When their turn

finally came, they stepped up to the yellow line, handed the woman their passports and waited. Her hand was a blur as she rubber-stamped the open books and waved them through. Eva let out the breath she'd been holding and they headed toward the gate. Each step they were taking was moving her closer and closer to Houston. As much as she hated to think of what that meant, she'd wanted even less to be thrown in an Argentinean jail for using a fake passport.

A nervous hour later, they boarded the plane, a 747 with an upstairs first-class section. The flight attendant led them up the narrow, spiraling steps and into the row nearest the cockpit. They settled into their seats, then Eva looked out the window beside her.

The twinkling lights of Buenos Aires sparkled beyond the airport, the Río de la Plata beside it, a dark ribbon that stretched for miles. On the other side of the water was Uruguay. Remote, empty, another place where she could have gotten lost.

The plane lurched forward, then began to taxi down the runway. She stared out the window and accepted reality. Getting lost was no longer an option.

IT WAS ALMOST 2:00 a.m. by the time the dinner service was finished, the dishes put away and the last bottle of wine served and removed. When the cabin lights dimmed, everyone settled in and prepared themselves for the long night ahead.

Everyone but Eva. Her mind was a tangled knot of unanswered questions and unspoken fears, the rest of the flight stretching interminably before her. Obviously untroubled, Daniel had no such worries. He was deep in dreamland, covered in blue blankets and curled up with pillows tucked around him on the three empty seats in front of them. Michael seemed equally at ease. As he rested beside her, his eyes were closed and his face relaxed. Breathing evenly, he looked fast asleep.

Until she moved.

His eyes shot open almost instantly, and his fingers gripped her wrist before she had a chance to stand. He looked down in surprise at his hand locked on her arm, then he loosened his hold, his touch turning into a caress instead of a handcuff.

"Sorry," he said. "I react, and then I wake up. An old military habit, I guess." He rubbed the inside of her wrist with his thumb.

Once her heart had resumed a normal pace, she let the warmth of his touch lull her and, for the space of a second, pretended they were nothing more than lovers, learning about each other. "You were in the military?" Her voice was curious.

He leaned his head back against the padded seat. "I caught the end of Vietnam with a low draft number and nowhere else to go. Did two tours."

"You were young."

"Eighteen—but not young. At least, not by the time it was over."

The dim light, the close surroundings, the intimacy

of the hours they'd spent in his bed cocooned them.
She pressed ahead, knowing he wasn't the kind of
man who answered questions but might now.
"Where were you based?"

"Everywhere." He paused. "Nowhere."

That told her more than she wanted to know. He'd
probably ended up in black ops. That was the military term for situations that had happened…but not
really, according to the records. She'd get no more
from him than that. "And afterward?"

"Afterward, I went to Washington. And joined the
Treasury Department."

Surprise caught her, stole her speech for just a moment. She blinked. "You worked for the department!
You never told me that before. I had no idea.…"

He turned his head against the seat, the leather
whispering with his movement. "Where do you think
my jobs come from? The department doesn't hire
strangers—you know that."

"I…I guess I hadn't thought about it," she said,
her mind slowly adjusting to this new piece of information. "How long—"

"Long enough," he said, cutting off her question.
"I left after Amy, my wife, was killed. That's when
I started my company."

Eva remembered the picture, the golden woman.
She looked at Michael. He'd closed his eyes again.
A sign to tell her to keep quiet? If it was, she ignored
it.

"You loved her a lot." Eva's voice was low; the
words came out without her thinking.

"Yes, I did." He sighed, eyes still closed. "We married right after college. I'd survived Vietnam, had just been hired by the department, had a woman who believed in me. I thought I had the world by the tail."

"But you didn't really?"

"Oh, no, I had it all right." He turned and looked at her. "But my work started meaning more to me than anything else. My punishment for being that blind was losing everything. I didn't understand until then what I'd had, how lucky I'd been. While it was there, I didn't have a clue."

His voice was calm, but beneath it there was an edge, a dangerously sharp edge. It was waiting just out of sight, but it was there, and Eva knew it. Who would be cut the deepest by it? Michael, or the people who loved him? She was afraid she knew the answer.

"What happened?"

He took so long to answer she didn't think he would. Finally, he spoke, his voice barely audible above the steady drone of the jet's engines.

"I was working on a case. Some tough guys out of New Orleans who worked a very rough trade."

"Guns?"

"Guns were the least of it." His lips pressed together, granitelike now, no hint of their earlier softness visible at all. "I took risks I shouldn't have, got in deeper with them than I'd planned. There was a rivalry going on between them and some guys out of Miami, control for some of the things they moved. I managed to get in the middle of it. They called a meeting one night to decide what to do, and they wanted me there. Amy begged me not to go, but I ignored her. I told her I had to—that it was my job.'' He swallowed, his throat moving up and down. ''The truth was, I *wanted* to go. I wanted the rush, the adrenaline, the high being in the middle gave me. While I was gone, someone broke into our house and killed her.''

He said the words as if he were an observer, not someone who was personally involved in the tragedy.

''She was three months pregnant. It would have been our first child. She'd been trying to get pregnant for years.''

Eva pulled in a breath and held it. She could feel his pain—it radiated from him like heat from the sun. Reaching out, she released her breath and put her hand on his arm, her heart cracking at the cold detachment in his voice. It was the only way he could stand to tell the story, she realized, the only way he could stand to live his life. At her touch, he started talking again.

''He beat her to death...for a television and the piddling amount of cash she kept for groceries.''

''Did the police make an arrest?''

He nodded. ''Yeah. They got lucky and tracked him from the pawnshop down the road where he'd tried to hock the TV. Unfortunately, he died before he could go to trial.''

Her eyes jerked to his face, and she prayed he couldn't read her mind. ''What happened to him?''

"He got some bad dope. Died of a drug over-dose." He stared at his boots stretched out under the seat in front of him. "It wasn't a good way to go. I saw the body."

Her mouth went dry. "How...strange. That he would die like that...right after the murder, I mean."

His eyes cut to hers, and too late she realized he knew *exactly* what she was thinking. She might as well have spoken her suspicions out loud.

"I had nothing to do with it."

She nodded.

"But I wish I had...."

She should have been shocked, she thought, but deep down, she actually understood. If there was any way she could get her hands on the men who'd killed Thomas and Sally... She sat beside Michael, her fingers on his arm. He seemed to drift away from her, to go into a private world where no one was allowed except himself. After a moment, he roused himself and looked at her. The detached expression he'd worn until now had crumbled a bit around the edges.

"It was all my fault. I shouldn't have left her. Because of my case, we'd had to settle into a neighborhood that was changing, going bad. Amy had begged me to move several times, but I told her we couldn't. It wasn't open to discussion. I had to be there for my job and that was that." His voice was full of guilt. "A punk wielded the weapon, but I killed my wife. Me and me alone."

She stared at him speechlessly, then finally found

her voice. "Th-that's ridiculous, Michael. To feel responsible is crazy—"

"She was my wife, dammit. I should have been there for her. I should have listened to her. I should never have moved us into that damned neighborhood."

"'You had no idea what was going to happen there!'"

"But I *should* have. She'd told me about things she saw and heard during the day when I was gone, warned me about what went on after dark. She wanted out of there. I ignored everything she said, and she paid for my refusal to listen. She paid—and my child paid. They were my responsibility, and I should have been able to protect them. Instead, I got them killed."

Stunned by his intensity, Eva sat perfectly still. Guilt lingered on his face, contorting the angular planes and stonelike jaw into lines of agonized self-recrimination and remorse.

"Sometimes things just happen, Michael. You were doing your job, doing what you thought was right, and things just went wrong. It doesn't mean you were responsible for them." Her eyes searched his face for agreement, but he only stared at her. She tried again. "Do you really think Amy would want you blaming yourself like this? Ruining your life over it?"

"She's not here to tell us, is she?" His voice was a harsh slash through the hum of the engines.

"No, she isn't. But I refuse to believe she'd blame

you and see it as totally your responsibility. You were doing your job the best way you knew how and taking care of her that way.''

''Well, my best wasn't good enough. All I can do now is make sure it never happens again.''

THERE WAS NOTHING she could say or do after that. He turned his head and closed his eyes once more, effectively ending the conversation.

But Eva's mind refused to settle. It was more than clear to her what Michael was doing.

He hadn't saved Amy, so he was saving her and Daniel.

And destroying himself in the process. By controlling his emotions and controlling his life, he wasn't planning for emergencies—he was killing his feelings. Wrapping her and Daniel up and delivering them to the protection program was his way of making sure they were safe—*and* his way of dealing with the change in their relationship. It had been doomed from the start, of course, but had the situation been different, he still would have ended it somehow.

If he didn't feel, *couldn't* feel, then he wouldn't hurt. It was just that simple.

And just that complicated.

Eva turned and stared out the window. Beyond the wing and its glowing red tip, empty blackness stretched to infinity. Michael had managed to effectively block out all his emotions, all his feelings, until she and Daniel had come along. They'd triggered everything, and now, to keep them safe, he felt he had to give them up. Logic meant nothing, her proof meant nothing. Whether they needed it or not, he had to save them or lose himself in the process.

THEY BEGAN THEIR DESCENT into Miami just as dawn broke. The motion of the plane and burgeoning activity inside the cabin woke Michael. He rubbed his unshaven cheeks and glanced over at Eva. She was twisted into a ball and tucked against the curvature of the plane's inner wall, as far away from Michael as she could get.

And who could blame her? He'd tracked her down, forced her to leave her home, lied to her, then made love to her without any promises to go with it. Now, she knew about Amy's death and his part in it, too. What woman in her right mind would want to get close to him?

Eva Solis was as smart as she was beautiful and sexy. She knew better than to get emotionally involved with someone like him.

He reached over and tightened her seat belt, then stood and made sure Daniel's was secure, too. Sitting back down, Michael pulled his own belt tight as the big plane gradually nosed down.

Half an hour later, they were walking down the jet way and into the bright, airy corridors of the Miami airport. Daniel and Eva both seemed stunned. The past few days had wiped them out, it was clear. Daniel shuffled beside Michael while Eva slowly followed behind.

The gray-haired man behind the immigration desk

was the complete opposite from his counterpart in Buenos Aires. He smiled cheerfully at Michael and commented sympathetically about Daniel's obvious exhaustion. Staring longer than Michael would have wanted at Eva's passport, the agent finally stamped it and waved them through. Michael could have dealt with any trouble here by simply calling Washington, but the hassle would have been incredible.

They trudged downstairs and went quickly through customs, Thomas's briefcase their only piece of luggage. Two hours later, they were on another plane and heading for Houston.

Michael glanced at Eva and tried not to think about the brief but searing passion they'd shared in BA. It was something that would never happen again, and shouldn't have happened then. He'd let his senses be overrun. The silk of her skin, the fragrant allure of her body, the simple prospect of losing himself—if only for a moment—were excuses and nothing more. They'd each needed something, one from the other. As much as he hated to admit it, Michael knew this.

He wouldn't entertain the possibility that he was starting to love her. Like failure, love wasn't an option.

He closed his eyes and went to sleep. His last thought was of Eva.

WHEN THE GREEN PATCHWORK of the Texas countryside came into view, Eva felt her heart lurch. It was a sight she hadn't expected to ever enjoy again, and as much as she hated what she knew was coming, a part of her rejoiced at the beautiful scene spreading out beneath the airplane's wings. Within seconds, she saw the tall spires of downtown Houston, then the Galleria and beyond. The airport came up quickly.

She glanced toward the opposite seat. Daniel was playing quietly with a new Game Boy they'd bought in the Miami airport. His eyelids were growing heavy again, though, and he was nodding off. Beside her, Michael sat quietly. They hadn't exchanged two words since he'd talked to her in the dimly lit cabin at three in the morning.

"He's worn-out," she said, glancing toward Daniel. He had finally given up and was stretched out on the seat.

Michael shook his head. "Poor kid. He's been through a lot. He needs the sleep."

"So do you," she answered. "You look exhausted, too."

"I'm fine. There'll be time to rest later."

"Are we going straight to the safe house?"

He nodded. "An agent from the Houston office is meeting us."

"Who?"

"Ridley Holt."

Mixed emotions assaulted her. Ridley meant home. Ridley meant memories of Thomas. "He was my brother's best friend. He knows we're coming in?"

For a second, Michael looked surprised, then he recovered. "I called him from Miami. He'll take you and Daniel to the safe house. I don't even know where the current one is.''

''And you?''

''I'll find a temporary place.''

That word—temporary—dropped on her like a stone, heavy and unexpected. It took a moment for her breath to come back. ''And after...after it's all over? Where will you go?''

''Home.''

''Washington?''

When he spoke, his voice was unexpectedly gentle, almost apologetic. ''I keep a house there, yes, but I don't call it home.''

Time seemed to speed up, and suddenly she felt desperate to know more about him. This might be her final chance. ''Where is home?''

''I live in Buenos Aires.''

Her eyes widened as the words sank in. ''The house we were in—''

''It's mine.''

Oh, God... No wonder his expression had been so pained when he'd seen her in the robe and gown. They'd belonged to his wife.

''I...I had no idea.'' The words sounded lame even to her ears. ''The gown...it...it was in a box. I didn't know...''

''It's all right,'' he said, his understanding reflected in his dark eyes. ''You looked incredible in it, and she never wore it. I'm glad you did.''

Leaning closer, he seemed to have made a decision—to allow her one final look into the real Michael Masters.

"I'll never forget what happened between us, Eva. We both knew it could be nothing more, but you gave me one single night that will stay with me always. I want you to know that."

Her eyes locked on his, and the words came out impulsively. "Does it have to be that? One single night?"

"Yes," he said softly, his expression tinged with regret. "It has to be that way...and you know why."

She let herself drown in his eyes, those dark, endless eyes, then slowly she hardened her heart. He was right.

They *were* lost to each other, one way or the other. It had always been that way and it always would be.

To save her, he had to give her up.

To stay alive, she had to run.

CHAPTER SIXTEEN

THE THICK HOUSTON AIR wrapped itself around Eva like a soggy blanket, the humidity sticking to her clothing and hair and pulling at her with clammy fingers. After the cool fall weather of Buenos Aires, the Texas climate, never nature at her best, was twice as hard to handle.

Eva turned to Michael. He stood beside her under the canopy outside the international terminal. He was holding Daniel in his arms. Ridley had gone to get his truck after meeting them at the gate. A sudden wave of anxiety hit her, but she managed to keep it hidden. She spoke stiffly. "You really can't come with us now?"

"No." He shook his head. "It's a safe house. That means safe from everyone, including me. You still won't be able to run, though. Jack will have plenty of agents there."

"Running never crossed my mind."

"I'm sure it didn't," he said dryly.

"You'll meet us tomorrow, though?"

"Yes. We'll see Jack at nine. Ridley will bring you, but I wrote my mobile number down and stuck it in Daniel's pocket if you need me for any reason before then."

"I can't think of any reason I should call you."

He shrugged. "You never know. You won't be alone, one way or the other. Like I said, there'll be plenty of agents there."

She turned away and stared out at the pavement. "No telling what lies Jack has told them about me by now—"

"They're federal agents, Eva. Good, honest people. If you were right and Jack *was* going to pull something, he wouldn't do it at the safe house." His tone told her just how much credence he had put in her proof regarding Finely. "We're in more danger standing here than you'll be at that safe house."

Ridley pulled up, his black Bronco sleek and polished. Eva blinked rapidly as the sun hit the windshield and the glare bounced back into her eyes, tears temporarily welling up at the brightness. Or so she told herself.

Ridley jumped out and opened the rear door. Michael laid the still-sleeping Daniel down, then turned back to Eva while Ridley fussed with something on the edge of the door.

Michael put his hands on Eva's shoulders. The weight of them was heavy, but not reassuring. "You'll be all right," he said gruffly. "Everything will work out, and you'll see this is all for the best. It was right to come back."

"Nothing about this is right," she said, shaking her head. "I should never have let you bring us back."

"Let me? I tried to make sure you didn't have a choice."

"We should have run in Chile," she murmured, almost to herself. "I just have this awful feeling...."

"It's nerves." He paused and glanced toward Ridley, his expression shuttered tightly. For just a second, she thought she saw something that looked like hesitation cross Michael's face, then it was gone.

"All righty!" Ridley's Texas drawl interrupted any more conversation. "It's time to get this show on the road. You ready, Eva?"

She heard him, but she didn't move. She suddenly seemed paralyzed. Michael looked down at her for one long second, then made a sound of involuntary surrender and pulled her into his arms. He crushed her to him, lifting her chin with one hand and pressing his lips to hers in a kiss that didn't stop.

A kiss that said everything he couldn't.

That he wanted her, that he cared for her, that she'd made him feel alive again and he couldn't afford that at all costs.

That he loved her, even if he couldn't admit it.

Despite her best intentions, she answered him. Winding her arms around his neck, she kissed him deeply, her breasts tight against his chest, the very air leaving her lungs. She clung to him and let her body answer his.

For several long minutes, they stayed that way, wrapped in each other's arms and lost in each other's emotions. Michael came to his senses first and pulled back.

"Go," he said hoarsely. "Go now before I change my mind and do something I shouldn't."

She looked into his eyes, his image swimming as her own gaze filled with tears.

As if he wanted to burn the moment into his memory, he stared back at her, then without another word, he stepped abruptly from her, turned around and strode away.

BY THE TIME THEY LEFT the airport and headed south on Interstate 45, the rain had begun. By the time they reached the downtown, water was pouring from above in horizontal sheets, lightning splitting the sky and thunder rolling behind it. Eva barely noticed. She stared out the window and saw only Michael's face, the angles and curves, the darkness and the light. Her fingers went to her lips as she remembered his kiss.

"Regular gullywasher, huh?" Ridley looked across the front seat at Eva and smiled. "Bet you didn't see this much rain down there in ole South America?"

They were in an awkward situation, and he was trying his best to make her feel comfortable and ordinary—as if they were out for an afternoon drive instead of the two of them being guard and prisoner. Appreciating the effort but not up to participating in it, Eva smiled weakly, then glanced at Daniel in the back seat. He was sleeping like a log.

Billboards flashed by, their letters blurred by the rain. The sky turned darker.

"It's got to be pretty cold down there right now.

Seem weird to you, being spring here and everything?''

Ridley was determined to make conversation, she realized. Well, if they were going to talk, then she was going to make it count. She looked across the seat and waited for him to look back. When their eyes met, she said bluntly, ''You lied to me about Michael.''

His face took on a wounded expression. ''I wouldn't call it a lie now, Evie—''

''I would. I asked you about him, and you told me he was a salesman.''

''What the heck was I supposed to do? Tell you he was down there just to snatch you and bring you back? You would have hightailed it outta there faster than a six-legged jackrabbit.''

''I thought you were my friend. *Thomas's best friend.*''

He shot her a sharp glance. ''I am, darlin'…and I was. I miss him like I'd miss my own right arm.''

Rain pounded the roof of the truck. She wanted to talk to him about Jack, maybe even enlist his help, but something held her back. What if Ridley hadn't been the agent to tell Thomas the truth about Jack? If he wasn't, he wouldn't believe her any more than Michael had. It *had* to have been Ridley, but months of caution kept her silent. ''Have there been any arrests?''

He shook his head. ''No clues, no suspects, no arrests. Why do you think Jack wanted you back so badly? You and ole Danny there are the only leads we got." His voice dropped, turned confidential and comforting. He was an old friend, just asking for help. "What didya really see, Evie? We ain't got squat right now."

As soon as he spoke, she was forced to accept the truth. Clearly, he knew nothing—someone else must have been Thomas's informant. She couldn't hold back her disappointment. An ally—just one—would have been nice.

She looked out the window. Between the bruising rain and the darkly tinted glass, it looked like night outside the truck. She stared straight ahead, trying to get her bearings and decide what to say all at the same time. They'd exited near Shepherd Drive and were winding their way through the mansions and bungalows that surrounded nearby Rice University.

"I saw enough," she said quietly, finally. "And what I didn't see doesn't matter because I can fill in the blanks. I have proof." Her eyes went involuntarily to the briefcase on her lap, her fingers gripping the sides tightly.

"Well, now..." Ridley drew the words out until they held four syllables. "That puts quite a different spin on everything. What kinda proof you talking 'bout, sweetheart?"

"The only kind that's any good," she answered. "Irrefutable. How's that?"

"Dead men don't tell lies, huh?"

She jerked her gaze to his and realized he was staring at Thomas's briefcase. He'd obviously recognized the unique eelskin case. She remembered now how Ridley had teased Thomas over the intricately patterned leather that she and Sally had taken such pains to select. Eva had told herself a thousand times to give up the case and replace it with a cheap one, but she hadn't been able to. It was the only thing of Thomas's she still had. How could she just throw it away?

Her hands flattened protectively against the leather. "I don't know anything about that," she said. "I just know what I know."

He wheeled the black Bronco down a side street, then turned into an alley. A few seconds later, he pulled up to a garage in a row of about twelve and pressed a transmitter lying on his dashboard. The door went up, and he eased the truck inside, the sudden silence deafening as they escaped the rain. Inside the garage, a side door opened immediately, and a stocky blond man appeared in silhouette. She recognized him as one of the younger agents from the office, Bill something or other. A rookie who'd drawn baby-sitter duty, she thought wryly.

"Well, this is it." Ridley turned to look at her, his arm across the seat. "Your home for the next few months. It's a town house for security reasons, but I think you'll like it and settle right in."

Not likely was all she could think.

The other man approached the Bronco. Seeing Daniel sleeping on the back seat, he opened the door. Turning to Eva, he asked, "Can I carry him up for you?"

She jumped from the front seat and opened the

rear door on her side of the Bronco. "I'll do it." She reached in for Daniel and almost pulled him out of the young agent's hands.

He gave her a startled look.

"H-he doesn't know you," she explained lamely. "He might get scared."

Daniel murmured as she lifted him up into her arms. He was heavy, but she wasn't about to turn him over to anyone else. Then she remembered. Daniel in Michael's arms, resting his head against that broad, strong shoulder. Her heart cracked open a little wider as she forced away the image.

Daniel eyed Eva sleepily and blinked, the overhead fluorescent lights a bright contrast to the rainy darkness. He yawned sleepily.

She patted him on the back. "We're in Houston. In a safe place."

"Wh-where's Michael? I want him to carry me."

The knot inside her chest tied itself tighter. "He's not here right now. We'll see him later," she promised.

He accepted the answer, his eyelids drifting shut once more after a quick glance in Ridley's direction.

Awkwardly gripping Thomas's briefcase in her free hand, Eva followed the young agent and Ridley inside. She found herself in a newly decorated kitchen with wide marble countertops and gleaming white cabinets, a cheerful blue-and-yellow-striped wallpaper coloring the walls. Even with the rain still pouring outside, the room gave off a feeling of comfort. At a table in the center, a woman sat, a *Houston*

Chronicle open before her to the crossword puzzle. She was doing it in red ink.

Ridley made the introductions. "This is Maureen Singletary, Eva. She's new in the Houston office. She'll be helping you while you're here."

Helping you? Eva wanted to scream at the euphemism, but she smiled and nodded in the woman's direction. She was slim and young and attractive with long brown hair and sparkling eyes to match.

They greeted each other as Ridley moved to an arched opening at the end of the kitchen, then paused. "C'mon, Eva. I'll show you the bedrooms and you can put him down."

She followed him out of the kitchen, feeling Maureen's and Bill's eyes on her back. What had Jack told them about her? That she was a killer, that she'd set her brother up? If he had, they were good actors. There had been no accusations in their eyes when they'd met her.

The rest of the house was as nicely decorated as the kitchen, but the details hardly registered. They headed up the stairs, Eva beginning to feel the effects of the long journey, Daniel's weight a burden almost too much to handle. Ridley led her into a small bedroom with twin beds at the rear of the house. She laid Daniel down, then smoothed his hair. After giving the boy one last look, she walked out with Ridley and eased the door shut behind them.

"I have to go back to the office," Ridley told her, "but if there's anything you need, Evie, you just let me know. Maureen and Bill down there are good folks—they'll take care of you even if they are a little green." He paused, his blue eyes apologetic as he acknowledged the real situation for the very first time. "I'm sorry it's gotta be this way, sweetheart." He rested a sympathetic hand on her shoulder. "I know you don't like it."

"It won't be forever."

His gaze sharpened for a moment, then he seemed to relax. "You're right, it won't last forever. As soon as you talk to the boss man and show him all your proof, we'll make an arrest and get this thing straightened out once and for all. We'll get the sons a bitches who killed Tommy, and you can start a brand-new life."

"You make it sound so easy."

He smiled reassuringly. "Life *is* easy, sweetheart. I make it that way. Black and white. Rich and poor. Left and right. There aren't too many decisions when you get right down to it."

Outside, the rain continued. She could hear it more clearly upstairs, the sound muffled but still there as it relentlessly battered the tile roof. She looked up at Ridley.

"I used to think that way, too." An image intruded into her mind. A pair of dark eyes, two slow hands, a hard-muscled body drawn tightly against hers. "But I've decided it's all a little more complicated than that."

HER BATH WAS AS HOT AS she could stand it. Eva sank into the huge whirlpool in the master bathroom until her head was the only thing above the steaming water. Closing her eyes, she let the stinging heat sap the tension from her body and the tautness from her muscles.

If only it could quiet her mind, as well.

Images of Michael kept haunting her, refusing to leave. His dark eyes glancing over at her in the plane. His strong arms holding Daniel. His generous lips pressing against her own. After tomorrow, would she never see him again? Probably not. How could she? If she actually ended up in the witness protection program, her life wouldn't be her own. He wouldn't have any idea of where she was and there would be no way for her to even get in touch with him. As she soaked away her stiffness, she tried not to think about what that really meant.

Outside in the hallway, she could hear Maureen's voice. She and Bill were talking about their schedule. Eva caught only a bit of the conversation—but enough to realize Maureen would be the one watching the late night TV while Bill would be catching the morning cartoons. A second later, a soft knock sounded and the outer door of the bathroom opened slightly.

"I brought you a nightgown, Eva. I'm putting it out here on the counter, okay?" Maureen's voice was low—she knew Daniel was sleeping in the bedroom down the hall. "I'll be downstairs, so you call if you need anything else."

Eva swallowed. What she needed only one man could give her—and he was lost to her now.

"Thank you," she answered faintly.

Seconds later, the door closed with a faint click. Eva let her eyes drift shut again as a welcome lassitude crept over her. There was nothing else she could do tonight but try to rest. Maybe a miracle would occur tomorrow, and she'd figure a way out of the mess her life had become.

Ten minutes later, a faint noise sounded in the outer dressing room, and she came awake with a start, her heart pounding an anxious rhythm. She'd dropped off, the water too soothing to resist, her body too exhausted to try. Lying perfectly still, she listened for a moment, but there was nothing to hear. Only the faint drip, drip, drip of the faucet broke the silence. Standing up, she reached for a towel, then straightened, her gaze jumping to the doorway as a sudden movement caught her eye.

CHAPTER SEVENTEEN

MICHAEL STOOD in the doorway and stared.

She clutched the towel to her dripping body and found her voice. "M-Michael! My God, you scared me half to death! What are you doing here?"

He held one finger to his lips and motioned her to be quiet.

She dropped her voice. "Does Maureen know you're—"

He shook his head, then moved past her and turned on the shower full force. He put his hands on her slick shoulders and spoke into her ear, his breath warm and urgent against her cheek. "I followed Ridley's car. I thought it might be a good idea to know where you were."

"How'd you get inside?"

His thumbs eased their way up and down the sides of her arms. The touch made her shiver. "The window in Daniel's room faces the garage roof. He let me in...then hid me under his bed when the alarm beeped downstairs. He told Maureen he needed fresh air."

"I can't believe he—"

Michael's hand came up to caress her face, cutting off her protest. She found herself turning into his palm, her lips pressing into the center of his hand, the familiar smell of his skin reaching deep inside her. They stayed that way for a few moments, then Michael lifted her chin with his fingers. His eyes were black and intense. They held a mixture of regret and resignation. "I couldn't stay away, Eva. I had to come see you."

Emotions she couldn't hold back swept over her at his words. "I'm glad you came," she said honestly.

"Are you?" He searched her face. "Are you really?"

She nodded, her fingers going to the plane of his jaw. "I...I don't understand it, but all I can think about is you. I've got a million problems right now, and the only thing in my mind is the time we've spent together. Do you feel the same way? Is that why you're here?"

He looked into her eyes and tried to memorize their image. He had no answer to her questions—he only knew that when she and Ridley had driven off, part of him had gone with her, and he couldn't stand the empty feeling he'd been left with. He'd immediately flagged down a cab and followed the truck through the teeming rain. Waiting outside until the Bronco had left and the lights had gone out one by one, he'd studied the town house and had easily spotted the window over the garage. It was sheer luck that Daniel was the one asleep in the room.

Sheer luck and sheer craziness. What in the hell did he think he was doing?

He didn't know...and he didn't care.

Pulling Eva closer to him, he felt complete once more, and he didn't want to stop and analyze why— he simply wanted to experience it. She clung to him, the wet towel between them, their bodies already heating as the steam swirled around them. He bent down and angled his head toward hers. Their lips met and ignited a higher, hotter flame.

Any hesitation she might have felt left at that point. He could feel her body respond just as he felt his own grow hard with desire. Dropping his hands from her shoulders, he let his fingers trace a pattern down her still-wet back as he deepened his kiss, his tongue darting into her mouth and caressing the warm wetness with thrusting movements.

She shivered against him, her body a slick, smooth column of heated desire. Steam rose around them, fogging the mirrors and sleeking his hair. With an almost frantic intensity, Eva reached for the buttons of his shirt and began to undress him as their kiss continued unabated. Within seconds, he was nude, the evidence of his own desire in full view of them both. She dropped her hands between them and cradled his erection in her fingers. He groaned at the touch, her hands two smooth gloves encasing him and moving up and down. After a few exquisite moments, he reached out and stopped her.

"You'd better quit that unless you're totally unselfish." His words were a harsh, dull whisper in the foggy vapor surrounding them.

Her eyes narrowed with passion, their dark depths

heating with excitement. "I could be...but not right now," she said. Closing her eyes, she pressed against him, her full, taut breasts and tightly pebbled nipples thrusting against him.

He groaned and reached down to lift her into his arms, the full length of her body now held against his own. Her eyes rounded, then her head fell back and she exposed the slim ivory line of her neck to his gaze. He gave in to the temptation it presented, nibbling up and down the sweet flesh, his tongue snaking out to lick the drops of moisture still clinging to her. She moaned as his teeth grazed against her.

Taking two steps, he closed the distance between the tub and the marble countertop, Eva's arms clinging to his neck, her naked body slick and wet in his arms. When she felt the edge of the marble against the backs of her legs, she eased her weight from his arms but didn't release him.

Instead, she pulled him closer, her legs wrapping around his waist, her heels gently drawing him closer as they pressed against his buttocks.

He needed no urging.

He came to her freely, urgently, his passionate need for Eva going outside the boundaries of what he'd ever allowed himself to feel for anyone, including Amy. The swirling, roiling hunger scared him, but there was nothing he could do to stop it.

His arms went around her and he dragged her to the very edge of the marble, his hands digging into the sweet flesh of her waist, his mouth going to her nipples, tasting first one and then the other. His hands slipped lower as she moaned beneath him. When his fingers found the sweetest point of all, her groan grew louder. He covered her mouth with his own and kissed into silence the sounds of her desire. As she pressed herself into his hand, he moved his fingers against her, bringing her the pleasure he knew she'd bring him, as well.

Their lovemaking had a wildness to it. Eva was a passionate woman to begin with, but this was more than passion, more than desire. She lost herself in Michael. Totally. Completely. She seemed intent on blocking out everything but his touch, his mouth, his own urgent needs. Nothing else mattered to her at that moment. Part of him knew it was a way for her to forget—for just a minute—but part of him suspected she would always be like this with him, regardless.

As he would be with her.

He worked his way down with his mouth—his lips kissing, his teeth tugging, his tongue caressing—the smooth, beautiful body beneath him. Everything about her was perfect, and even the dreams he'd had since their first time together paled in comparison with the reality. His own arousal was becoming almost painful when she arched her back and cried out. He quickly put his hand over her lips and she bit against his palm, the sharp edges of her teeth no less a pleasure to him than the slick wetness beneath him.

She pulled away from him, then tugged at his shoulders. "Please," she said, pulling him closer. "Please, Michael. I...I want you inside me. Now."

Their eyes locked, and in that moment, a silent message was sent and received. They both understood what it meant and accepted it. There would be no going back after this. No returning to the way things had been.

He entered her, and the passions—but more important, the emotions—he'd been keeping at bay could no longer be controlled. With every thrust, he loved her more. With every push, she loved him back. They sealed the moment the only way they could—with their bodies and hearts—the words no longer necessary.

SHE WAS STILL CLINGING to him when the knock sounded on the door. Above the running water, a woman's voice, barely audible, called Eva's name.

Eva held her breath as she stared at Michael. He held his finger to his lips just as he had when he'd first come into the room, then he leaned toward her. "Shut off the water. Ask what she wants."

Immediately, Eva slid off the countertop and twisted the tap, her heart pounding erratically. She grabbed a towel, wrapped it around her, then went to the outer door. "Maureen? Is…is that you?"

"Yes." The voice that came back was concerned. "Are you okay? The water's been running forever."

"I…I'm fine. It's just been so long since I had a really hot bath—I guess I got carried away."

There was a moment's silence, then the voice changed. From concern to sternness. "Open the door, please." Eva shot a look over her shoulder. Michael was out of view. She hesitated. "Now, Eva. Open the door."

She reached out with trembling fingers and twisted the brass knob. Maureen was on the other side, her own hand in the process of going inside her jacket. She stopped and looked as Eva pulled the door open wider. "Is there a problem?"

Maureen's eyes darted suspiciously past Eva's innocent look and into the steamy room behind her. "I thought I heard voices." Her gaze came back and she studied Eva's face. "You are alone, aren't you?"

Eva held out her hands, the towel tucked around her naked and still-quivering body. Her voice was shaky, but not too bad, considering everything. "Who do you think I'd be hiding in here, Maureen? Did someone slip past you downstairs?"

The woman's expression turned tighter. "Well, I thought I heard something...."

"Please..." Eva shook her head. "I'd like to finish my bath in peace, then go to bed."

For a moment, the agent looked ambivalent. Clearly, she didn't want to anger Eva, but she *was* a professional. A second later, she pushed past Eva and walked into the dressing area. Glancing around, she went into the other part of the bath. Eva's legs threatened to go out from under her, but there was nothing she could do. She waited nervously.

Two seconds later, Maureen turned around and brushed past a trembling Eva. Her throat was so dry she could hardly swallow. Where was Michael? How had he hidden in that tiny room?

Maureen spoke brusquely. "I'll be downstairs if you need me."

The young woman turned and started down the stairs, but at the landing midway down, she stopped and looked up at Eva—who hadn't moved an inch. Their eyes met and held. Eva's still-thundering pulse leaped even higher into her throat at the agent's stare—she was sure she looked guilty. After one long moment, though, the agent continued down the stairs to disappear into the kitchen.

Eva closed the bathroom door and leaned against it weakly. When she opened her eyes, Michael was standing beside her. He was dressed again, his black slacks and shirt a shadow of darkness in the steamy confines of the tiny dressing room.

She grabbed at his shirt. To connect *and* to hold herself upright. "Where'd you go? Where were you?"

"There's access to the attic in the ceiling. I went up there." He reached up and covered her hands with his. "I should never have come here, Eva. It was stupid. Stupid and dangerous."

"Dangerous?" She stared at him, her own gaze locking on his. "Dangerous for whom? Me...or you?"

He didn't answer her. Instead, he bent down and kissed her fiercely, his mouth hot and demanding. When he lifted his head, her breath was gone.

A moment later, he was, too.

THE HOUSE SETTLED into sleep, but Eva couldn't.

She tossed and turned trying to find a comfortable

spot in the bed, but it was an impossible task...not because of the bed, but because of her thoughts. Michael's sudden unexpected appearance had brought into focus how desperate her situation really was. If she couldn't prove Jack's guilt enough to get him convicted, she and Daniel would be on the run forever.

She'd been prepared to live this way when they'd fled to Argentina, but somehow, along the way, things had changed. Michael had changed them. Now she was no longer certain living that kind of life was a good idea, especially for Daniel. Especially for her...

Turning onto her left side and punching her pillow, she thought about Daniel in the room next door. Before getting into her own bed, she'd checked on him, and he'd been wide-awake, lying still, his arms behind his head as he'd stared at the ceiling.

"What are you doing?" she'd asked. "You're supposed to be asleep by now."

Hearing her voice, he'd immediately sat up, leaning on one elbow, his eyes gleaming with excitement when she entered the room. "Is Michael still here? I was looking out the window for shooting stars and he just popped right up. It scared me till I saw who it was."

"Shh." She held her finger up and glanced over her shoulder. "He's gone."

"But you saw him?"

All she could do was nod.

"Is he gonna get us outta here?"

She sat down on the edge of the bed. "I think you're forgetting something, aren't you?" Not waiting for an answer, she continued, "He's the one who *brought* us here. Why would he come get us?"

"I think he's changed his mind. We talked about it when he came in the window. I think he knows the bad guys are here, and he's gonna come back and rescue us."

"The bad guys?" Suddenly alarmed, she stared at him in the darkness. "Did you see someone, Daniel? Someone you recognized?"

His demeanor slipped into defensiveness. "No! If I did, I woulda said something."

She made her voice calm, but on the inside she was trembling. "Of course you would have," she said quietly. "If you'd been completely, one hundred percent positive. But if you hadn't been..."

He looked up at her, his expression guarded. "Yeah?"

"Well, if you hadn't been sure, you might not have said something because you were afraid to make a mistake. I feel that way sometimes."

"You do?"

"Sure I do. Everyone does. Nobody likes to make mistakes. Of course, it might not be a mistake, either, and then you'll have wished you said something." She took a deep breath and slowly let it out. "*Did* you see someone you thought you recognized?"

"I don't know. I—I might have...."

Her heart started a slow, uneasy pounding. "When?" she whispered. "Who?"

"In the garage when you carried me in." She could hear the apprehension in his voice. "I was asleep, so I thought I was dreaming, but maybe... maybe I wasn't."

She held her breath. "Are you talking about the young guy? The one with blond hair?"

He shook his head.

"The woman?"

Another quick shake.

"That only leaves Ridley," she said, her voice puzzled. "He was the tall one with dark hair. Is that who you think you might have seen?"

He bit his bottom lip. "I think so, but I'm not sure. I was sorta scared, so I—I closed my eyes real tight and didn't look again." He dropped his gaze, an embarrassed expression on his face.

"Oh, honey, it's okay." Feeling relieved, she wrapped her arms around the little boy and hugged him tightly. "It couldn't have been Ridley, sweetheart. He was your daddy's best friend. He would never do anything to hurt us."

"He was Dad's friend?" Eyes wide, he stared at her through the darkness, wanting to believe her.

"Yes, they were best friends at work. He's a good guy, believe me."

She'd gone back to her room after that, but why had she bothered? She certainly wasn't sleeping. With a sigh, she threw off the covers and stood up.

Maybe a glass of milk would help. She'd check on Daniel one more time, then go down to the kitchen.

Throwing on the robe Maureen had left her, Eva slipped down the hall toward Daniel's room. She quietly opened his door and started inside, then froze.

Her reaction was automatic.

She screamed.

THE DARK, DAMP AIR was sticky and humid, full of crickets and the call of an occasional night bird. Michael stood in the shelter of a pecan tree a few houses over from the row of homes where he'd left Eva.

He was taking a risk. Standing on a street corner in the dead of night was not a good thing to do in Houston, even in a neighborhood like West University.

But taking risks was becoming a way of life for him as long as Eva was around. He didn't care, though. He couldn't leave her.

He'd walked away from the house a half-dozen times. Each time, he'd returned, his feet apparently incapable of taking him more than a block away. Giving up, he walked to a park the size of a postage stamp at the end of the block, settled himself on a bench in the shadows and prepared to wait.

For what, he had no idea.

Through a crack in the drapes, he caught the glimmer of a light as it came on in the master bedroom. He briefly closed his eyes and imagined Eva slipping in between the sheets. It didn't take much imagination—he'd seen it a thousand times already in his dreams. These were the same impossible dreams where he let himself think about the three of them— Eva, Daniel and himself—being a family. It was a fantasy, pure and simple. No one knew better than Michael that it would never turn into reality. He'd given up those kinds of possibilities a long time ago. But somehow...that didn't stop the images from forming in his mind.

He watched the house settle into darkness and thought about the promises he'd made her in Buenos Aires. He'd said he'd find out if Finely was behind her brother's death, but the more he thought about Eva's accusations, the more Michael had come to realize how impossible they really were. Not only was Jack not that kind of guy, the facts just didn't add up.

Finely had had no way of knowing where Thomas was that day. According to Eva, Thomas had left the office telling no one about their destination. Sure, Jack could have had someone follow him, but Solis was smart. He would have spotted a tail.

Michael thought about it some more, his mind going over all the angles. He considered and rejected a dozen ideas, but each time he kept coming back to one single thing.

Thomas was a responsible, thorough agent who would have felt uncomfortable just disappearing. He *had* to have told someone where he was going.

And who would he tell but his best friend?

The friend who'd fed him all his information.

The friend who'd assured him Jack was to blame.

The friend who'd been Michael's contact all along—Ridley Holt.

Michael sat immobile on the wet park bench and stared through the darkness at Eva's bedroom window. He'd been shocked to learn Ridley Holt had been Thomas's best friend and confidant. Holt had always acted as if he hardly knew Thomas, but obviously that wasn't the case. Why had Holt kept their relationship a secret? That was suspicious in and of itself.

Then there was Daniel's behavior. The little boy had tried to act casual, but underneath the acting, there had been fear. After Michael climbed through his window, Daniel had asked him who was downstairs guarding them. As soon as Michael said it was a woman, Daniel had visibly relaxed. He'd refused to say more even though Michael tried to press him.

Michael had dismissed the conversation, but now he rethought it. Had the little boy seen someone he'd recognized from that horrible day? Someone he knew as a friend of his dad from the office, but nothing more?

Michael closed his eyes and took a deep breath. The men who'd shadowed Eva and Daniel in Comodoro, the men who'd eventually tried to kill them— he hadn't seen them until after his first call to Houston. He thought long and hard about that conversation. Had he told Ridley where he was? No, he finally decided, he hadn't. But he hadn't bothered to time the call, either. With some decent equipment—and the department had plenty—Ridley could have traced the call and figured out where they were. A private plane, already stationed in Latin America, could have easily gotten there the next day.

Jack could have done all these things, too. But Jack hadn't been his contact, had he? Michael had spoken to Ridley and no one else. He'd been Michael's connection all along.

And Michael had been his.

His chest growing tight, he remembered the last time they'd talked. Calling from Chile, Michael had told the agent that the two men who'd been after Eva were no longer an issue. His plan was to drive them to Santiago, but Ridley had insisted that Michael bring them back to Houston. He'd arranged for the plane.

Arranged to bring them in as quickly as possible...before he and Eva could talk about the situation anymore. Before she could convince him. Before they could each realize who'd really been responsible.

Shaking his head in the darkness, Michael swore. He'd ignored Eva's pleas and tossed her concerns aside. Just as he'd done with Amy. Instead of listening, he'd led Eva and Daniel straight back to the one man they needed to avoid at all costs—the man who'd killed Thomas.

The man who would now be more determined than ever to kill them both.

THE MAN BESIDE Daniel's bed turned around as Eva's cry split the tiny room.

He smiled and held up his hands. "Eva! Eva! It's me—Ridley! Everything's okay. No cause for alarm."

She jerked a hand upward to put it against her chest. Her heart was galloping beneath her fingers. "Damn, Ridley! What in the hell are you doing here? You scared the fire out of me!"

His accent seemed more pronounced in the darkened room, and he held himself stiffly, nervously. "Well, there's been...a little problem, guess you could say."

"A problem? What kind of problem?" She waited for his answer, her mind swirling. Where was Maureen? Hadn't the agent heard Eva's scream? Was she asleep, for heaven's sake? And what about Bill? Where was he? Surely he'd heard her—he was on this same floor. Eva's uneasiness went up another notch.

"The house has been compromised. Gotta move you out." He waved a hand behind him toward the bed where Daniel was rubbing his eyes sleepily. "I was gettin' Danny here, then I was gonna come after you."

"Compromised?" Alarmed, she edged closer to Daniel's bed, moving quickly past Ridley's tall form. He stood between her and the little boy with his back to the bed. She reached over and flipped on the bedside lamp, then glanced down, trying to reassure Daniel with her eyes. Ridley slowly turned to face them both.

And Daniel screamed. A reflexive cry as loud as

Eva's had been, but holding even more terror. Reaching blindly for Eva, he grabbed her arm and pulled wildly at her, jumping up in the bed.

"It's him," he screamed. "It's him. It's the bad guy, Aunt Eva."

Without thinking, Eva wrapped her arms around Daniel and tried to calm him. He continued to scream and fight her, his cries only getting more and more frantic. His ferociousness even sent Ridley a step back from the bed.

"It's okay, baby. It's okay!" She put her hands on either side of his face and tried to force him into stillness.

"It's *not* okay," he screamed. Pointing a shaky finger in Ridley's direction, he started to cry. "H-he's the one I saw the night Daddy was killed. H-he was driving the big black truck."

Big black truck? Her eyes widened. Ridley had been driving a black Bronco when he'd picked them up. She'd seen a black *Explorer* that night. It had been an Explorer, hadn't it? Her pulse quickened despite herself.

"I think you're making a mistake, sweetheart," she found herself saying anyway. "This is Mr. Holt—he was your dad's friend, remember? I explained that earlier."

"I don't care what you said," Daniel cried, his eyes wild. "I'm telling the truth! He's the one." His sobs echoed in the tiny room as Eva lifted her eyes and met Ridley's blue stare.

The hair on Eva's arms suddenly stood up, and a

cold haze of fear settled over her at his expression. She tightened her arms protectively around Daniel as Ridley began to speak.

"I'm afraid the little fella's right," he said with a smile, his drawl more friendly and Southern than usual. "I'm the one. I'm the bad guy."

CHAPTER EIGHTEEN

EVA STOOD PERFECTLY STILL. Nothing about her was moving except her pulse, and it had slowed with disbelief and shock. She stared at Ridley numbly. "Wh-what are you saying?"

He smirked. "You always were kinda slow, darlin'. Time and time again I tried to explain to poor ole Thomas why I wasn't quite captivated by your charms, but he just never understood. I like my women with some brains—keeps things interesting."

His insults didn't even register. "D-did you kill my brother?"

He measured her with his look. "I didn't kill your brother. Those damn gunrunners from Mexico did. I'll prove it, too. Just like I'll prove they were the ones who broke into the safe house and killed you and the boy here—along with the agents on duty."

Daniel buried his face in her neck and began to whimper. Eva wished she could do the same—she knew now why Maureen and Bill hadn't responded. Her stomach rolled over in fear and loathing.

"Why?" she whispered hoarsely, her hand on the little boy's head. "Why are you doing this?"

"Why?" His eyes glittered coldly. "Because your brother couldn't leave well enough alone. He had to keep digging and digging. He knew the gunners had someone on the inside—too many raids were turning out unsuccessful. I told him it was Jack, and he bought it for a little while. Then...he had to start digging again. Sooner or later, he was gonna figure out it was me. I had to make sure he didn't.''

''And Sally?''

''She got in the way.'' He shrugged and lifted one eyebrow. ''I'm makin' some serious money here, darlin'. Nobody's gonna get between me and my green.''

A red mist formed behind Eva's eyes. She blinked, but the rage remained. ''You took away my only family—this child's father and mother—for money?''

''You know what they say.'' His stare turned into blue ice. ''Money makes the world go round.''

''That's 'love,''' she said fiercely. ''It's *love* that makes the world go round.''

He laughed. It was a cold, hollow bark of a sound. ''Love? Sure...right. That's what sent Masters chasing you halfway across the world, wasn't it? I promised him plenty of *love* so he headed off to Argentina to find you and Danny boy here. It wasn't that big fat check from the department, no sirree.'' His leering grin gained width. ''After seeing you two at the airport the other day, I'm suspectin' he's getting some of the real thing, though, along with my dollars, isn't he?''

She stared at him, unable to say a word.

An expression of regret, totally false, came across

his face. "Too bad, too. 'Cause he's about to be in love with another dead woman." He reached behind him and she tensed. His hand came back holding a wicked-looking pistol. She couldn't tell for sure in the dim light, but it looked like a Ruger. "First, you and me are gonna take a little walk back to your bedroom. You've got something there I gotta have."

He smirked at her startled look. "I'm talking about your brother's briefcase, honey. I'm not interested in your virtue...or what's left of it." From the night-stand he picked up a rope and tossed it to her. "Tie him up."

She caught the rope, but just barely. Her hands were numb; Daniel had been keeping a tight grasp on her arms. She looked down at him. His eyes were huge with fear. "It'll be okay," she said softly. He started to cry again, and Ridley made a sound of disgust. She raised one hand to the boy's face and wiped off the tears. "C'mon, sweetie, everything will be all right. Y-you just lie here and look out the window." She gave him a piercing look. "Watch for shooting stars, okay?"

"Cut the crap. Tie him to the bed, and let's get on with it."

Daniel sniffed, but his gaze told her he understood. "I—I'll watch."

She nodded encouragingly. "You do that. I won't be gone that long, I promise." Her fingers fumbled, but she twisted the rope around his ankles and then his wrists. When she finished, Ridley made a show of pulling on the loose ends of the rope as if to check the knots. When they held, he seemed satisfied.

He stuck the gun in her back and pushed. "Let's go, sweetheart."

Sending Daniel one last look of reassurance, Eva headed toward the door.

MICHAEL MADE HIS WAY slowly along the garage, every foot bringing him closer to the window of Daniel's room. A dim square of light told him the boy was up, but he didn't need that to know trouble had already hit. He'd looked in the window downstairs. The woman who'd searched Eva's bathroom after they'd made love was slumped at the kitchen table, a bloody stain already spreading across the navy blazer she was wearing. As Michael crawled even closer to the window, his senses went on full alert. It was open already. Even if he hadn't seen the woman downstairs, he would have known something wasn't right. No one in Houston slept with the windows open; if the heat didn't kill you, the mosquitoes would.

He reached the window, took a deep breath, then inched his way up until he could see over.

Daniel's head popped up at the very same time, filling Michael's vision and eliciting a painfully graphic curse. When his heart started again, Michael grated, "Dammit it to hell, boy, what are you doing? You nearly gave me a—"

"The bad guy's here." Daniel interrupted Michael's curse without even acknowledging it. "He's got Aunt Eva. They went to her room. I got out of the ropes and opened the window. I hoped maybe you'd—''

Michael's body went cold. He reached through the window and gripped Daniel's arms, shaking him lightly into silence. "Who is it?" he asked urgently. "Who exactly has her?"

"It's the bad guy. Mr. Hold or something. He came in my room and he was gonna kidnap me!"

Michael slipped through the window as the little boy continued to whisper excitedly. He stopped to draw a breath, then his eyes grew huge when he saw the sleek black pistol in Michael's hand.

Michael bent down to Daniel's eye level. "I'm going to your aunt's room. I want you to scoot out onto the roof and stay there. Right beside the window. Don't go any farther and don't come back into the room no matter what you hear. I want your Scout's honor."

Daniel's eyes shot to the window, then gleamed with excitement. "Okay. Scout's honor." He quickly crossed his chest, then held up his fingers.

Michael smiled. "Good boy." He helped him up, then pushed him out to the roof. "Don't come in till you hear my voice."

Daniel nodded, then Michael slowly eased down the window. If he didn't come back, at least Ridley wouldn't find him.

Michael turned and headed toward the hall.

EVA SLID THE BRIEFCASE out from under her bed and stood up. With its sharp metal corners and the extra weight of Thomas's laptop in it, the leather case made a formidable weapon. Unfortunately, Ridley realized the same thing at about the same time. He pulled it roughly from her hands and threw it on the bed. Keeping one eye on her and his pistol balanced in his hand, he flipped back the brass clasps. They'd been broken in the wreck, making it impossible for her to lock it.

He eyed the computer. "His notes are in there, right?"

She nodded, expecting him to tell her to power it up.

"Any copies? Floppies? Printouts?"

"No."

"Sure." Ridley lifted his upper lip in a sneer. "I don't guess it matters much, though, does it? In a few more minutes, you won't be around to tell anybody about copies anyway."

Raising the gun and pointing it at the computer, he fired off two rounds. The flat bark of the silencer kept the noise down, but the unmistakable sound of a discharging weapon echoed in the room as black plastic flew up all around them.

Eva was still gasping when the bedroom door flew open, hit the opposite wall and bounced. Immediately, Ridley grabbed her, putting his gun to her head and yanking her against him—just as Michael filled the doorway.

As relief flooded her, Ridley jerked her to one side, the gun's barrel grazing her forehead in a painful swipe. She cried out. Michael sent her a quick glance, then his eyes locked on Ridley's.

"Release her." Michael's words were knives, slicing into the room. "Right now, Holt. I'm a better shot than you. I can drop you in a second."

"And I'll shoot her going down." Ridley tightened his arm around her midsection, cutting off her air. Black dots starting swimming in front of her eyes. "I know the drill as well as you do, Masters. My finger's on the trigger. It'll be reflexive."

Michael's expression was cold as he edged into the room. "You think I care? All I'm interested in is you. If I can bring you in before you run, it's money in the bank for me. Jack knows everything, but he wants to hear it from you."

Ridley pulled in a quick breath of surprise, but he bluffed anyway. "Finely knows shit."

"He knows everything. I told him." Michael picked up the receiver to the nearby phone. "Call him and ask him if you don't believe me."

Ridley swore, his arm jerking again.

"Give her up." Michael's voice was matter-of-fact. "She's just going to complicate things."

Ridley started toward the doorway, pulling Eva with him. She cried out and reached for Michael, but he didn't move—couldn't move. A quick flicker of his eyes in her direction gave her hope, though. Their dark depths were filled with love and fear and promises.

"You're making a mistake, Holt." Michael followed them as they entered the hall.

"The only mistake I made was telling you to bring her back," Ridley answered. "I should have gone down there myself as soon as I knew where you were. Instead, I told the gunners. They sent those two fools who managed to completely screw things up."

Shaking so hard she could barely stand, Eva briefly closed her eyes. If he dragged her into Daniel's room, it would be all over. Ridley was getting desperate—he was starting to tremble as badly as she was. He'd shoot them both without hesitating whether Michael had a gun on him or not. The thought of seeing Daniel's eyes if that happened was more than she could bear. She hadn't protected him this long to give in now.

Pulling her down the carpeted hallway, Ridley stumbled against the wall. His gun knocked against her forehead, and a dull reverberation of agony echoed the length of her body. She blinked back the pain and tried to concentrate instead. They reached the edge of the stairs, and Eva realized this might be her only chance.

If she jumped up, then fell backward—actually used her own weight against Ridley to make him fall—it could be just the diversion Michael needed. She'd fall, too, but what was better? A broken neck or a shot through the head?

She didn't stop to answer. Just as they came even with the stairs, she took a deep breath, then jumped up from the carpet and threw her weight against Ridley, her back connecting solidly with his chest.

The air escaped from his lungs with a rush. His

body resisted for just a moment, and they both seemed to hang in the air above the top step.

In that one quick second, she shot a last desperate look in Michael's direction, sending him all her love, all her feelings, all her heart. Their eyes connected with a jolt, then it was over.

She and Ridley tumbled backward, head over heels, into empty, painful space.

CHAPTER NINETEEN

FLASHING LIGHTS of different colors illuminated the brick facade of the town house. Red for the police, white for the ambulances, blue for the department. From her gurney, in a daze of pain and disbelief, Eva watched as a crowd of people, some in uniform but most in suits, scurried over the front lawn.

The immediate moments after her fall were all a blur. One second, she'd been in the air, and the next thing she knew, dozens of people were swarming around her, including Daniel. His green eyes had been huge with fear until Michael had reassured him everything was okay and led him away to a nearby female officer. The woman had kept him close but distracted. With relief, Eva realized she could see them both from the corner of her eye.

She squirmed a bit on the gurney, groaning automatically as her sore body protested the movement. The EMS team had assured her none of her injuries was too serious, but that, she'd decided, was a matter of perspective. If one of them had been lying here in her place, it might be a different story.

Then again, maybe they *were* right. Michael's perfect aim had sent a bullet neatly through Ridley's left shoulder as they'd fallen. His ambulance had disappeared down Shepherd only seconds before. Unlike Eva, he was heading for surgery.

Then jail.

The thought brought an abrupt lightness to Eva's spirit, and for the first time in months, the burdens she'd been carrying seemed to float away. She was left with a remarkable feeling of freedom and choice.

She didn't have to hide anymore. She could do anything she wanted. She and Daniel were free! As the reality soaked in, Michael appeared by her side. His touch was gentle and comforting as he placed his hand on hers—the only part of her body, it seemed, that wasn't in pain or turning black and blue. She smiled widely at him, plans for their future playing like a movie inside her head.

He met her expression with a warm smile of his own, and her heart lifted even higher. Had she ever really thought she could live without this man?

"I know you're hurting," Michael said, smoothing back a lock of her hair, "but would you mind talking to Jack? He just got here and wants to see you before you go to the hospital."

She nodded despite her pain. With Michael beside her, she could do anything. He turned and motioned to someone behind her, then Jack stepped into view.

Jack Finely's thin, ascetic face looked even more severe than usual in the eerie-colored lights. He was dressed impeccably, his navy suit pressed, his white cotton shirt spotless. Even in the dead of night...Eva thought wryly.

"You're a very lucky woman, Eva," he said without preamble. "You could have been killed tonight."

She squeezed Michael's fingers and smiled again. "But I wasn't. Everything turned out great."

"So far. Next time, it might not turn out the same way. I've assigned two shifts of two agents each. You'll be covered night and day until the trial, and then—"

"Whoa, whoa. Wait a minute," she said, a sudden and awful panic coming over her. "Wh-what do you mean you've assigned two shifts? Ridley's not going to do anything in the shape he's in, and once the trial is over—"

"Once the trial is over, you'll be in even more danger than before. Ridley's out of commission, thanks to you. The men who were buying his information will not be happy about that. Not to mention the fact that you were involved in the killing of one of their own—the man who ran you off the road outside Comodoro. You also saw the ones who were with Ridley when Thomas was killed. That's three good reasons they have to come after you. I talked to Williams in Washington and he agrees. It's too dangerous for you now." His thin blade of a nose wrinkled slightly. "You didn't really think you were going to go about your merry way, did you?"

"But I—I thought..." She looked at Michael, who'd stepped to the foot of the gurney to make way for Jack. Her eyes beseeched him to somehow contradict the man, but Michael said nothing. Standing stiffly, he was staring at Finely, avoiding her gaze, his expression closed. Had Michael known this was coming? A knot formed in her chest as Finely began to speak again.

"These are international gunrunners, Eva. Ridley's arrest can't keep them from you. I assumed you knew that all along."

"I thought it was over. All over."

"It'll never be over—for you. In fact, it's even more important that you go into the witness protection program now. Men like this do not fool around, believe me."

Thomas's words echoed in her mind. It was as if he were standing right beside her. *"These guys are dangerous as hell. They'd just as soon kill you as look at you."*

A black hole opened up in the vicinity of her heart. She slid slowly toward it, the plans she'd had—for only a moment—of life with Michael, slowly vanishing into the abyss before her.

Hanging on to the edges of her sanity by a thread, she tried to voice her protest even though she knew it was useless. "But I—I can't do that. I can't go into the program. Not now—"

"You don't have a choice, Eva. You've got Daniel to consider. If you want to live—*if you want your nephew to live*—then you're disappearing. There are no other options."

The moment stretched and built into a tense silence that was broken only by the voices of the men behind them. Down the street, in the early-morning silence, the sharp tap of a car's horn sounded. Someone trying to leave for work, she thought distractedly.

Finely's voice broke into her thoughts. "We'll get you into the program as soon as we can. It's the only way."

She stared at him. He was right, of course. Absolutely right. There was nothing else she could do.

Her eyes full of tears, Eva turned toward the end of the gurney, but the spot where Michael had been standing was empty. He was gone. Her heart tipped over and fell into the hole.

"THE DOCTORS SAY you're going to be okay. As soon as that ankle gets a bit more rest, you'll be good as new."

Michael stood beside Eva's hospital bed, his gaze going over her face, then her body. When his eyes reached the bottom of the bed and her elevated and wrapped ankle, his heart twisted. Thank God her injuries weren't any more serious. When he'd seen her fly off those stairs, he'd almost died himself. Even worse had been that split-second moment when he'd looked over the railing at her sprawling body lying next to Ridley's bleeding one. At that moment, Michael hadn't known if she was dead or alive, but he'd known one thing. He hadn't been able to protect her. He'd failed her—just as he'd failed Amy.

In the past twenty-four hours, Michael had examined the situation from every possible angle, but he'd come up with no solution. He'd let Eva down. That was all there was to it. His only choice now was to distance himself from her. He had to. For his own protection and hers, as well. Despite Finely's pronouncement, she'd let herself hope there was still a chance for a real relationship between them. Michael had seen it in her eyes.

But he knew better.

There could be nothing between them. If there was, she'd never leave. And if she never left, she'd die. She'd die because he couldn't protect her. He'd more than proven that. When the inevitable attack happened—and it would if she stayed—he'd fail her. Again.

Nothing had changed. He had to give her up to save her life.

"How's Daniel doing?" Eva's voice broke into his thoughts.

"He's okay. He was building a fort under the Finelys' dining-room table this morning. Apparently, he and Jack's daughter are getting along great."

"I can't believe Jack and his wife are actually keeping him for me."

"It's the safest place he could be. And Zilla's great. I don't know how she got hooked up with Jack."

"Opposites attract."

Their eyes met and locked. Tension formed in the gap between them, rising up and separating them as effectively as a brick wall.

Eva spoke awkwardly, breaking the moment. "I— I suddenly realized last night you never told me why you came back to the house. How did you know?"

"I started thinking and everything just came to-gether." He shrugged. "I saw the whole picture. If I'd had any sense, I would have seen it much ear-lier."

She started to say something, but he held his hand up and stopped her. In the instant that followed, he took one final look and memorized her face—the curve of her mouth, the tilt of her nose, the ivory sheen of her skin. She wore an expectant expression that dug painfully into his already broken heart.

"I'm starting to see a lot of things I should have seen earlier," he said, deliberately making his voice rough. Stepping away from the bed, he took a deep breath and spoke quickly so he wouldn't back out. "I don't know how this situation got so out of hand, but it's not going any further. It's stopping. Right here. Right now."

Eva stared at him, almost unable to breathe. She'd known this was going to happen. She'd tried to pre-pare herself for it. Still, hearing his voice—so calm and cold—and seeing his expression—so resolute and determined—made her heart skip a beat. She au-tomatically lifted her hand to the base of her throat as if somehow protecting herself. "Wh-what are you saying?"

"I'm going home to Buenos Aires. My flight to Miami leaves at 6:00 p.m. tonight."

She leaned back against her pillows, feeling the color drain from her face.

"You don't need me anymore. Jack has everything under control and he'll see that the marshals do their job. As soon as Ridley recovers, his trial will begin. After you testify, it'll all be over for you and Daniel. You can go into the program, and everything will be fine."

Fine? How could anything be fine if they were thousands of miles apart and she had no idea where he was or what he was doing? *Fine?* How could that be if they weren't together?

She could only assume her expression reflected her agony. He crossed the room to stand beside her bed, the planes of his face softening minutely as he gazed at her. Something electrical passed between them even though he didn't touch her.

"It's for the best, Eva."

Her voice cracked, then broke. "Th-the best for who?"

"For both of us. I'm not the kind of man you need in your life."

"Can't I be the judge of that?"

"In normal times, yes." He didn't move, but there was a sudden distance between them, a bigger gap than ever before. "But not now. Right now you see the person you want me to be—not the person I am. I told you before you don't know who I am and that hasn't changed." His voice turned harsher. "Don't make the mistake of thinking you understand me."

She couldn't help it. Her anger flared. "I understand you better than you do, and I know exactly what I'm looking at. I see a man who saved my life. A man who saved my nephew's life. I see a man who cares. That's who you really are—you just can't admit it.''

"You're wrong. I *can't* love you, Eva. That part of me is gone, it's dead. Even if I could get it back, I wouldn't want it." His black eyes turned abruptly angry and cold. "I don't *want* to love you. And I don't want you loving me."

His words rang out, echoing around the room, and suddenly she couldn't breathe at all. Her heart cooperated, too, standing still and slowing her pulse until she was completely paralyzed. The pain was so intense, so blinding, that for just a moment, she prayed it was real. She actually hoped her heart would never start again and that she wouldn't have to face a life on her own without this man. Then she realized how silly that was. She would live. She *wanted* to live. She would make a life for herself and for Daniel. She'd done it before. She could do it again. She inhaled. The pain stayed.

''I'm sorry it has to end this way." His words held no real meaning. They were flat and empty, stones that fell on her bruised heart. "But I'm going back alone. I want it that way and you should, too."

The door whispered shut behind him. She stared at the place where he'd stood, then she turned her head against the pillow, her eyes going to the window across the room. The sky outside was a fragile shade of blue, as deserted and empty as she was. She could have been anywhere. She could have been nowhere…and soon enough, she would be.

HE WATCHED HER LEAVE Finely's house a week later, Daniel at her side. Eva had no idea he was there, of course, but Michael's eyes never left her as she and the boy climbed into the marshal's vehicle with their luggage, her inherent grace obvious even though her ankle was still wrapped and clearly painful.

A week after that, he was still sitting in his hotel room in Houston. The tickets to BA had been issued and changed half a dozen times already. The last time he'd called Aerolineas Argentinas, he'd simply canceled the reservation. He didn't ask himself why; he only knew he couldn't leave. Not yet anyway.

When he found himself at the cemetery one muggy evening several days after that, Michael knew he was no longer capable of fighting his emotions. He couldn't just go back to BA and pretend none of this had happened. The torturous conflict was too great to deny. It had grown into an elephant sitting on his shoulder, demanding attention, demanding answers.

A heavy green silence enveloped him as he stared at the headstone. Shaded by an ancient magnolia tree and guarded by two angels whose stony expressions begged comment, the pink Texas granite glinted in the evening sun. Michael closed his eyes and repeated the words he knew by heart. "Amy Delouise Masters. Beloved daughter, cherished wife."

Two simple lines to sum up a life that had touched his in a way he'd never forget.

He sat down heavily on the bench at the foot of

the grave, a wash of regret and grief threatening to overtake him.

He'd loved her. Loved her so much it hurt. Amy had been more than a wife to him—she'd represented everything he'd always valued. Honesty, goodness, beauty. Then he'd allowed his job to consume him and he'd lost her.

Was he going to let that happen again? Was he prepared to repeat the agony of loss? When he'd watched Ridley Holt's gun press into Eva's delicate skin, Michael had thought he was going to die himself. He'd lost all sense of direction, all concept of right and wrong. All he'd wanted, at that instant, was to kill Holt, to commit a cold-blooded murder and never look back. When Michael had actually pulled the trigger, it was only at the very last moment that he'd adjusted his aim—for Holt's shoulder instead of his heart.

Michael stared at the dappled light hitting the granite, then brought a hand up to cover his eyes. The motion didn't remove the image from his mind. Eva's face had appeared as clearly as if she were standing in front of him. Dark, loving eyes, hair like black silk, sympathy and caring radiating from her. He dropped his head into his hands.

A week after that, he knew he no longer had a choice. He couldn't lie to himself anymore. He loved Eva Solis. He loved her beauty, her strength, her character, her deep sensual side. There was nothing about her that didn't call out to him and make him want her...but he didn't deserve her or her love. He never had and he never would, and the sooner he began to accept that fact, the better off he'd be.

ANOTHER ENDING. Another plane. Another beginning.

They'd been in the air almost two hours and would be landing soon. Eva's gaze went to the seat opposite her own where Daniel sat. He was playing with a magic kit she'd gotten him before they'd left Houston, practicing the art of making coins disappear. She wished he could do the same with her emotions. They felt raw and exposed. A certain kind of numbness had sustained her throughout the trial, but when Ridley had been convicted, that blessed lethargy had disappeared. Reality had settled in, and now she felt as though she were walking through fire. The U.S. Marshal's words replayed in her memory, laying out the details.

"We've gotten you a job at an energy company. It's a large firm, and they do a lot of international business. You'll be on their staff of translators. Daniel's already been enrolled at a local private school. It's a good one, and we feel sure he'll fit right in. Your apartment's already been rented. It's at 5334 Cascade Drive. You'll like Arizona…"

The speed of the plane changed as it lowered its thrust and started its descent. She looked out the window. The ground rising up to meet them was barren and dry, heat coming off the asphalt landing strip in undulating waves. In the baking sun of the early afternoon, everything in the landscape was the same color and it stretched for miles. Brown. She closed her eyes, and the image of Michael's face filled her mind.

She'd never see him again.

She and Daniel were on their own once more, the wonderful security of Michael's arms a thing of the past. She'd thought a lot in the previous few months, sitting in the courtroom, watching Ridley day after day as the trial had played out. Not only had he taken her past by killing Thomas and Sally, he'd stolen her future, as well. Never again would she feel Michael's skin, experience his warmth, have his love. It was gone, all gone.

She'd tried at first to convince herself that in a normal situation they wouldn't have fallen for each other. Their time together had been crazy, extraordinary. Nothing like they would experience in a conventional life. After a while, she was sure they'd find out how incompatible they really were. But the more she thought about it, the more she realized the truth.

It didn't matter. She would have loved Michael no matter what.

He possessed a kind of intensity, a vibrancy, that she knew she'd never forget. She could spend the rest of her life looking for a man with the same passion for life—passion for *her*—and she'd never find him because he didn't exist. Michael was the only one who had it.

And he was the only man she'd ever love.

She told herself she was lucky to have had him the short time she did. A lot of women never experienced the kind of love they'd shared. Never. At least she knew now what it was like, even if it was gone forever. She turned once more to the window as the wheels of the jet touched down on the desert floor.

Like Finely had said, she was a lucky woman. Very lucky.

Right.

Weeks later
Somewhere in Arizona

DANIEL SAW HIM FIRST. He climbed out of the apartment's swimming pool with a scream and shot toward the fence, a wet ball of energy, delight and screaming disbelief.

"Omigosh! Omigosh! I don't believe it! You're here!" He turned to Eva and yelled, "Look, look!"

From the other side of the elaborate swimming area where she was sunning, Eva sat up abruptly, her heart leaping into her throat. Pulling her wide-brimmed hat from her head and shading her eyes with her hand, she stared with shock across the deck.

It couldn't be.

But it was.

He crossed the distance between the pool's edge and Eva's chair before she could blink, Daniel at his side. Putting his hand out, Michael steadied her as she jumped from the chair, the feel of his fingers beneath her arm sending a current upward through her body and straight into the center of her existence.

She pulled off her sunglasses with shaking fingers and stared. His black eyes were as intense as ever, but an aura of subtle hesitation hovered around him just out of sight. If she hadn't loved him, she would never have noticed. His stare raked over her with a greediness that stole her breath.

"H-how in the world…?" She couldn't even get the rest of the words out.

Daniel supplied them. "How'd you find us? Mr. Finely said no one in the world would ever be able to track us down."

Michael's eyes never left Eva. "I find people," he said. "That's my job."

She searched his expression for clues. Why was he here? What did he want? Her heart began to thump furiously and a damning weakness came into her legs. She turned to Daniel. "I—I think Michael and I need to talk privately for a little bit. Why don't you go get something to drink? There's lemonade in the refrigerator. When we finish, you can come back and visit with him."

"For as long as I want?"

She glanced at Michael. "For as long as he has time."

Daniel's green eyes shone with excitement and he stuck out his hand. "Deal?"

She shook his hand. "Deal."

Grinning and clearly pleased, he shot Michael another look, then took off down the deck beside the pool. Eva turned back to Michael. The conversation with Daniel had allowed her to regain a measure of control, but not enough.

"How *did* you find us?" she asked, her hand fluttering to the V neck of her black one-piece bathing suit. "We have new names, new stories..."

He reached out and took her hand, his fingers brushing over the swell of her breasts before he brought her palm to his mouth and kissed it. "I know some people in the U.S. Marshal's office. They didn't come right out and give me your address, but they gave me enough hints. Enough to lead me here."

His touch made her weak. "The last time we spoke, I got the impression you didn't care to find me. Ever again."

"I thought that's what I wanted, but I was wrong," he said bluntly. "Dead wrong. I couldn't leave Houston. Every time I went to the airport, I ended up watching the plane leave instead of being on it."

Her eyes studied his face. She waited for more.

"Then I went to Amy's grave. It was the first time I'd been there since the funeral."

Her heart melted. "That must have been hard."

"At first, yes. Then I went back the next day, then the next one, too. After a while, something happened to me sitting there...."

She let the silence build, not knowing what to say.

He lifted his head, his eyes sweeping her face. "I began to understand what I've been doing all this time." He stopped and looked toward the sparkling pool, the bright Arizona sun glinting diamonds off the water. "I've been so stupid," he said, shaking his head.

She wanted to wrap her arms around him, but she made herself sit still. "You're not stupid. You're just a man…a man who hasn't allowed his feelings out in the light of day for way too long."

"I was afraid of what I'd see."

"We all are. But sometimes we surprise ourselves."

"It's been so long…so long since I've let myself love. Do you think I can do it again?"

She took a deep breath. "I think you can do anything you put your mind to. You're the most remarkable man I've ever known—and the only one I've ever thought I really needed." She dropped her gaze and gathered her courage. When she looked up, she knew her emotions were plain to see, leaving her open and vulnerable. "I love you, Michael, love you more than I've ever loved anyone. You're everything I've always wanted…and needed, but I—I can't ask you to stay. You'd have to give up your whole life…become someone else. I can't ask you to do that for us."

"Good—because if you asked me, you'd be too late." He grinned. "I've already joined the program, and I've got a new job lined up. You're looking at Arizona's newest state security consultant—Capt. John Benson. I'm your neighbor and a very old friend. In case you've forgotten, we were quite close at one time…and I have a feeling we'll be even more so in the future." Her mouth dropped open in surprise, but before she could say anything, Michael gathered her into his arms. "I love you, Eva. You're the most important thing in the world to me, and I'm going to spend the rest of my life proving that to you over and over again. You have to promise me one thing, though."

Still stunned, she looked up at him. "Anything. Anything at all."

"Promise me you'll never run again." His eyes pinned hers. "I don't want to repeat this kind of torture again. Ever."

Her heart thumped, almost painfully. "There's nowhere to hide from you. Even if there was…I wouldn't want to. Not anymore. I promise."

He cupped her face with his hands, then lowered his mouth to hers. Their kiss was sweet and long.

Then a loud giggle shattered the moment. They looked up in unison. Grinning widely, Daniel stood beside them, his green eyes sparkling.

"Hey, Michael. Does this mean you're gonna stay?"

Holding Eva with one arm, Michael reached out and embraced Daniel with the other. "There's nothing that could keep me away, buddy. We're going to be a family—forever and always."

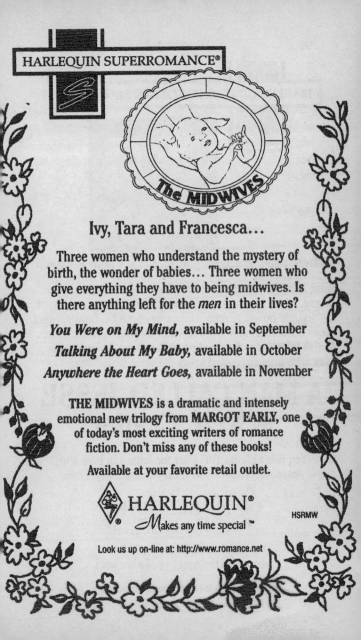

MEN at WORK

All work and no play?
Not these men!

July 1998
MACKENZIE'S LADY by Dallas Schulze

Undercover agent Mackenzie Donahue's
lazy smile and deep blue eyes were his best
weapons. But after rescuing—and kissing!—
damsel in distress Holly Reynolds, how could
he betray her by spying on her brother?

August 1998
MISS LIZ'S PASSION by Sherryl Woods

Todd Lewis could put up a building with ease,
but quailed at the sight of a classroom! Still,
Liz Gentry, his son's teacher, was no battle-ax,
and soon Todd started planning some
extracurricular activities of his own....

September 1998
A CLASSIC ENCOUNTER
by Emilie Richards

Doctor Chris Matthews was intelligent, sexy
and *very* good with his hands—which made
him all the more dangerous to single mom
Lizette St. Hilaire. So how long could she
resist Chris's special brand of TLC?

Available at your favorite retail outlet!

MEN AT WORK™

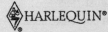 

Look us up on-line at: http://www.romance.net   PMAW2

Glamorous, hot, seductive...

THE AUSTRALIANS

Stories of romance Australian-style guaranteed to
fulfill that sense of adventure!

September 1998, look for
Playboy Lover
by Lindsay Armstrong

When Rory and Dominique met at a party the attraction was
magnetic, but all Dominique's instincts told her to resist him.
Not easy as they'd be working together in the steamy tropics
of Australia's Gold Coast. When they were thrown together in
a wild and reckless experience, obsessive passion flared—but
had she found her Mr. Right, or had she fallen for yet another
playboy?

*The Wonder from Down Under: where spirited women win
the hearts of Australia's most independent men!*

Available September 1998 at your favorite retail outlet.

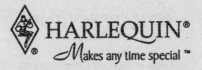

HARLEQUIN®
Makes any time special ™

HARLEQUIN SUPERROMANCE®

MONTHS LATER

DEBORAH'S SON

by award-winning author
Rebecca Winters

Deborah's pregnant. The man she loves—the baby's father—doesn't know. He's withdrawn from her for reasons she doesn't understand. But she has to tell him. *Wants* to tell him. She wants them to be a family.

Available in October
wherever Harlequin books are sold.

HSR9ML